SLUGFEST

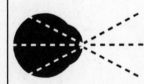

This Large Print Book carries the
Seal of Approval of N.A.V.H.

A DIRTY BUSINESS MYSTERY

SLUGFEST

ROSEMARY HARRIS

THORNDIKE PRESS

A part of Gale, Cengage Learning

GALE
CENGAGE Learning

Detroit • New York • San Francisco • New Haven, Conn • Waterville, Maine • London

GALE
CENGAGE Learning™

LIBRARY OF CONGRESS CATALOGING-IN-PUBLICATION DATA

Harris, Rosemary.
  Slugfest : a dirty business mystery / by Rosemary Harris.
    p. cm. — (Thorndike Press large print mystery)
  ISBN-13: 978-1-4104-3950-5 (hardcover)
  ISBN-10: 1-4104-3950-X (hardcover)
  1. Holliday, Paula (Fictitious character)—Fiction. 2. Women gardeners—Fiction. 3. New York (N.Y.)—Fiction. 4. Large type books. I. Title.
PS3608.A78328S58 2011b
813'.6—dc22   2011014777

Published in 2011 by arrangement with St. Martin's Press, LLC.

Printed in the United States of America
1 2 3 4 5 6 7 15 14 13 12 11

For Mary M. Simari
1921–2010
Whose favorite saying was
"Watch your back!"

ACKNOWLEDGMENTS

Special thanks to NYPD Det. Marco Conelli; bestselling author and NYC medical examiner Jonathan Hayes; Ed MacFarlane; Margaret Norton; and my fellow volunteers at the Philadelphia International Flower Show, Cheryl Carter, Laura DiPreta; and to all the beekeepers I know. I've learned so much from all of you. Thanks for letting me pick your brains.

Many thanks to David Baldeosingh Rotstein for another inventive cover for a book with an unusual title, to my editor, Allison Strobel, for her support and insightful comments, and to my amazing copy editor, Martha Schwartz.

And as always, thanks to Bruce.

Flowers always make people better,
happier, and more helpful; they are
sunshine, food and medicine to the soul.
— Luther Burbank

A cynic is a man who, when he smells
flowers, looks around for a coffin.
— H. L. Mencken

ONE

When I was eight, I was convinced I could disappear. It's not as crazy as it sounds. It wasn't as if I saw dead people or thought I could beam myself to another planet. I did it all the time. Grown-ups and teachers would smile and glide past me to torture another poor kid who hadn't cultivated this valuable skill.

It had been years since I'd thought about this long-neglected talent, but I prayed it was like riding a bicycle as I crouched in a shed, hoping the person who'd already killed two people would not see me or the women I was hiding.

"You in there, little girl . . . ?"

Four days earlier . . .

Rolanda Knox was formidable. I could attest to that. I pictured her laying out her uniform with all the pomp and ceremony of a warrior going into battle. Freshly pressed dark blue material. Shoes, belt buckle, and badge so shiny she could start fires with them if she needed to. This would be a grueling assignment and she'd need all her patience, experience, and powers of observation to ensure things went smoothly. Not that they ever did. No matter how prepared you were, something or someone always came along to gum up the works.

My name's Paula Holliday. Rolanda Knox, who in my mind had earned the nickname "Fort," had stared me down with a surprising ferocity two days before. Her actual words were "talk to the hand," an expression I've never really understood but which commands a certain respect when the hand in question is almost as big as your own head.

I wasn't listed in the official show directory, only in the addendum, and from her post at the entrance to Hall E, Rolanda had interrogated me as if I'd been trying to gate-crash the Pentagon. She'd even subjected the printed insert in my badge holder to the low-tech spit-and-rub test to make sure it wasn't counterfeit. All weekend long I'd bear the traces of her smeared thumbprint. Knox was a security guard; and in this day and age, no one was getting into her convention center without proper documentation no matter how long it took and who was tapping her toes and glaring from the back of the line.

The young man Rolanda was talking to must not have had his papers in order, but he was persistent. He'd be no match for her if it came to a physical confrontation — but that was unlikely. He didn't look stupid, just young and cocky in a T-shirt and baggy pants — too certain the quick smile and boyish charm, which had probably earned him a 90 percent return rate elsewhere, would work on this woman, too. He was mistaken.

The wall of polyester dared him to pass. It wasn't just the wide expanse of fabric covering a well-muscled figure. And it wasn't the badge. Who was impressed by authority anymore? It was a steely look in the woman's eyes that conveyed her dead serious attitude. Stopping this boy would be no big deal. She'd be like a water buffalo swatting at a cattle egret: barely breaking a sweat. Then, something the kid said caused a slight chink in the woman's armor, but she held her ground.

"Absolutely nothing," she said. "Now, get that chicken chest out of my sight." But this time she dismissed him the way you'd shoo away a pesky child.

He looked vaguely familiar — pale, with straw-colored hair and a mischievous Tom Sawyer expression on his face that could get you to paint the fence for him and thank him for it. The faded T-shirt read Happy Valley, and tied around his waist was a denim jacket covered with dozens of souvenir patches. He could have been any of the young workers hustling around the Wagner Center on Manhattan's West Side on this early spring morning, but he wasn't.

The boy scoped out the crowd, looking for an entrance with a less imposing gatekeeper or a sucker. He found me, just as my eyes lingered on him a second too long, struggling to remember where I'd seen him.

"Yo, Adrian."

That was it. The art museum. The morning before I'd been jogging near the museum and couldn't resist the urge to run up the steps and wave my hands over my head Rocky Balboa–style. To my utter humiliation the spectacle of a thirtysomething-year-old woman pretending to be Sylvester Stallone had been witnessed by someone who peered out of the shadows and applauded. He was huddled in the doorway, surrounded by bags. Something told me he wasn't waiting for the Matisse exhibit to open.

I assumed he was a runaway. His belongings had been clustered around his ankles and his backpack had been punched down, probably used as a pillow. Like the jacket he'd been wearing, one of the bags bore patches from colorful destinations not generally frequented by runaways and homeless kids.

"She's tough," he said, walking over to me and motioning toward Rolanda.

"She lightened up toward the end. I thought you had her. What did you say?"

"I asked if last night had meant nothing to her." He shrugged. "It was worth a try. Humor sometimes works wonders with authority figures." He said it like a kid who had experience getting around people with equal parts of charm and flattery applied liberally with a shovel.

It would hardly have affected national security to let him slip into the convention center; but, in fairness, Fort Knox was just doing her job. Who wanted to be the one to let in the psycho-killer because he seemed harmless and had playfully suggested they'd had a tryst the night before? The show would open to the public in two days. I advised him to wait until then and buy a ticket.

"Can't. I need to see one of the exhibitors before the show starts," he said. "It's *super* important."

What constituted "super important" for someone halfway between skateboard age and first-real-job age was anyone's guess. How urgent could it be? Knox shot us a look that warned *don't try any funny business,* and I aborted the sales pitch before it came.

"I don't have any extra badges. I'm a one-woman show. Just manning a booth for a friend. And I don't know anyone else at the show well enough to ask."

"I know a couple," he said, looking around, "but they don't know I'm here." He eyeballed the rest of the exhibitors in line, preoccupied, furiously fingering Black-Berrys or sucking on coffees to help them wake up. He quickly calculated the odds and stuck with me.

"If you can't get me in, will you deliver a note for me?" He took my silent intake of breath as assent. "Perfect." He dropped his things on the floor and rummaged through his backpack until he found a scratch pad, pilfered from a budget hotel chain a half step up from the museum's doorway. He pointed to my thick show directory. "Can I borrow that to write on?" He scribbled his note, then folded it over four times. "It's private. You can't tell anyone."

Two

Why was I such a softie? Where was the ruthless media exec who had trampled corn-fed kids like this on her way to the board room or edit suite in a previous lifetime? "Okay, who gets it?" I asked, holding out my hand for the note and the directory.

"The company's new. I'm not sure which name they've settled on, so I need to look it up." He stood up and clumsily juggled the note, the directory, and his bags. The throng of exhibitors waiting to set up condensed, and we slid a few feet closer to the door, the way you do at Disneyland or airport security when you need to feel like you're getting somewhere but in fact aren't. I picked up one of his bags to keep his belongings together. While he searched the bricklike book for his friend's name, I inspected the patches on the bag. I'd been to a lot of the same places — Hong Kong,

Rome, Utah. As he flipped through the pages, the crowd clustered around Rolanda until the doors were opened and a gold-rush-like sweep of people attempted to enter the halls all at once. Credentials were checked carefully at every door and we inched up to the door of Hall E until it was our turn.

"I know he doesn't work for you, missy." Rolanda Knox peered at my badge to let me know she'd remember me. *Miss Holliday, Primo's Outdoor Art.* And you, Mr. Happy Valley, how many times do I have to tell you, you ain't going nowhere? How do I know you don't have an incendiary device in those bags? Or an envelope of anthrax?"

I was still holding the guy's bag and reflexively held it out toward him. Great. I'd be collateral damage and an unwitting accomplice to a terrorist act or some obscure ecological protest like Free the Albino Tree Frogs. Passionate and ready to take a stand, a handful of antichemical demonstrators with placards were stationed outside the convention center. For all we knew, this kid was one of them. He made a move to open the bag with his free hand.

"Don't do that, fool. I don't want to see your dirty laundry. You never heard of a rhetorical question? I was simply illustrating a point. No badge, no entry."

We'd stepped aside to let in a slight man in a black cotton outfit, who'd obligingly raised his badge up to Rolanda's eye level, when a bloodcurdling scream ripped through the cavernous convention center.

"What the . . ."

THREE

All heads turned to see what the commotion was. Other security guards and exhibitors rushed in, only some running toward the screams that had now escalated into wails. Rolanda held her arms out wide, but it was like trying to hold back the ocean or a surging crowd of European soccer fans.

"Oh, hell." She dropped her arms and sprinted, as much as a large woman can sprint, in the direction of the cries. Rolanda was the largest and most intimidating of the Wagner Center staff, and the crowd parted for her. The shrieks were coming from the direction of my booth, so I rode in her slipstream.

Near a grass shack, under a banner that read *Connie's Brooklyn Beach Garden,* was a blond woman dressed in an outfit that suggested she'd raided the closet of the Little Mermaid's promiscuous older sister. The top was a shrunken Sergeant Pepper–style vest with two small fabric lobsters instead of epaulets on the shoulders and scallop shell appliques cupping her breasts. Across the back was an octopus whose tentacles reached to the front, grabbing the wearer around the waist. Someone spent hours of his or her life creating this garment. It was impossible not to stare.

"My veronica. My veronica's dead."

Two women from nearby booths brought a conch-shaped chair from the back of her display. Without thinking, the woman I assumed was Connie sat down heavily on the papier-mâché chair, and it collapsed, eliciting a ripple of laughter from some teenagers on the fringes of the group. A woman in overalls, who wasn't much older than they, gave them a stern look; but it wasn't easy to maintain since she was chuckling herself.

A trade show volunteer in a bright yellow pinny fanned the woman with a straw hat, and a weather-beaten exhibitor in a smock produced a pack of cigarettes that the woman smacked away. The smoker stood with her arms folded as if to say, *In that case, I'll just enjoy the meltdown.* She scanned the crowd and fixed an accusatory gaze on the teenagers that shut them up more effectively than their companion had.

Rolanda explored the partial ruins of a

cloyingly sweet flower bed filled with a staggering number of cardboard fish and plaster crustaceans. In the rear, a painted sign paid homage to Nathan's Famous hot dogs and thick-cut fries, two Coney Island staples.

The woman's eye makeup spread out like a Rorschach test. The creator of a nearby Zen garden drifted over to console her. "Sometimes plants die," he said. "It's a circle."

"Listen, grasshopper, circle this. My garden looks like it's been kissed by a blowtorch. Don't talk to me about impermanence. I'm not shopping for enlightenment right now, so why don't you just scurry back to your little hut and rake the sand again?" Ouch. The pajama-clad man backed away.

Any sympathy the shrieking blonde might have garnered evaporated. She'd been rude to the hat fanner, the smoker, and now a Zen gardener. It was as if she'd trashed the Dalai Lama. The Little Mermaid's less nice sibling fiddled with her cell phone and jutted her chin in the direction of an exuberant display garden, prejudged and already festooned with ribbons. It belonged to a Mrs. Jean Moffitt.

"That old dame practically has armed sentries stationed at *her* displays. Where are my sentries? I've ruined five nail wraps on this exhibit, and someone has sabotaged it. And don't think I don't know why." She held the phone to her ear and waited for it to come to life.

"There's no one here," the security guard said, after a thorough check around the display and inside and behind the fake grass beach house.

"Veronica, veronica," the woman persisted. She raised a freshly manicured hand and pointed to a mound of desiccated plants. Formerly blue, formerly tall and willowy.

Under her breath, Rolanda Knox muttered, "Welcome to the Big Apple Flower Show."

FOUR

Connie Anzalone stared down the few remaining bystanders with a slightly less friendly look than she'd given the Zen gardener and they wisely scattered, leaving just Rolanda and me. Rolanda was paid to stick around, but what was my excuse? In addition to being mesmerized by the outfit, I was drawn to the spectacle of a grown woman throwing a tantrum over a few dead plants. Her veronicas had gone to that great compost heap in the sky. It happened: the little suckers don't always do as they're told. You feed them, you water them, and do they thank you? No. Sometimes they gave it up to pests, bacteria, fungus, or a good stiff wind and they didn't even say good-bye. I kept silent while Rolanda tried to do what the Zen gardener couldn't.

"Calm down, ma'am. I'll alert someone from show management, and I'm sure they'll mount a complete investigation."

I couldn't tell if the guard was joking, but within minutes a frosty woman of about thirty arrived to defuse the situation. She introduced herself as Kristi Reynolds, director of the Big Apple Flower Show.

She had a Bluetooth implant in her head and I would have bet there were two larger implants farther south. I could visualize her standing in front of a weather map, making sweeping motions with her arms and maintaining the same manic smile whether she was forecasting sunshine or tsunami.

Much like the kid who'd tried to sneak in, Kristi was a smooth talker. She assured the woman that should anyone be found responsible, they would be prosecuted to the fullest extent of the law.

"For what," I muttered. "Herbicide?" Kristi glared in my direction. Her eyes traveled to the name on my badge but all the while she kept the same smile, the smile facial expression.

Either another emergency call had come in or Kristi had perfected the artful exit. She tilted her head and nodded to an unseen speaker, fluttering her eyelids — the only sign that the caller was delivering bad news.

"Oh, dear. I'll be right there," she said. "Seems someone has borrowed a baseball bat from the Bambi-no booth and decapitated a gnome. I must fly. And you, Rolanda, need to get back to your post. Those fanatical protesters could be pouring in right now, ready to do more damage. Let's get Otis to clean this up." The two women exchanged forced smiles before Kristi turned on her heels and clacked away.

"Otis works at night," Rolanda said, under her breath and out of earshot. "She doesn't even know who's on duty at her own event."

"Bambi-no?"

"Another one of you lunatic vendors. The man's dressed like Babe Ruth. What the hell that has to do with gardening I don't know." I nodded sympathetically.

I trailed Rolanda back to her post, still holding the gatecrasher's bag. I could tell she was disappointed in herself for abandoning her station, so I waited for an appropriate moment to give her the boy's bag. At the door I saw that my exhibitor's directory had been placed on Rolanda's chair. The Happy Valley kid was long gone, presumably inside the hallowed halls without the all-important exhibitor's badge. Whoever it was he needed to reach, he'd do it without my help.

"You see why I can't let unauthorized people in?" Rolanda said. "People like you think I'm a martinet, checking papers like I'm the border patrol, but the rules are the rules. The minute anything goes wrong, you got hysterical people like the Fish Lady and Ms. Reynolds screaming conspiracy."

I silently agreed and moved to hand her the bag.

"I don't want that thing," she said, pushing my hand away. "What am I supposed to do with it?"

"Isn't there a lost and found?"

"It doesn't open officially until the show does. Just hold on to it. You'll probably see the little peckerwood before I do, wandering around, stealing stuff. My job is to stand here for eight hours with one forty-five minute lunch break and two informal bathroom breaks, so that's what I'm going to do. You tell your friend if I see him again, I'll bounce him out on his Happy Valley butt."

"If he comes back looking for the bag, my booth number is eleven forty-two."

"Wait — let me write that down. Don't you think I can find you if I need to?"

I said nothing, but retrieved my directory and headed to the curtained thirty-by-ten plot that would be my home until the show closed.

Another shriek split the air, but this time I

didn't bite. Given the high-strung nature of the flower show participants, it could have been a slug or a leaf miner. I had the luxury of ignoring it and going for coffee, but Rolanda didn't.

Now what? she muttered.

FIVE

After the bigger shows in Philly and Boston, the Big Apple Flower Show was the Northeast's oldest and most prestigious, sponsored by a consortium of local garden clubs. I'd only been once before and not as an exhibitor. I'm a gardener. It's been three years since I hung out my shingle in Springfield, Connecticut: Dirty Business Garden Solutions. Quite a change from my former job producing videos for a boutique production company in lower Manhattan — just as much dirt but of a different sort. At least that's how I started. More recently, only some of the solutions have been garden related. I've developed a reputation as something of a problem solver.

I wouldn't have been at the Big Apple show if it hadn't been for Babe Chinnery and an eccentric artist named Primo Dunstan. Babe owned the Paradise Diner, where I spent more time and ate more carbs than

I should since moving from New York to Connecticut.

Primo was her pal. And he was a character. No one referred to him as strange or antisocial, although he was certainly both, and no one spoke of him as the town hermit either, although he lived alone in the house his parents had left him surrounded by two acres full of scrap iron, broken lawn furniture, and machine and auto parts that made his yard look like the innards of an old television set or that stretch of New Jersey highway that resembles a giant computer motherboard.

Primo had startled some young girls on their way to school one morning and there'd been an ugly rumor until one of the girls recanted. After that, he rarely ventured out except to ride his bicycle around town, filling two hand-wrought wire baskets with interesting junk he obtained foraging through garbage. That was how he'd met Babe, behind her diner.

The good ladies of Springfield worried about Primo and were pondering their humanitarian course of action when one day he showed up at the diner with a five-foot-long iron dragonfly he'd hoped to barter for food.

Babe was appreciative and happily fixed

Primo lunch while he and Babe's boyfriend, Neil, soldered the oversized darning needle onto the diner's neon marquee. The next day, she got a slew of offers for the unusual sculpture but turned them all down. Instead, she encouraged Dunstan to bring in smaller works she'd display and sell in the diner. That's how Babe's makeshift gallery was created. That was when Primo's status was elevated from weirdo to a "character," code for a weirdo with money or an artistic bent.

Since then, Primo's found-materials sculptures had gotten modest press, giving him a reprieve from the do-gooders who wanted to fix whatever it was they thought was wrong with him — his hair, his clothing, and his social life or lack of one. Some said he had Asperger's, but Babe insisted he had just never gotten around to cultivating his social skills. She was the one who had the bright idea Primo should exhibit at the flower show with me managing the booth, since he was far too shy to do it himself. Like I said — I'm a sucker.

Six

When Babe wasn't finding work for me, she was trying to fix me up. The jury was still out on her latest matchmaking effort: Hank Mossdale, a stable owner in Springfield. We had met over a mountain of manure he'd generously offered on Freecycle, an online bulletin board where people found takers for their unwanted stuff. I was the only nibble. Hank and I had shared a few diner meals but no actual dates until Babe donned her matchmaker hat and suggested he drive to New York on Monday, to help me deliver Primo's unsold items to a library in Ridgewood, where she had arranged for a private showing the following week. Surprisingly, Hank said yes.

During the flower show, I would crash at Lucy Cavanaugh's apartment. She was my oldest friend and one of my last real connections to my life in New York. I had no serious regrets about leaving the big city, just the occasional twinge when Lucy jetted off to some exotic place and I found myself shoveling compost or dining alone with my seed catalogs.

This time Lucy was somewhere in Central America for work. She was delighted to let me use her place and anything in her closets, since in her fashionista math it would bring down the cost per wear of any clothes I borrowed. Always happy to be of service, I arrived a few days early.

My booth neighbors at the flower show were David Heller, one half of a Brooklyn Heights couple who made light fixtures with botanical motifs, and Nikki Bingham, a chatty antiques dealer from upstate New York. Nikki and her much-mentioned but never-seen husband specialized in vintage and reproduction garden furniture.

Both she and David subscribed to the notion that food is love, and it was abundantly clear that every morning and afternoon would be punctuated with a platter of rich, breadlike substances in which we would all be encouraged to partake lest we be considered antisocial. She came over and held open a white cardboard box, and the smell of cinnamon filled my booth.

"Crumb cakes," she said. "I made them myself."

"I had a big breakfast," I fibbed. I set down my things and pitched the gatecrasher's bag in my booth under a standard trade-show rental, a six-foot table tastefully stapled with royal blue plastic. "Maybe later."

David Heller didn't have an ounce of fat on his rangy body and had no such reservations about the crumb cakes. He plucked a thick square from the box and a gust of brown powder escaped.

"Quite an outburst this morning. Anyone know what happened?" David licked cinnamon sugar from his fingers one at a time.

Nikki launched into a detailed re-creation of events, including a very good, if unkind imitation of Connie Anzalone's hysterics. "I wasn't there, but I heard about it in the ladies' room. That's where you get all the best info."

"Her garden didn't look that bad, but she was pretty upset," I said. Why kick the woman when she was down? Connie Anzalone was an easy target. The Little Mermaid outfit didn't help.

"She'll recover," Nikki said, mouth full. "And you watch, two guys named Paulie and Vito will be guarding her booth tonight." She flicked her nose with her index finger, leaving a trail of cinnamon on her left nostril.

David's eyebrows rose over hipster, tortoiseshell frames. "Do you know her?"

"A little bird told me. Her husband's *connected,* if you know what I mean." Nikki had already downed two pieces of cinnamon cake, so she settled for picking at the topping on her third. "Apparently you don't get your lawn mowed in her neighborhood without Connie's husband's say-so."

SEVEN

Michelangelo, da Vinci, Puccini, and all my Italian ancestors were banging on the inside of my head, urging me to uphold the honor of my people. Or at least half my people; the Irish half didn't mind a bit.

"I think everyone whose name ends in a vowel has to deny they're in the mob, at least once in their lives," I said.

"I only know what I was told." Nikki sniffed. Having denuded the third piece of cake she put it out of its misery and polished off what was left. "You have to admit, she *is* a fish out of water in this atmosphere." She paused, and then snorted at her own unintentional joke.

With or without the garish costume, Connie Anzalone *was* a fish out of water. Apart from her, the Big Apple crowd was comprised of Mayflower bluebloods who probably never touched dirt themselves, smooth-talking hucksters selling Hansel and Gretel–

like sheds and sunrooms (Is there no one left selling electric organs in suburban malls?), and garden club doyennes with big hats and short white gloves. With her long nails, white-blond hair, and — shall we say — salty language, Ms. Anzalone was a breath of fresh air. Although her fashion and landscaping choices weren't my style, she'd managed to get here, and if she didn't have a right to verbally abuse her neighbors, she did have a right to be pissed off if she thought her garden had been intentionally sabotaged.

I identified with that fish-out-of-water feeling. I'd felt it many times in Springfield, especially on days when money was tight, the phone didn't ring, and I wondered if I'd made the right decision to leave everything and everyone I knew and move to the suburbs. But all it took was one person to make me feel welcome. I promised myself — and my Italian ancestors — I'd swing by Connie's booth to say *ciao* and *buona fortuna* before the end of the day.

For the rest of the day we shared box cutters, duct tape, and crumb cake, and critiqued one another's displays. Placement was everything — one inch to the left or right could change destinies, or so I was told. Primo's sculptures didn't need much attention, but it took hours to unwrap, assemble, store the bubble wrap, and find the proper arrangement to make them irresistible.

As heavy as Primo's sculptures were, they would have cost a small fortune to ship, so once again Babe had enlisted the help of friends. If they wanted to stay on Babe's good side, truckers passing through New York allowed themselves to be shanghai'ed into delivering pieces to the convention center. It had been going on for the past three days, ever since the earliest exhibitors with the most elaborate displays arrived. The good news was that the shipping was free. The bad news was that I was never sure when items would arrive, so I had to be there every day since setup began. Most likely I'd be moving things the next day to make room for new arrivals, so I tried not to obsess about placement. Hopefully all the pieces would arrive by Friday morning in time for that evening's reception. If not I had a slide show on my laptop, including pieces too big or too expensive to ship.

A veteran of these events, David had his own displays that showed off his chandeliers, sconces, and table lamps to best advantage. He also had a giant copper tub that held hundreds of pinecone-shaped nightlights, his bestselling item.

"We're all hoping for that one big score," he said, "but you'll see, I'll be refilling this tub all weekend. It makes people feel like they've *been* somewhere if they buy something. And a five-dollar nightlight is easier to say yes to than a torchère in the shape of a weeping cherry tree."

He had a point. It also explained the popularity of those T-shirts with *Someone Went on a Cruise and All I Got Was This Lousy T-shirt* inscriptions.

After perfecting her own booth, Nikki set her sights on mine. "You need a real tablecloth. Did you bring one? No worries. I have one you can use."

All Primo's pieces were named, and I was busy labeling them when Nikki came over to help.

"You know, if you move this piece to the left — see it lines up with the *P* in *Primo* on the sign — the arrangement will be more symmetrical." She stepped back to admire her handiwork. I failed to see how that would improve sales but thanked her anyway.

Our three booths were in a ghetto, but a nice, arty one. The smaller, nonfloral exhibits were relegated to an area known as the Garden Shop. If the display gardens got all the publicity and the photo ops, the shops did the real business and paid for the show. Prefab gazebos, fertilizers, and antique pots shared space with what must have been an entire container-load of merchandise from China — chimes, resin figures of St. Anthony, and a hundred different items with hummingbirds or frogs plastered on them. And curly willow. It would be a small miracle if no one was impaled or had an eye put out by one of the ubiquitous corkscrew branches.

Purists grumbled that Kristi Reynolds had no low bar and anyone who put an X on a check could exhibit at the show, but that was generally a sentiment shared by those who didn't accept that gardening was a multibillion-dollar business and wasn't just about pretty flowers and afternoon tea on the veranda. A large part of that business involved the systematic genocide of deer, chipmunks, squirrels, and slugs — creatures made lovable by the likes of Walt Disney, Chuck Jones, and various children's book authors but much reviled by any gardener who's had her heart broken when her tulips, hostas, and bird food disappeared. Someone once said that gardening was all about sex and death. He might well have added murder.

EIGHT

This year's most ballyhooed product was SlugFest, a supposedly guaranteed slug repellent. While that might not register high on the wish lists of most people, to a gardener, it ranked right up there with world peace. And if it worked, its creators could make a fortune — gardeners were constantly looking for a magic bullet to keep the little critters from munching expensive plants and leaving silvery trails all over the garden like so many chalk-outlined bodies. Copper wire, baking soda, beer in shallow containers — the last was my favorite method for dispatching the little buggers. Showing no preference for imported or domestic beer, they slithered into the containers and died with a buzz on. On one hand, plenty of humans wouldn't mind going out that way, and it beat being crushed under the heel of a garden clog. On the other, disposing of a container of bloated, decomposing slugs was not one of the most fun things I'd ever had to do. Where do you put them? Do you bury them? Say a few words? Leave them out for the birds to deal with? I did that once and then worried I'd caused a nest of chickadees to be born with fetal alcohol syndrome or the avian equivalent.

SlugFest's booth was six times the size of Primo's, but as of Wednesday, no one had seen anything other than their rotating hologram, a slug inching toward a hosta and then vanishing, and half a dozen female employees, decked out in salmon-colored polo shirts and khaki pants so unflattering it was a wonder any of them took the job.

Rumor had it that Scott Reiger, the company's founder, was close to a major distribution deal with an international chemical company, but no samples were on display and no one had gotten as much as a whiff of the actual product for fear that it would be ripped off.

"We're in a good spot, strategically," Nikki said. "He'll bring a lot of action our way." That's what we all wanted — action.

NINE

After three hours I called it a day. I stored the packing materials, leaving one box intact for box cutters, water bottles, and whatever supplies I'd need during the show. I tucked a piece of bubble wrap around the bag I was babysitting to make it less attractive to potential thieves. It was a drawstring bag with some of the same patches I'd noticed on the kid's jacket. I wasn't normally a suspicious person, but why tempt anyone? I was surprised the kid hadn't come back for it, but perhaps he'd run into another security guard with the same SWAT team training and dedication Rolanda Knox had. When the lost and found opened, I'd dump it.

In the meantime I headed to the ladies' room to wash up. Two women entered, whispering conspicuously in a fashion guaranteed to attract attention. One of them I'd seen at this morning's excitement; she was the charmer who'd offered Connie Anzalone the cigarette.

Her badge read Allegra Douglas, Riverdale Garden Club. Allegra was all of four foot eleven in ballet flats, slim black slacks, and a black smock not unlike the ones worn by employees at department store makeup counters. Her short gray hair looked like half a dozen steel wool pads had been knitted together to form an unbecoming cap, and her eyes were rimmed with a black pencil liner in a style that no doubt suited her better in her youth. Her companion was a jolly woman in frameless glasses, a white turtleneck, and a novelty sweater bearing the image of an enormous golden retriever and the message *Prince of Pups.* She had the same sloppy, puppylike demeanor as a golden, and if she'd been any shorter, I'd have been sorely tempted to bend down and scratch her behind the ears.

We mumbled hellos and I continued scrubbing my hands with a small nailbrush and a bar of gardener's soap I'd brought from home. I was stunned when Allegra blissfully ignored the Thank You for Not Smoking sign, produced a pack of Winstons, and lit up. She inhaled deeply, then released a plume of smoke that drifted my way. I imagined her forty years younger, hand on hip in a slinky dress. The only things missing were the cigarette holder and a martini glass.

"All I know is the exhibitors' committee opened a Pandora's box when they started allowing *that* element into the competition. This is the second year, and it's changed the entire complexion of the event." She dragged on her cigarette again, and her cheeks and the wizened, red scar that was her mouth were sucked into her skull.

"You'd know," the retrieverlike friend agreed. A perfect straight man.

The smoke was getting to me, but I was nosy enough to want to know who they were discussing. I dried my hands and fished in my bag for an emery board I knew I didn't have. I kept listening.

"For one hundred years, this show has kept to the highest standards, and now . . ." Allegra didn't finish her sentence but made a sweeping gesture with her right hand as if her friend and I could see the obvious destruction in our midst. Was it possible she'd been exhibiting that long? Could be.

She squinted and tipped her helmet head back, trying to read the name on my badge to see if I was one of the interlopers. I abandoned my phony search and turned to face the tiny despot full-on. "Excuse me," I said, "you seem to know so much about the show. This is my first time exhibiting."

"Oh, please don't take anything Allegra said personally," the friend said. "She didn't mean *you*."

It hadn't even occurred to me that they might be talking about me, but if she felt like apologizing, I'd accept it on behalf of whomever they were maligning.

"It's the public school exhibit," the friend said, lowering her voice. "Allegra feels some of the students aren't taking the show seriously."

That's right, heaven forbid anyone have fun at a flower show. I had seen the teenagers near Connie's beach garden but assumed they were volunteers or kids pressed into service as some sort of punishment, not fledgling gardeners. Apparently, they were exhibiting.

"And if you ask me," Allegra said, running the tap to douse her cigarette after a few more hearty puffs, "someone should talk to *them* about these little mishaps we've been having this year."

"Mishaps?" I asked.

"The headless gnomes? The crew cut on Mrs. Hamilton's dwarf bamboo?" They were stunned by my ignorance. "Ask anyone in the members' lounge," Allegra said,

46

knowing full well I wasn't a member. The door flapped as she strode out of the ladies' room, her meek friend and the stench of stale smoke trailing behind her. On their way out they all but knocked down the young woman in overalls I'd seen earlier. She closed her eyes as if counting to ten.

TEN

"I tell my students high school is only four years — what's happening now is just one brief chapter in their lives. Then I meet a woman like that and I'm beamed back to my own high school days. Mean girls. Even when they get old, they stay mean girls."

"True," I said. "Although I doubt if anyone has referred to Allegra Douglas as a *girl* in quite some time." I introduced myself.

"Lauryn Peete. I'd shake but my hands are grubby." She held them up as if it were a stickup. Other than that, she looked tidy in ironed overalls and a clean, long-sleeved T-shirt with the sleeves pushed up. Her hair was almost entirely covered by a wide headband; just a soft, lamblike fuzz escaped out the back.

Lauryn told me she taught at High School 240 and still loved the job now as much as she had that first day when one of her students brought in a plant and pretended not to know it was a marijuana seedling. "They must have thought I was going to run crying to the principal," she said. Instead the pot plant inspired her to start a garden project with her homeroom class.

That year they grudgingly planted annuals in the front of the school, mostly bedraggled flats that Lauryn had wheedled out of a local supermarket. The following semester they started seeds on the windowsill. Easy stuff — basil, parsley, morning glories. Seeds almost guaranteed to germinate because Lauryn didn't want her students' early efforts not to bear fruit. "They're good kids, despite what that Ms. Douglas thinks."

Of course, some kids couldn't be bothered. This was real life, not some touchy-feely after-school movie. But every year four or five students got into it, enough to convince the principal and the school board to front them the money to enter a borough-wide contest that they ended up winning. Jamal Harrington was among them.

At least one of her fellow teachers thought Jamal was too much of a favorite and secretly suggested Lauryn's botanical teachings were helping Jamal cultivate a garden less likely to result in an appearance on *Martha Stewart* and more likely an appearance before a judge — charged with growing and intending to distribute a controlled substance — but Lauryn took the high road and ignored them, even though Jamal had been in trouble in the past.

Not all the Big Apple participants had appreciated the lifelike rubber rat Jamal had used to adorn his part of the school's garden exhibit — a fire escape trellis. According to Lauryn, he had thrown himself into the project and had even confided his dreams of becoming an artist or set designer. But that wasn't something he wanted spread around. In Jamal's neighborhood that kind of talk could get the crap knocked out of you.

I thought the fake rat sounded clever, but apparently it had been responsible for a few rapid heartbeats during setup, so the students were personae non gratae with some attendees, including Allegra Douglas.

"To paraphrase Jamal, these other entrants think their manure smells better than ours does." After my own encounter with Allegra, I tended to agree with Jamal. Forewarned about the rat, I promised to check on their exhibit the next day.

On the way out, we bumped into a woman who was dressed like an extra from the film *A League of Their Own* — baseball cap with the bill worn high like a 1950s gas pump jockey and a peach-colored romper that suggested gym bloomers from the same time period. Maybe her own. She gave us a tired smile and kept walking.

"What's up with the retro baseball outfit?" Lauryn said, once the woman had passed.

"She's selling something. I'm sure she'd be happy to tell us at great length. Want to go back?" Neither of us did.

ELEVEN

The really huge New York conventions —
the boat shows and the car shows — were
held at the Javits Center. The Big Apple
Flower Show had remained at the more
intimate Wagner Center, and that was probably what had kept both alive. If the Javits
Center was all glass and as much natural
light as possible, the Wagner was a throw-
back, dark and stuccoed. Some considered
it a landmark, one of the last vestiges of an
early postmodern era. Others found it an
eyesore, an unfortunate reminder of a bleak
time in American architecture and a blight
on its up-and-coming neighborhood now
filled with as many galleries and event
spaces as there were taxi companies, auto
repair shops, and one-room Caribbean
music studios. Lucy's apartment was ten
blocks south of the Wagner, and I looked
forward to walking and people watching on
the way back to her place.

Every once in a while I felt the pull of the city — the excitement, the stores and the styles changing, the hot new show or restaurant. The newest thing in Springfield was a garden shop two friends were opening and the girls' high school soccer team, which was faring pretty well considering their star player's recent bout with bulimia. Soccer was the great equalizer in the suburbs. In the city it was still something foreigners did, except every few years when the World Cup was played and hipsters tried to show how cool they were by pretending to be interested.

I returned to the booth for my laptop and before leaving, stopped at a concession stand for an afternoon caffeine fix. The octopus caught my eye instantly. Connie Anzalone stood in line ahead of me. Her body language screamed almost as loudly as she had that morning, only this time it was saying, *Stay the hell away.*

The ancestors advised me to try anyway.

"How are you doing?" I asked. No answer. I repeated it in case she hadn't heard me.

"Just peachy." She barely turned her head to see who'd spoken.

Last time I listen to a bunch of dead people. I'd overheard security guards saying the flower show crowd was proving to be

53

just as cutthroat as the dog show people had been the week before — "just two-legged b*tches not four-legged ones." I stared straight ahead, studying the items on the blackboard menu as if there were going to be a quiz. When it was Connie's turn, she placed her order in a small, childlike voice at odds with the snappish tone she'd just used with me. She thanked the cashier and left a bill in the cardboard tip cup. Moments later, on my way down the escalator to street level, someone touched my arm. I was startled and sloshed hot coffee on my gloved hand.

"I'm so sorry. Are you okay? That was terribly rude of me, upstairs. I don't know what's come over me. I'm not usually like this. Most people think I'm nice. I *am* nice." The tough-girl mask had fallen away, and Connie's face had totally changed. For a minute she looked like a girl playing dress up in her mother's clothes and makeup, much younger than the heavy paint job and cotton candy hair suggested.

We reached the street level and stepped over to a counter, where I peeled off the wet glove, turned it inside out, and shoved it in my pocket.

"I'll replace those."

"No need. Three dollars from any street

vendor except when it's really cold. Then the price goes up to five."

"This is my first time. Some of the others have been, well, mean to me. One of the exhibitors even made a comment about seeing too much when I bent down. Muffin top."

It was a more personal remark than I expected. "If you've got muffin top, it's a low-fat minimuffin," I said. "It's not you. There seems to be an acceptable level of hostility toward the newbies. Some sort of horticultural hazing ritual."

Connie looked at me as if I were speaking a foreign language.

"Gardeners can be compulsive. Everyone gets so crazed about their booths and their entries. It's business, not personal." Did I really say that to a woman who looked like a Mafia princess? She burst out laughing, and so did I. Maybe in the city, *The Godfather* was the great equalizer.

"Let me make it up to you," she said. "How about something stronger than coffee? Can I buy you a glass of champagne? My husband, Guy, says it's the only thing I can drink without getting loopy." Loopy? Not a word you hear every day in that context.

Perhaps I should listen to the dead relatives more often. Five minutes ago, I thought she was going to hand me a smackdown. Now she wanted to buy me a drink, and I rarely say no to champagne — especially when someone else is buying.

"I'd like that," I said, "but I can't tonight. I'm just settling in at my friend's apartment. Can I get a rain check?"

Most people would have recognized the gentle brush-off, but Connie pressed the issue and I found myself agreeing to meet her for a drink the following night.

TWELVE

The cool early evening air off the river gave me more of a second wind than the coffee. Even at that hour I could see a dusting of electric-green buds in some of the trees, specks of pink or white in others. It was that time of year when changes in the cityscape were evident every day, sometimes every few hours.

I walked across the street from the park. New York was one of the safest big cities in the world and had been for as long as I could remember, as long as you didn't do anything stupid. And I prided myself on not doing too many stupid things. I resurrected my New York walk — fast, no sightseeing or window shopping, don't smile too much lest someone think you're drunk or stupid, which would make you easy prey. New Yorkers could navigate a crowd of tourists like sea lions, slipping in and out quickly but never touching one another.

57

I couldn't remember a time before Korean groceries dotted every available corner in New York City with canned goods, salad bars, pre-cut fruit, extensive selections of energy drinks, and fresh flowers twelve months of the year. No doubt there are names on leases and health department certificates, but to most people they are just the Koreans on Twenty-eighth or the Koreans on Seventeenth, et cetera. I headed for the Koreans on Eighth Avenue about three blocks from Lucy's. The outside flower stand was shielded by heavy plastic sheets to protect the merchandise, and I brushed aside the cold, clear panels to get to the front door. I sensed someone behind me, so I held the flaps open for an extra second but, seeing no one, I let them go. Inside the small market, I stocked up on provisions for the weekend.

When I'd arrived, Lucy's nearly empty kitchen had reminded me she was a single woman who generally ate out and probably hadn't stocked her pantry since a world-class Mardi Gras party thrown two years earlier attended by members of the Preservation Hall Band and half the New Orleans Saints bench. She still had foil packets of Pat O'Brien's Hurricane mix on the refrigerator door. Inexplicably, she also had ten or twelve envelopes of Orville Redenbacher's. I wasn't a good enough cook to turn sweet pink powder and popcorn into a meal, so I'd been replenishing at the Koreans one or two bags at a time.

After less than a block, the plastic I Love NY bag handles were stretched thin and cutting off the circulation in my fingers. I walked carefully, hoping the bags wouldn't break and I wouldn't have wasted forty dollars on chickpea and tuna salads the pigeons would be feasting on the next morning. I regrouped and changed hands while waiting for the traffic light to change.

Once again, I felt someone walking just a little too close behind me. There wasn't much traffic; a Lincoln Town Car idled on the other side of the street. That was good. I wasn't alone. In the same way flight attendants and fire drill captains always know their exit strategies, women who occasionally have to walk in New York at night develop a survival strategy. It was second nature.

We knew when to cross the street to avoid an unsavory character. We knew not to recite our telephone or credit card numbers out loud in a crowded bar, not to flash cash at an ATM, and not to leave half a drink on a table and then come back and drink it.

These are in the collective New York memories, the way farm kids automatically know cow stuff and children in seaside towns know about the tides. At least we do most of the time.

In addition to two salads, which wouldn't make very effective weapons, I was packing heat — four twelve-ounce cans of diet Red Bull that could put a sizeable dent in someone's Adam's apple if he messed with me. I'd taken a self-defense class once, and it was one of the few things I remembered. Go for the vulnerable spots — throat, groin, shins, eyes. I doubt the manufacturers had that in mind when they introduced the new, larger cans, but it was reassuring as I walked the rest of the way home.

THIRTEEN

Lucy's building was a five-story limestone next door to a church that housed a soup kitchen in its basement. Two mornings in a row I'd seen men lined up as early as six A.M.

There were a few steps down to the vestibule, where the mailboxes were, and then a locked glass front door that led to the lobby and to the apartments upstairs. Lucy lived on the fifth floor, in two studio apartments bought and combined a few years back when prices were down and she'd gotten a bonus for doing a highly rated story on the unscrupulous owners of a Long Island puppy mill. I had talked her out of adopting the three Havanese she fell in love with and now I regretted it; they'd have been good company in her absence.

My fingers were numb from the heavy bags, so I took a quick break on the third floor to switch hands and get the circulation back. That's when I heard someone jiggling the doorknob on the inside door, downstairs. I stopped to listen. There was a frustrated push against the door, all the glass panes shaking, then the sound of a person ringing all the doorbells in an attempt to get someone, anyone, to let him in. No one took the bait. I hurried up to the next landing, banging the bag that held the cans against my right shin. One of the vulnerable parts. Ouch, that would leave a mark.

On four, I caught a glimpse of a woman through the one-inch opening between her door and the chain that held it closed. She eyed me suspiciously.

"Hi," I said. "I'm Lucy's friend." Then I remembered where I was. In large cities people didn't always know their neighbors' names. Maybe it wasn't a geographical thing, just the times. You could have eight thousand Facebook friends but not know the name of the person living right on top of you. And as much as Lucy traveled, it was no surprise that her downstairs neighbor barely recognized her name.

"Lucy Cavanaugh, the woman on five. I'm apartment sitting while she's away. I'm here for the flower show." That struck a chord. The woman undid the chain and opened the door a bit more to take a closer look. She had a few decades on me, with straight blunt-cut hair, flecked with gray, that said, *I'm too serious to color my hair or have it styled.*

She wore a black sweatshirt and sweatpants and held a long metal rod that could have inflicted serious damage. If I didn't know better, I'd have thought she was an aging ninja warrior with an iron pugil stick, but I recognized the bar as part of an old-fashioned door lock, the kind where one end slips into a hole in the floor and the other into a bolt on the door. Only the oldest apartments in New York still had them.

A white Persian cat slipped out of her apartment and crept around her bare ankles to see what was going on.

"Get back inside, Tommy." She nudged the cat with her bare toes, but he didn't budge. "Technically this is three and your friend is on four. They don't count the first floor in this building for some reason. Absentee Italian owners, some European thing. Did you ring my bell?"

"No, ma'am." I dangled Lucy's keys so she could see I wasn't the culprit. As long as she held that iron bar I wasn't taking any chances. The cat hissed.

"Beautiful cat." I hoped complimenting

her cat would disarm her, literally and figuratively.

"Beautiful but deaf as a post. That's why I named him Tommy. Can't hear a thing. But I heard something. Probably the menu deliverymen. When I first moved here it was Jehovah's Witnesses who left stacks of literature in the hallway. No one wants to feed the soul anymore. Now it's all about the food. I shred the menus and use them in the litter boxes."

A second cat ran into the hallway and sniffed the plastic bags I'd placed on the steps while the woman and I spoke.

"That's Moochie. He thinks he owns the building. Always running around, looking for food. You'd think he was a stray. Come on, Mooch."

I bent down to play with the cat, then looked up to see if it was okay. The woman nodded. Rules of engagement: if you love my pet, you're probably all right.

She eyed the bags. "Supermarket on Ninth delivers. They're cheaper than the Koreans, too. Even with the delivery charges."

I thanked her for the tip, said good-bye to Moochie, and finished my way up the stairs to the sound of multiple door locks being thrown. With the bags hoisted on one hip like a baby I unlocked Lucy's door, then reenacted the same ritual the woman below me had — chain, bolt, bolt. I piled the groceries and my backpack on the aluminum kitchen set and collapsed on Lucy's sofa.

The apartment had originally been a floor-through cut up into studios, two per floor, by the building's previous owner. Lucy's plan was to knock down the dividing wall, restoring it to a larger one bedroom; but the renovation had hit a snag after she'd had an argument with her contractor. (Never sleep with your contractor until the work is finished or at least at the punch list stage.) Now the place looked like a deranged person had taken a sledgehammer to the wall or, in the words of Rolanda Knox, "an incendiary device" had gone off. It had been that way for months, and Lucy had turned it into a focal point.

I felt a powerful desire to climb into bed and pull the covers over my head, but knew that would only have me up and ravenous at 2 A.M. so I forced myself to stow the perishables and crack open one or two of the pint containers. I fiddled with the remote for five minutes before stumbling upon the magic combination and sequence of button pushing that turned on the television. Mission accomplished, I sank into the love seat with a teaspoon and a plastic bowl of chickpea salad. If good food took time, mine was all ready. I was watching an improbable garden makeover when my cell rang.

"Don't you pick up messages?"

"Why would I want to talk to someone whose first words to me are a reproach?"

"You're right. Hey, Paula, it's been ages. Don't you pick up messages?" It was Babe Chinnery. She'd been leaving messages on my cell and at my home in Springfield. Someone had been trying to reach the woman at booth 1142 at the flower show, and since Babe's name was on the registration, whoever it was had dialed her number. Babe thought the caller might be a buyer.

"He said he met you at the convention center. I didn't want to give him your number. If you'd wanted him to have it, you'd have given it to him, right? Getting his name was like pulling teeth. Garland Bleimeister. Do you know him?"

The name meant nothing to me.

"Hank Mossdale was in the diner tonight. I told him some young stud was tracking you down. I think he was jealous. Guy on the phone sounded young. Are you finally taking my advice and going for some young blood?"

I'd only met one young guy at the show. I wasn't looking for a date and I didn't know his name but I had his bag stashed under the cheap royal blue tablecloth at Primo's booth.

FOURTEEN

The next morning I left a message for Bleimeister at the number Babe had given me. At the convention center Rolanda Knox was marginally more civil than she'd been the first few days. I thought of asking if she'd seen the young man who'd tried to sneak in, but I didn't want to bring up a painful subject. I smiled, flashed my badge, and headed for my booth, threading my way through union workers still laying down carpet and hopeful contestants spritzing and pruning their floral entries.

I was expecting another delivery for the prejudged specimen plant categories and braced myself for the notorious trade show issue of *drayage*. A word that seldom crops up in most conversations. To cut short the six pages of convention mumbo jumbo, your boxes, like Elvis, may be in the building, but until some guy who looks like a member of ZZ Top says so, it's anyone's guess when

68

you'll see them. And new exhibitors were low men on the totem pole who had to dangle candy, free goods, and occasionally cash to light a fire under them. You made your peace with it and thanked them profusely when your merchandise arrived.

I stopped at the concession stand to refuel. The barista had just arrived and it would be five or ten minutes before the coffee was ready, so I took a spin around the floor. Nursery pots and electrical cables had been camouflaged with literally tons of pine bark mulch. Timed mistings kept everything moist, and consequently the entire building smelled like a national park or the woods after a spring rain. Incongruously, the air was also filled with the incessant beeping of service vehicles backing up. When had that become mandatory? If you can see the vehicle, you don't need that hideous noise; and if you can't, how will it help?

The beeping died down, first one chirping machine, then another, like quitting time at a factory. Then it stopped entirely and was replaced by footsteps and a flurry of activity. Two men with walkie-talkies materialized and sprinted to a set of escalators at the rear of the convention center. Rolanda and three other guards barreled past me, wearing their game faces and trying not to look alarmed. I followed at a discreet distance. Whatever it was, it was bound to be more interesting than waiting for coffee to brew. Had a deer been spotted? A vole?

A dozen or so onlookers were clustered at the top of the escalator. Below, near an exhibit of storage sheds, more gawkers stood outside a red ten-by-ten unit with faux gingerbread detailing and vinyl hanging planters on the windows. Thirty-seven hundred bucks — I'd talked a client out of buying one by telling her she'd also have to hire seven dwarves to go with it to get the full effect. The white resin planters outside the shed were slightly askew and a trio of smaller pots overturned.

When the guards reached the lower level, the crowd parted and that gave me a somewhat better view down the nonworking escalator. All I saw were two Timberland boots, feet splayed in an awkward pose that didn't look comfortable and didn't look healthy.

The convention center's emergency staff, two handymen with a defibrillator, were quick on the scene, but they looked nervous, inexperienced, and in over their heads. Onlookers stepped aside to let them do their work, but when the real deal arrived in the form of a New York City emergency medi-

cal team, the Wagner staff was visibly relieved and moved on to crowd control, a
role for which they were better suited. I
bumped into Nikki on the way back to our
aisle.

"What's the hubbub this time?" she asked.

"Doesn't look good. Someone collapsed
or maybe had an accident on the escalator."
I considered telling her what I really thought
— that the person was as dead as Connie
Anzalone's veronicas — but why jinx him if
he was still alive? And why upset her if he
wasn't? I'd seen a man fall over dead during a keynote speech at another trade show
once. It wasn't *that* dull a talk. He was
whisked away and the speaker went right on
yakking. Most people didn't even know
about it until they read about someone
who'd taken ill in the show daily the next
morning. As heartless as it sounded, one
monkey don't stop no show. A brief announcement over the loudspeakers stated
the rear escalators were not in service. No
reason was given, but Nikki Bingham already had a theory.

"Connie's husband probably found out
who nuked her veronicas and had the
person killed."

FIFTEEN

"That's a little harsh," I said.

"I didn't mean it. I guess I'm not feeling warm and fuzzy this morning." *I'd just met the woman two days ago. Please tell me she isn't going to pour her heart out to me.*

"Pay no attention to me," she said. "Momentary lapse."

We reached our aisle and Nikki got to work, rearranging everything she'd pronounced perfect the day before. David arrived bearing gifts — a Box o' Joe from Dunkin' Donuts and an aluminum-foil-covered platter that held a homemade frittata he'd warmed in the microwave in the members' lounge.

"I could get to like this," I said, helping myself to a slice. Nikki looked hurt. First I'd refused her crumb cake, then her attempt to get something off her chest, now I was scarfing down someone else's culinary accomplishment. I'd have to remember to

72

skip breakfast tomorrow and gush over whatever Nikki brought to keep the peace.

Babe had said three more pieces were coming but I couldn't do much until the final shipment arrived, so I busied myself tweaking my laptop presentation. The computer battery needed recharging, so I crouched down to find the ridiculously expensive power source we'd had to order. I was on my hands and knees, peeling back corners of the rented carpet trying to find it, and half listening to David discuss what some exhibitors were now calling the Javits Curse.

They had decided it was the late New York senator's way of steering business to the sleek, glass structure farther north that bore his name instead of the building we were in that honored a former mayor. If the flower show's organizers took the bait and left or, worse, succumbed, it could be the final nail in the coffin for the Wagner Center and it could put a lot of people out of work. And invite the wrecking ball so a newer, bigger structure would take its place. It was prize real estate. Needless to say, there were interested parties on both sides.

"If it's not the curse," David said, "and it's just another mishap, that makes six. The members' lounge was buzzing this morning. Mostly that viper Allegra Douglas. She's already pointing fingers." According to David, more than a few longtime flower show denizens didn't approve of the new crop of exhibitors, although most weren't as vocal as Allegra.

"There's one of the old-timers now," he said. His voice dropped. "Uh-oh, she's coming this way. Big pencil at eleven o'clock . . . and something tells me she's not looking for pinecone nightlights. Command performance, ladies."

I hadn't heard the term *big pencil* to denote a big buyer since my days in the video business, and from my crouched position I craned my neck to see. The low whirr of a machine was followed by a shaky voice behind me. "Redecorating?" I bolted upright, and made eye contact with . . . no one until I shifted my gaze downward to Jean Moffitt's wheelchair.

"Just joking. Don't get up on my account."

She wore a cherry red suit tricked out with more gold buttons and braid than a character from a Gilbert and Sullivan production, and her thin, storklike legs were partially wrapped in a luscious shawl I pegged as Loro Piana. Very Italian and very expensive. At the chair's controls was a young man with watery blue eyes and sandy blond hair cropped in very short, almost military fashion. A light-colored polo shirt stretched across a well-defined set of pecs, and his chinos looked as if they'd been ironed. Definitely military. He was comfortable enough with the old woman to have been a relative but maybe not. There was also a little reserve.

"Rick and I should come back when you've finished setting up," Mrs. Moffitt said.

Perhaps this was how it was done. The on-the-floor business was window dressing; all the big deals were made at off-hours. "No, no, just testing my computer presentation," I said, kicking into salesman mode. "May I show it to you?" She looked at me as if I'd suggested she view my vacation pictures from the last ten years.

I'd seen the Moffitt name on a dozen items at the flower show from containers to window boxes to specimen plants — each entry adorned with a ribbon. David had told us about her. Jean Moffitt's late husband was a wealthy industrialist who'd been a big supporter of the show. No one ever said that's why she always won, but there were some who thought she was guaranteed a certain number of prizes every year. If the show had been around for a hundred years, Jean Moffitt had been there for most of them, and her sitting room was lined with glass cases filled with blue ribbons to prove it.

This year's theme was "A New York State of Mind," and Mrs. Moffitt's entry, A Sleepy Hollow Garden, was the odds-on favorite to take first prize Friday night when the biggest awards were given for best overall display garden. The Moffitt garden was a masterpiece worthy of a Las Vegas theme park. Playing on the Washington Irving short story, it featured marble tombstones, rotting tree trunks, and numerous specimens of Harry Lauder's Walking Stick, which looked like dead, gnarled limbs but were very much alive. She had planned to have a headless horseman galloping through the Friday night reception but at the eleventh hour had learned it would be a building code violation. Her attorneys were still working on getting the variance, and hoped it would come through before the final judging.

"My gardener was here yesterday," she said. "He seems to think some of your pieces might suit one of our gardens." How many did she have?

"They're not mine," I said. "They're the

work of a friend." I launched into my spiel and fidgeted with the flash drive, plugging it into the laptop and continuing my pitch — but I'd never located the power source and my battery was at 20 percent, so nothing much was happening on the screen.

"I'm so sorry," I said. "I'm a little electrically challenged right now." I dropped down again to check for the outlet and was at eye level with the woman.

"That's all right, dear. We'll stop by during the reception." I saw my sale rolling away and was pressing for a firmer commitment and a specific time to meet when Lauryn Peete and two young girls walked by, balancing three vintage streetlights on a too-small dolly whose casters were being uncooperative. The dolly snagged on a cable, and one of the streetlights teetered dangerously close to Lauryn's head. Rick sprang into action and averted disaster, although the light did guillotine an amaryllis. The kids cheered, "Hey, the marines are here."

Mrs. Moffitt and I watched as her companion picked up the fixtures at the middle and carried them like lightweight barbells to the school's display garden.

"Rick won't like that at all. He was at the Air Force Academy," Mrs. Moffitt said, keeping an eye on him.

I didn't know much about the various branches of the armed forces, but I knew you had to be recommended for the Air Force Academy by a congressman. That bit of information came to me courtesy of a snowboarder in Colorado who thought it would help him get to first base. It did. After a short while, Rick jogged back to us, full of unnecessary apologies to me and Mrs. Moffitt.

"Nonsense. You did what any red-blooded American boy would do — you helped a pretty woman in distress."

His ears flushed bright red, and I took the brief silence as an opportunity to get back to the business at hand. "Was there any one piece that particularly struck your fancy?" I asked her, while looking at him.

"Don't ask him," she laughed, patting his hand. "This child wouldn't know a weed from an orchid. Rick is my physical therapist, my chauffeur, and frequent dining companion. Mr. Jensen is my gardener. He's not here now; he's arranging for our last few accoutrements to be delivered." I wondered if he was interviewing headless horsemen.

She was describing the pieces Jensen had mentioned seeing, when Jamal Harrington, he of the rubber rat, shuffled by swinging the empty dolly in a manner that could have been considered aggressive. He glared at Rick as if he were trying to burn a hole in him. Rick didn't flinch.

"We will come back," Mrs. Moffitt said. "I promise. But now I must go and check out my competition. Jensen says there are one or two quite original gardens that may give me a run for my money this year. He's always looking after me. Come along, Rick."

As he wheeled her away I overheard her say, "There certainly is an odd crop of entrants this year."

SIXTEEN

I breathed easier when the last of Primo's pieces arrived. With Nikki's help they were test-driven in every possible location until the arrangement met with her approval. Her own booth looked ready for a glossy magazine shoot with dried flowers and decorative throws artfully dropped around the vintage tools and furniture. I'd seen at least one photographer strolling the halls, taking pictures during setup, and there were sure to be others on opening night.

The central element of Nikki's booth was a sarcophagus topped with a decorative iron grate to be used — if you owned a property big enough — as an outdoor dining table. There was no rearranging that baby, so Nikki contented herself with tweaking everything else she'd brought: a wrought iron bistro set, antique plant stands, Japanese lanterns, carved stone pots, and a hundred smaller items — busts, birdbaths, and vintage tools — for those of us who didn't live on huge properties but still wanted to feel like the chatelaines of great estates. Then she moved on to Primo's pieces.

"If Mrs. Moffitt comes back to see you and happens to also buy my sarcophagus, I will give you anything in my booth as a commission. You're going to bring me luck, I can feel it. Last year I was next to a couple selling Alaskan fish fertilizer. It was awful," she said. "Stray cats followed me home."

After staging his light fixtures, David had a minor crisis when the power in our aisle died. It was as if the Christmas tree in Rockefeller Center had failed to light. It was impossible to appreciate the detail and intricacy of his work without a warm light glowing behind the shades and sconces. Forty minutes and a fifty-dollar tip later, all was well, and we wondered if it was the Javits Curse again or one last attempt by Wagner employees to squeeze additional baksheesh out of frantic exhibitors.

When the public address announcer made his first feeble attempt to eject us, all the kinks had been ironed out. The heavy machinery was gone, the carpets were in place, and the industrial-looking building had been transformed into the series of New

York gardens the organizers had hoped to inspire.

And while we'd been tinkering with our displays, Cinderella's mice had been hard at work. Temporary bars and buffet tables had materialized, and in twenty-four hours they'd be filled with finger foods and beverages of every stripe. If Connie Anzalone was correct, some attendees were already laying out their clothing. I hadn't seen her all day and secretly hoped she'd forgotten my promise to have a drink with her.

"Leave business cards out," David said, as he packed up. "Business-to-business sales are key. Other exhibitors walk around at off-hours, and they can be some of your best customers." It was a good tip, and I spent the last fifteen minutes before lights-out doing as David had advised.

I wandered haphazardly and found myself in an aisle dedicated to single plant specimens — the Gloxinia Society, the Hosta Association. The plants were impossibly perfect, like pictures in a White Flower Farm or Park Seed catalog — no brown edges, no yellowing leaves, and no telltale nibbles. Like a kid, I wanted to touch them to see if they were real.

Connie was gone, so I poked around and inspected her garden entry. Coney Island was one of the most famous beaches in the world, although it was anyone's guess whether or not the creatures and plants Connie depicted could be found there. It didn't matter. The display was fanciful, whimsical, and the tiniest bit tacky, like the woman herself. As I leaned in for a closer look at her botanical version of a Whack-A-Mole game, I noticed two men in the shadows checking me out. Maybe they were the mob bodyguards Nikki thought Connie's husband would bring in to protect her plants from human pests. Both men were slim enough to be almost hidden by the trio of rosemary topiaries from a penthouse garden display. I moved on.

There was no major category without a Moffitt entry. I didn't see how she found the time to submit all the entries I saw. I had only covered one quarter of the room before a loud slam and a dimming of lights told me it really was time to leave.

The two men had disappeared. Only one other person was in sight, a young girl in a polo shirt and khakis taking pictures of a booth designed to re-create the Feast of San Gennaro. I didn't buy the white hydrangeas as zeppole, but gave the entry extra points for imagination.

On my way out, I swung by the horticultural information booth for handouts on deer-resistant plants and others on hostas, amaryllis, and clivia. I grabbed another called "Poisonous to Pets" as a goodwill gesture to Lucy's downstairs neighbor. I was tucking them in the outer pocket of my laptop case when a woman I hadn't seen approached. She shoved handfuls of assorted flyers in her canvas bag. I realized I was staring.

"Getting some for friends?" I asked.

"Stacking them at my own booth as a service to show attendees." She sounded defensive, as if I were going to report her to the flyer police. Hell, I didn't care.

"Good idea," I said.

"Just doing whatever it takes."

She handed me her card and proceeded to tell me her story.

SEVENTEEN

The woman's name was Terry Ward, Bagua Designs, certified feng shui practitioner, Dix Hills, New York.

In the 1980s, as feng shui worked its way into America's lexicon, Terry thought she'd struck gold. She'd always known her obsessive desire to move the furniture was more than just neurotic behavior. It was her struggle to, in her words, perfect her surroundings. And now there was a name for it. If only her husband were still around so she could say I told you so.

Terry had signed up for a three-session course at the Learning Annex, and before it even ended she'd ordered cards for her new venture. Back then, it was easy to be considered an expert when few people could even pronounce *feng shui*, much less tell you which way they thought their *chi* should be flowing.

She worked the flower, crafts, and flea

markets in New York, New Jersey, and Connecticut and the fairs in all five boroughs and Long Island, cobbling together a business from the sale of a staple-bound self-published book and bits and pieces collected from tag and yard sales.

On one fateful trip to the Elephant's Trunk flea market in Connecticut, Terry reconnected with an old high school friend Kyle DiMucci, who in a fruitless attempt to escape his churlish wife, Doreen, traveled to all markets, preferring the ones farthest from home, where he sold classic television ephemera, mostly lunch boxes and board games. One thing led to another. When Kyle's wife found out, she threatened to divorce him and torch what remained of his beloved *Dark Shadows* memorabilia collection. That dried up the flea market scene for Terry.

To refill her pipeline with low-cost feng shui–like tchotchkes Terry found a Chinese wholesaler of resin fountains, chimes, and mirrors. The merchandise had a smaller profit margin than the junk she had bought for a dollar and resold for ten, but avoiding flea markets greatly reduced the chances of bumping into the incendiary Mrs. DiMucci.

"You gotta leave, ladies." The security guard looked tired and bored. She swung

86

her badge and lanyard around mindlessly over and over again. Unlike Rolanda, she appeared to be an uninterested part-timer filling the extended hours. I didn't think she cared one lick if we got locked in or backed up a trailer and left with a load of stolen merchandise. But Terry must have been worried she'd get in trouble for taking the flyers, so she scurried off without even saying good-bye.

I walked through the empty convention center hallway to the down escalator and saw Rolanda Knox leaving the security office. "Wait up," she yelled, but my gloved hand was already on the moving handrail and I'd already started descending. She couldn't possibly need to see my credentials now. I tapped my fingers and pretended to inspect my coffee-stained glove.

She hurried down the escalator and caught up with me at the bottom.

"Underneath this jacket, I swear, I'm wearing my badge."

"You crazy?" she said. "I want to ask you something. You ever see that kid again — the one from yesterday who tried to sneak in?"

I'd almost asked her the same question. "Why?"

She waited for me to answer.

"I haven't, but it's possible he called me."
I told her about the phone messages Babe
had delivered and the one I'd left him.

Rolanda asked if I'd checked the message
board.

"I've been pretty busy today."

Rolanda took me by the arm and led me
to the up escalator. "Why are we doing
this?" I asked.

"I saw something that might interest you."

Upstairs, past the temporary bookstore,
the press room, and the members' lounge
was a long corkboard on the wall between
meeting rooms that would soon be filled
with people learning wreath-making and
bonsai techniques. Most of the notices were
four-color promotional materials for products or services with the occasional "Mary
Ellen, meet me at Herbaceous Perennials
101." Good place for an ad. I made a note
to print out a picture of one of Primo's
pieces and put it on the board with our
booth number. Rolanda was searching. "I
hope someone didn't pin anything on top
of it." Then I saw what she'd been looking
for.

Do you still have my bag?
Please call me. G.B.

Eighteen

"I don't get it. If he was here, why didn't he just find me? I left him my booth number."

" 'Cause he didn't have no badge. Do we need to go over that again? Another guard gave him the boot yesterday afternoon. I'm just glad the kid was here. I had a premonition about him. My mother had the gift. In our old neighborhood, she knew who was gonna die right before it happened."

Given Rolanda's size and temperament, it occurred to me her mom might have been a hit woman, but I kept that thought to myself.

"I have a little of it, too," she said. "The gift. You don't believe me, right?"

"What is it?" I asked, hoping I didn't look too skeptical and she didn't see whatever woo woo glow she'd seen around the kid around me.

"Hard to define," she said. "When I saw the accident this morning, I thought it might be the Happy Valley kid, but it was Otis Randolph, one of the overnight workers."

"Is he all right?"

She shook her head. "Didn't even make it to the hospital. Looks like he broke his neck. The escalator turns off automatically, so maybe he was on it and it jolted to a stop, throwing him down the stairs. The police aren't sure what happened — I'm just guessing."

"I'm sorry. That's horrible. Were you friends?"

"I knew him. At first when I saw the jeans and boots, I thought it might be our boy who sneaked in after the kerfluffle yesterday."

Kerfluffle. I liked that. And hadn't she referred to herself as a martinet the other day? Between her psychic abilities and her colorful vocabulary, Rolanda was getting more interesting.

I dialed the number on the bulletin board. The same one Babe had given me. It kicked into voice mail, and I left a message, saying the bag was at booth 1142, if he could get in (Rolanda was still within earshot). Otherwise he should call me and I'd arrange to meet him. Out of habit I left my cell phone and my home phone numbers.

90

"Look at this — you're a popular girl. Here's another one."

Rolanda plucked a pink index card from the board. It was from Connie.

Hi, Paula, Didn't have your number but hope you see this. Meet me at the St. George at 7 p.m. Connie A.

The *I*'s were dotted with circles. Instead of periods, she made little daisy-shaped characters. Aaaay.

I checked my watch. "You could pretend you didn't see it," Rolanda said.

"She'd know I was lying. I'm a terrible liar." The last thing I wanted to do was have drinks with a woman who made up her own punctuation marks, but it was a good hotel with a great bar and she was buying.

By that time the escalators had been turned off and Rolanda and I walked to the top of the staircase. The reception didn't start until 5:30 P.M. the next day, and I considered going back onto the floor for the bag, but Rolanda stopped me.

"Don't bother. These doors are locked."

"All right, since you have all the answers, what do people wear to this shindig tomorrow night?"

"Last year we had an international theme.

People had all sorts of getups. One woman wore a three-foot headdress that was supposed to be Brazilian. She had to sit in a chair and be carried in because she couldn't fit through the doorway standing up."

"Was she wearing her badge?"

"Damn skippy."

NINETEEN

The St. George had one of the best bars in the city. The murals; the low ceiling, which held in decades of New York life; the music; the fashionable cocktails of the time; and the cigarette and cigar smoke from bygone days that had yellowed the walls and given the room a warm, cavelike quality. It was the kind of place that made me want to order a sidecar or a sloe gin fizz, even though I had no idea what they were. And the St. George had the best mixed nuts of any establishment in the city. I loved the place, despite the fact that the house detective once took me for a hooker. That was the anecdote I used as an icebreaker when I joined Connie at her corner table.

"He thought *you* were a pro?" Connie asked, temporarily halting her low-key gum chewing.

Just out of school, I had been working as an assistant buyer for a catalog company.

An older salesman invited me for a drink, and I arrived early. I wasn't there five minutes when a portly, florid guy in a baggy gray suit asked if I was waiting for someone. I was too clueless to know what he was really asking. Luckily the friend showed up and rescued me.

"What a jerk," Connie said. "Nowadays, you could sue for that."

"Maybe it was the attire. Probably a Melrose Place suit with a teeny skirt." I let the wardrobe conversation dry up when I remembered who I was talking to. Tonight's package was wrapped in fluffy white Mongolian lamb that mercifully covered another scene of embroidered marine life. Clearly the dress code at the St. George had loosened up.

Connie had loosened up, too. Lubricated by two drinks, she gave me her life story in broad strokes — born in Brooklyn, she and Guy were neighborhood sweethearts who married when she was barely eighteen. She was quick to point out it was not a shotgun wedding; although I wouldn't have cared. She and Guy had two kids, but they came later at regulation intervals. Guy was making good money in his father's landscaping business and didn't see the need for more than two years of accounting classes at

Kingsborough Community College, so he dropped out. Then he started his own business.

"Interlocking tumbled blocks," she said. "It's the way of the future."

As a gardener I had a love-hate relationship with them. Lately it had been swinging to love. Most were obvious and plastic, kind of like fake boobs. And they came preweathered (the stones, not the boobs), like prewashed jeans. But recently manufacturers had improved the products, so they looked almost as good as the natural stone they replaced in gardens, driveways, and walls. Was I going over to the dark side?

Connie wriggled out of her jacket, revealing a tight white blouse with an oyster-shell design on each melon-sized breast. I did my best not to stare. She waved at the young waiter, this time ordering a full bottle. He was putty in her hands — clearly the man was a seafood fan. I nursed my first drink but made short work of the nuts. She signaled for another bowl, and in an instant they appeared.

Underneath the fish garb Connie Anzalone was an attractive woman in her early thirties with the figure of a Xena: Warrior Princess doll. Her wide blue eyes and pouty mouth all but guaranteed that wiggling her fingers was all she'd have to do to get whatever she wanted. It was fascinating to watch. Don't get me wrong, I like my looks, but really beautiful women were practically a different species. I think it was the casual power they wielded. And did they wake up that way every morning? Or did it, as a friend used to say, "take a village"? It took me twenty minutes just to dry my hair, and even then one side always looked better than the other, so I usually hid it all under a hat. The bottle arrived and was opened and poured in overtheatrical fashion, no doubt to impress Connie.

"Guy doesn't like me to drink so much at home, but I'm not home now, am I?"

No, she wasn't. Home for the Anzalones was Coney Island in Brooklyn. The nice part, she'd said, although I'd hardly know which area that was. I was born in Brooklyn, so I'd been to Coney Island. It was more than a Brooklyn landmark. It was a state of mind. When I was a kid I remembered a long stretch of beach from the aquarium to a dive arcade called Eddie's Fascination that had that seedy beach languor I'd since seen in resort towns from Bar Harbor to Miami and farther south in the Caribbean. The same sarongs, beach towels, and sunglass holders covered with flowers or imprinted with the town's name and all made in China. On every corner there were Italian restaurants, where old men sat outside on folding chairs doing who knew what. Twenty years later, it probably still looked the same.

Connie's husband, the Tumbled Stone King, made his fortune in landscaping, though he'd branched out into demolition and construction. She said it in a way that didn't lend itself to further elaboration and suggested the rumor about his involvement in illegal activities might be true. We returned to the safer subject of the flower show.

Her face lost all of its hardness and she lit up when she talked about gardening.

"It was the only work Guy would let me do — and even then he sent some men to help me plant things or move materials."

On my second drink and feeling comfortable, I pointed to her nails. "Gardening can't be easy with those."

"It's not! But Guy likes them, and he's, you know, king of the castle. I'm constantly taking them off and putting them on." That couldn't be healthy for the nail bed, but perhaps it was good for the *marriage* bed — and given the choice, most people would choose the latter.

"I think I'm helping the nail salon owner bring over her entire village. There used to be a real diamond on this one." She showed me the perfectly sculpted, shell-colored nail on her left ring finger, inches from a rock as big as a muscari bulb. "Then I lost it in the garden. I accidentally buried it when I was planting a row of allium last fall. When the shoots come up, I'll see if there's a bare spot and poke around. Maybe if I fertilize it'll grow into a tennis bracelet."

Connie had read an article about the Big Apple Flower Show and asked Guy if it would be all right if she tried to exhibit. She'd been fantasizing about the black-tie gala reception ever since she'd sent in the application and the way she talked about it, it may have been the only reason she wanted to participate.

"You could have knocked me over with a feather when Guy said yes. I did trick him, though. I kept talking about redecorating the master bathroom, so he figured it was cheaper to let me do this. Wasn't that clever? Now I'm finally here."

Wherever *here* was. She was Cinderella at last invited to the ball. I wasn't likely to make the society pages either, but I'd gone to black-tie galas — museum openings and screenings when I worked in television —

and they were generally no big deal.

"You know, those parties are more boring than they look. And it's not that hard to get invited. All you have to do is send a check to the organizations running them."

"I didn't realize." She poured another drink with such a practiced hand, I wouldn't have been surprised if she'd stood up and done a bunny dip.

"I'm usually good at making friends," she said, "but people have been so cold. First that man yesterday. Of course I didn't tell Guy about that. He'd have hit the ceiling, then hit the man. Then I overheard this nasty old broad — the one who smells like an ashtray but looks like she's giving make-overs at Saks — talking behind my back. I know my entry isn't the most sophisticated, but there must have been some reason the horticultural society accepted my application."

I wondered silently if her husband or his company had anything to do with it.

"Every garden doesn't have to look like Dr. Jekyll's, does it?"

My Robert Louis Stevenson was rusty but I was fairly sure neither of his most famous creations, the good Doctor Jekyll nor his evil alter ego, had had gardens.

"The English lady," Connie said.

The girl had done her homework, even if she did mangle the name. Should I correct her or let it go? Always a toss-up. "I think it's pronounced *Gee-kill,* Gertrude Jekyll," I said, gently, "just in case it comes up in conversation."

"See, you know so much. You're just the type of person I hoped I'd meet here."

Her eyes got watery, but instead of letting the tears spill over, she threw her head back and drained her glass. I was dazzled by her speedy recovery — and her apparently wooden leg.

I repeated what I'd heard — that there had been other mishaps at the show. She perked up and even laughed about a quartet of plaster gnomes that had given up their lives. We decided their ashes should be spread at the Taj Mahal or Eiffel Tower, where they'd had their pictures taken.

A commotion in the lobby caught our attention as a burly guy brushed aside the doorman, spun through the revolving door into the bar, and headed our way. Something told me she had called the Tumbled Stone King about today's mishap.

"Oh." With one finger she slid the champagne bottle a tiny bit closer to me, to suggest it was all mine.

"Did I not tell you? What did I tell you?"

he said. Connie shrank a bit as the man lumbered toward us. Towering over our booth, his hands on his bulky hips, he took a deep breath, then let it out in a blast of air that carried traces of Scotch and cigar smoke. He made a smoothing motion with his thick paws. "I don't mean to yell at you." He wiped his forehead with the heels of both hands. Then he motioned Connie out of the booth. "C'mon. We're going home."

She licked her lips, producing a pout I imagined she used whenever she wanted something. I felt like I should be taking notes.

"I just don't want you to get your feelings hurt, baby."

"For goodness sakes, Guy, all my things are upstairs. I overreacted. It was just a prank. Paula says there've been other incidents. It wasn't just me. They're calling it the Javits Curse. It has nothing to do with you."

I felt uncomfortable and got up to leave.

"Sit." He pointed, as if I were a dog he was training. I sat. What was next, rolling over?

"Look, I'm sorry. Please, don't go. I'm Connie's husband."

As if I couldn't tell.

Guy Anzalone motioned for the waiter,

ordered a Famous Grouse, and squeezed into the booth. I was sandwiched in between a woman dressed like Ariel and a Damon Runyon character from *Guys and Dolls*. I polished off my drink, and Connie quickly topped me off. I was going to need a lot more nuts.

TWENTY

It was simple. Anything that made Connie unhappy made Guy unhappy. Unhappiness was not a condition he handled well. All this was made clear over more drinks and a feisty exchange that was both comical and a little unsettling. Unlike Nikki, I didn't think Anzalone was a criminal just because he was rough around the edges, but there was something in his manner that screamed short fuse. And in Connie's, too.

"My girl needs looking after." He patted her hand. "She's a tough cupcake in her own milieu, but she's in a different world here. At the show, I mean. I don't want anyone to take advantage of her . . . naïveté."

"What's gonna happen to me at a flower show — I'm gonna get attacked by a man-eating plant?"

"Nothing's gonna happen. I've made sure of that. I sent Fat Frank and Cookie to look out for you."

103

"Don't you dare. I'll be mortified."

He put his fingers to his lips the way you'd silence a child. "It's already done. See, you didn't even know they were there. And this girl, this woman, is gonna help, too. What's your name again, hon?"

We'd already told him twice. Clearly I wasn't making much of an impression. Insult aside, did I want to be on a tag team with two guys named Fat Frank and Cookie? Were they the men I'd seen? But neither of them was fat. Would I be required to adopt a nickname, like "the Chin" or "Lips"? I felt the urge to get up again but suppressed it, since Guy weighed around 230 pounds, roughly double my size. Trying to muscle past him would be ridiculous.

I shook my head — dumb move since it magnified the buzz I was getting from the combination of champagne and no food except the nuts.

"I'm sure I can't improve on anything Fat Frank and Cookie can do." I struggled to keep a straight face when I said their names.

"My boys will make sure she's safe, but I want you to keep an eye on her. Make sure she's not lonely. That, you know, she's included in all the reindeer games." Connie protested, but Guy made it sound like a perfectly reasonable request. A big sister program.

Though I could have used their advice, Michelangelo, Leonardo, and the dead relatives were strangely silent on this issue. Perhaps I was channeling my inner cugine, or my inner Brooklyn girl, but I found myself agreeing. The show lasted just a few days and I didn't know many people there myself. Why not spend time with her? Everyone I knew in Springfield, apart from Babe and Caroline Sturgis, were so beige. It could be fun.

"I like Connie. You don't need to *recruit* friends for her," I said, not using the more obvious word — *pimp.*

"Good, well, that's settled," she said. "You'll help me decide what to wear to the reception. We can go shopping."

"No money to go shopping," I said. "Besides, I have to finish setting up. And don't you have last-minute primping to do?"

"Go shopping. Have a good time." He whipped out a roll of bills and left a stack on the table.

Connie said nothing, confident there'd be no serious objection to her shopping excursion, from either of us. "I have to go tinkle. Guy, make her say yes."

She playfully knocked Guy's elbow off the table on her way to the ladies' room, and his hand accidentally brushed my knee. At least, I hoped it was an accident, but it lingered longer than it needed to and unless I imagined it, Guy's pinkie finger trailed a good three inches up my thigh before he threw a pretend punch in Connie's direction and said, "Yeah, sure."

When Connie was safely out of earshot, he gave me his full attention. "So tell me what it is you're selling, hon."

My first sale. Maybe that old house detective knew something I didn't. I convinced myself playing kneesies with Guy Anzalone was an offer I couldn't refuse and was a small price to pay for the sizable purchase I'd pressure him to make. I'd take one for the team. Primo would sell a piece, Babe would be pleased, and I'd earn a commission. What could happen in a public place while his wife was in the ladies' room?

To keep the conversation professional I'd flipped open my laptop as soon as Connie left. Tactical error. Guy took that as an excuse to squeeze closer and reacquaint his hand with my knee. His thigh pressed against mine and it was surprisingly warm. I can't say I was aroused, but it was hard to ignore the heat. I repositioned the computer screen and crossed my legs to avoid contact.

By the time Connie returned, Guy's head

was inclined a little too close to mine and he had to pretend to be interested in a large wind device Primo had constructed out of two rusted lawn mowers. Served him right for hitting on a woman while his wife was twenty feet away and getting closer.

She peered over my other shoulder. "Ooohh, I like that one."

How much could I milk this? I clicked on another image. "Of course, if you have the space, you could go with this one, constructed from vintage tractor parts. It's much more impressive." And twice the cost. I shamelessly played to his vanity and her eagerness to impress. Say yes, please, I thought. I'll even go shopping with you if you buy this one.

Guy looked like a man who'd been caught with his hand in the cookie jar. Connie and I were about to deliver a five-thousand-dollar slap on that hand. Her lower lip started to quiver. His eyes softened. The checkbook was produced. Good grief. I didn't want to think about what I could have sold them if I'd actually let him cop a feel. I agreed to meet her the next morning for a fashion consultation and left the two lovebirds canoodling — or maybe it was arguing — in the hotel bar.

Twenty-One

As I recalled, that's what relationships were like — blowups, followed by makeups — though I imagined few were as animated or as expensive as the Anzalones'.

My last relationship ended when I was accused of being married to my job. Ironic, since I was fired soon after. It never occurred to me to call the man and tell him what happened. Some relationships have an expiration date, like milk, and that one had no longer passed the sniff test.

I'd been on my own for a while and, apart from the semiannual fix-up orchestrated by Babe or Lucy, I was content running my business, getting used to life in Springfield, and taking the occasional trip into the city to catch up with old friends. Apart from Hank Mossdale there had only been one other man on my radar — Mike O'Malley, a Springfield cop. But subtle signs were putting him into the confidant/brother camp and not the what-does-he-look-like-naked camp, and I was fine with that. In fact, I'd thought that he and Lucy might have some chemistry, but that flirtation was short-lived. He'd gotten her out of a jam and she was suitably grateful but, according to her — and she's the kind that tells — it never went any further.

When I got to her place, I picked up the mail and left the poisonous-to-pets info sheet and a brief note under the corner of the doormat of the woman on three. Or four, whatever it was. I would have slipped it under her door but worried she might automatically assume it was a menu and shred it and let her cats pee on it.

Once in the apartment, I hung on the refrigerator door, willing the remnants of the previous night's chickpea salad to miraculously turn into kung pao chicken or a slab of lasagna, but it didn't happen. The hurricane drink mix started to seem like a good idea but it went better with jambalaya than it did on an empty stomach.

I tiptoed down the stairs. As I passed the neighbor's apartment, the peephole cover moved, and I gave the woman behind the door a slight wave I knew she wouldn't return. The pet poison list was still outside. When I reached the ground floor, I held the inside door open with my stockinged foot. As the cat lady had predicted, any number of menus from local restaurants littered the floor. I had my choice of Chinese, Japanese, Italian, the intriguingly named Fusha Fusion, or a Greek diner, from which I could presumably get anything I wanted. This was New York at its best — anything you wanted brought to your door, 24-7. Food was the least of it.

The diner menus were just beyond my reach, stacked neatly by the outer door. Why did those guys have to be the neat ones? Everyone else had just flung theirs in the doorway and disappeared.

I stretched as far as I could and grazed the menus with my fingertips, but only succeeded in pushing them farther away. Then I got the bright idea to wedge the other menus between the door and the jamb, near the lock so the bolt wouldn't engage. Don't try this at home. The menus fell, the door locked. I was trapped in the drafty vestibule with no shoes, no jacket, no phone, and, more important, no keys. I stood there shivering, trying to decide what to do next.

One solution was to suck it up and walk to the bar on the corner and beg them to let me use their phone to call a locksmith. My free stay at Lucy's was going to cost me at least two hundred bucks unless prices had gone up since I'd moved to Connecticut. And she wouldn't be able to get into her own apartment when she returned. Not a good plan.

TWENTY-TWO

The only other person I'd seen in the building was the cat lady. I rang her bell and, as expected, she didn't answer. Nothing. I rang again. This time I heard the staticky crackle of the intercom, but no one spoke. This was a careful woman — after all, she answered the door with a door bar in her hand.

"Excuse me, ma'am. It's me. The woman on five, I mean four. Lucy's friend. I've locked myself out of the building." I heard nothing for a few minutes, then I looked through the glass panel and saw what looked like a thin periscope or a snake with a curved head. Next, a tanned hand and a slightly crepey wrist. The door opened.

"I brought my bar," she said. "Just in case."

"Thank you. That was smart." Paranoid, but smart. The cats, Tommy and Moochie, had followed her down and now trailed us back up the stairs. She unfolded my note and the pet poison flyer. "Did you leave this for me?" she asked.

I nodded.

"That was very thoughtful," she said, as though I'd donated a kidney. "Where are you from?"

I toyed with the idea of telling her I was from the Midwest or the South or the planet Zoran, which could be the only possible explanation for why I'd done something nice for a total stranger. But I decided the truth was the best way to go.

"Brooklyn."

So was she. In her book that made us kindred spirits. She looked at the menus. "I've got a tray of baked ziti in the oven. I could open a bottle of wine." Cooked food. Five minutes away. And it was baked ziti, which I hadn't eaten since my mother had inexplicably packed up and moved to Florida. There was no way I could really smell the oregano and tomato sauce, but I imagined I did. I said yes.

Her name was J. C. Kaufman. J. C.'s apartment was a marvel of efficiency. In one modestly sized studio she had a kitchen, a dining area, a living room with a working fireplace, and an office with a drafting table and two computer monitors. A tight spiral staircase led to a sleep loft. When I told her

I was a gardener, she insisted on showing me her garden, an eight-by-ten terrace lined with planters and punctuated with whiskey half barrels. Three of them held rhododendrons and two had evergreen shrubs that may have been *Pieris.*

"You can't tell now, but I have Japanese maples and clematis in the spring. Come back inside — it's still cold out here at night. I just wanted to show it to you."

J. C. was an editor. Videos, not books. She got started in the eighties, working on promotional tune-ins for the soaps. We swapped war stories.

"I've seen hundreds of these so-called stars come and go. The young ones — they all think they're the next Meryl Streep. They're not. It's all hair and lip gloss. And Botox. You could crack walnuts on their foreheads. Now, Susan Lucci, she's a class act. And even more beautiful in person. She does, of course, have a big head. They all do. All famous people."

I was regretting my decision to join her for dinner. I didn't know anything about soap stars or how big people's heads should be and didn't want to appear uninterested. She waved off my offer to help, put on a pair of silicone mitts, and took the ziti out of the oven, placing it on the butcher-block

114

cart that defined her kitchen area. The whole apartment filled with the fragrance of the stinking rose, and the top of the ziti was burnt in five or six places where the cheeses had bubbled up. J. C. pulled off the mitts and fetched a bottle of Barolo.

"I'll get glasses. You want to help, keep Moochie away from our dinner. I don't mind a few cat hairs on my food, but it turns some people off." She walked to a shallow china cabinet near the front door. Just as she suspected, Moochie made his move toward the sizzling baking dish the minute his mistress turned away. I was less worried about pet dander than I was about him burning his paws.

"Go on, Moochie." I tried to shoo him away. "Go on."

J. C.'s head poked around the corner. Her eyes were wide. She held two glasses and an index finger was pressed against her lips. At first I thought it was her special way of communicating with the cat. She motioned to the front door with her head; then I heard what she'd heard. Footsteps in the hallway, and they could only be heading upstairs to Lucy's apartment. Then we heard someone rummaging around. Had we left the downstairs door open? J. C. was frozen to the spot. She pointed to the phone on the far end of the wooden table, and I took the receiver out of the cradle and tiptoed toward the terrace, ready to dial 911. She viciously shook her head and pointed to the bathroom, where presumably it was less likely I'd be overheard than outside where the sound might drift up to where the intruders were.

By the time I'd hung up, two sets of footsteps had scrambled down the stairs and out the front door, which shut with a slam. We heard the tinkle of glass as one of the panels must have broken.

"Damn." J. C. finally moved and put down the glasses she'd been gripping during the entire incident. She looked like she was tempted to take a swig right from the bottle; instead she poured two large ones. "I'd say the wine's had time to breathe. Me, too." Neither of us minded that Moochie had started dinner without us.

When the cops knocked on J. C.'s door, we were startled, then realized if a glass panel had been broken in the front door, they wouldn't have needed to be buzzed in. Still, J. C. slid the metal disc that covered the door's peephole to one side and waited a full minute before putting her eye against the door to see who it was. "Old habit," she said, removing the bar and unlocking the door.

Officers Vargas and Wilson spent a few moments getting the story, then they went upstairs to search Lucy's apartment while we stayed at J. C.'s until they said it was safe.

"They really did some damage," Wilson said, leading the way through the door I'd foolishly left open. I didn't know what to think but followed him, expecting the worst. Nothing looked that different to me. The cops couldn't understand why I was so relieved. "It doesn't look that bad," I said. "Oh, that."

Vargas stood inside the hole in the wall Lucy's contractor boyfriend had started to join the apartments and never finished. One hand was on each side of the wall as if he were holding them up. "Looks like Iron Man crashed outta here."

TWENTY-THREE

I guess if you were a cop in New York City a sense of humor came in handy. Either I'd been stalked and had escaped grievous bodily harm, thanks to the siren call of oregano and baked ziti, or more likely J. C. and I had summoned the police to protect us from a couple of overzealous but harmless menu deliverymen. It was a toss-up.

J. C.'s cats explored Lucy's apartment while Wilson and Vargas took our statements. Then their walkie-talkies crackled with a more serious call, so they declined J. C.'s offer to stay for ziti. They cautioned me not to leave the front door open again — even for a quick trip downstairs — and recommended a buddy of Wilson's who did construction to finish the apartment renovation. Given Lucy's last contractor, I almost asked if the man was good-looking, but I didn't want the cops to get the wrong idea. The cop scribbled his friend's name and number on his own card.

"You decide if you want to call him. Tell him I sent you. He'll give you a price."

By this time I was less sociable and J. C. was perceptive enough to realize it, so she left soon after the cops did but returned minutes later with half a tray of pasta and the bottle of wine.

"I can't eat all this."

"Sure you can. Just don't eat it all tonight. And I think you need the wine more than I do. *Watch your back.*"

I would. I'd lost my appetite but not my thirst. I double-locked the door, put the ziti in the fridge, and poured myself a drink. I'd told Connie Anzalone that I'd help her choose an outfit for the Friday night reception, but I didn't have the first clue what I'd be wearing so I started rifling through Lucy's closet for something to borrow.

New York closets were notoriously small and Lucy had rather ingeniously installed a drapery rod and curtain that partitioned two feet from one end of the bedroom, thereby creating a giant closet. Presumably this was done without the help of her former paramour, since the number of holes in each side wall rivaled the number of holes at the Alamo. Still, it worked, especially if you didn't mind the occasional clump of dry wall. Maybe I'd be a really good houseguest and fill them in with Spackle.

Some women were inordinately proud of their linen closets or china cabinets. Others had rows of shoes lined up in formation like some phantom Busby Berkeley routine. Lucy could rightly be proud of this closet. Her clothes were arranged by color and length. Skirts, dresses, and slacks were hung with boutique precision on matching flat, black velvet hangers for maximum efficiency. I thought of my closet in Springfield: T-shirts, sweatshirts, painter's pants, and jeans folded in slightly listing stacks, the bulk of my work clothes from my previous life still in boxes and garment bags.

I hadn't had a nine-to-five job even when I worked in television, but occasionally I had to look professional and for me that meant jeans, boots, and a good jacket. It was all in the accessories. These days I was more likely to accessorize with a pair of nippers and Womanswork garden gloves than an Hermès scarf or pricey handbag, so shopping in Lucy's closet would be fun — and free.

Luckily we were about the same size. We even had the same coloring. Not that that mattered much. Ninety percent of the items in Lucy's closet were black — she did, after all, live in New York and work in the media. Three items that weren't black caught my eye. I put down the wineglass and stripped to my underwear to try on the first: a lilac one-shoulder number held together on the left side by sequined Velcro tabs. In its way, it looked fabulous. I could decorate the booth with lilacs from the Koreans and be color coordinated. But then I worried about the Velcro tabs opening and David having to duct-tape me back together, so I said no to the dress.

On and off quickly was a beige lace sheath. Pretty but practically see-through. The third nonblack item was a sleeveless red dress, short and made of spandex. I flashed on Scarlett O'Hara being forced to wear a red dress to Miss Melly's party after being caught in a clinch with Ashley Wilkes. And a brazen Bette Davis as Jezebel daring to wear red to the Olympus ball, even though uptight fiancé Henry Fonda warns she'll be ostracized. "But this is 1854 . . . 1854!" Bette trumped Henry; I had to try it on.

I wriggled into the dress and slipped off my panties to eliminate VPL, visible panty line. I went the whole nine yards with a pair of strappy stilettos. Jeez, the truckers at the Paradise Diner would have heart attacks if they saw me in this instead of my Old Navy tops and Columbia Sportswear bottoms. But could I really pull off this look? It was one thing to parade around in fancy dress in a fitting room or at home, quite another to go out into the world. I took a swig of wine for courage and did a modified runway walk in front of Lucy's full-length mirror. It was ridiculous enough when rail-thin models did it but downright impossible for a normal-sized woman. Ah, that's because we have thighs. I posed, I preened, I parted my lips and practiced looking lobotomized. I reached for the wine again with one hand on my hip, fingers splayed in the standard celebrity pose. Lucy's phone rang. I imagined it was her telling me which purse to wear with the dress.

"Hello?" There was silence for a beat. "Is this the guy from the convention center? Are you calling about the bag?"

There was a huge intake of phlegmy air and a gravelly voice said, "I prefer the red." Click.

It took me three full seconds to realize what had happened. I dropped the wine, kicked off the shoes, and ran downstairs to J. C.'s, banging on her door like a crazy woman. "Call nine one one, call nine one one!"

Wilson and Vargas were back in less than

thirty minutes. Once again, we received them in J. C.'s apartment, this time J. C. in her jammies, clutching her door bar, and me, barefoot and in a red spandex dress.

"If we'd known you were dressing for dinner we would have stayed for the ziti."

TWENTY-FOUR

Nothing could have induced me to sleep at Lucy's that night. Not J. C.'s offer of protection with her all-purpose weapon. Not Wilson and Vargas, who'd assured me they'd check in every two hours even after their shift ended in the morning. I wasn't the nervous type and it was true, nothing serious had happened. As if reciting from the manual, Vargas had said nine times out of ten prank calls were nothing more than bored kids getting their jollies.

If he'd said nine hundred and ninety-nine times out of a thousand I might have liked the odds better, but I wasn't going to get a good night's sleep, wondering if I was the unlucky tenth time out of ten. I didn't really think I'd be raped or murdered in Lucy's bed, but I needed a good night's sleep and that wasn't going to happen if I had to keep one eye open all night.

J. C. and the cops tried to talk me out of

it. She even offered me a spot on her sofa — an enormous concession from someone who greeted most strangers with a bar in hand — and I was grateful but adamant. The cops agreed to give me a ride to the St. George Hotel. I threw some essentials and Lucy's stilettos in a hard-sided suitcase with rotating wheels and an extending handle. I wasn't about to give a Peeping Tom another girlie show, so I left the red dress on. It was quite a look with my own sensible Merrells.

"Did you call us from this phone?" Wilson asked, as I finished packing.

"No. Why?"

Wilson pressed ★69 on Lucy's phone. He took out his pad and wrote down the number that appeared.

"Worth a try," he said, pleased with himself. He dialed the number, but there was no answer. He walked over to the window. "Come here," he said. I felt a sermon coming.

Lucy lived around the corner from a high-rise as big as one of those mammoth cruise ships with hundreds of little windows. If they'd wanted to, anyone from the fifth floor on up could see directly into Lucy's bedroom, where I'd been sashaying in my underwear and practicing for my turn on the catwalk. In the sliver of street between the apartment house and a movie complex was another line of sight and a bank of pay phones backlit by the theater's marquee.

"It's far away but could be one of those, too," Wilson said, looking at the traffic coming out of the theater. "Easy enough to find out."

"I didn't know there still *were* pay phones."

"Yeah. And there are still people who don't have E-Z-Pass and know how to parallel park. Where are you from?" I wasn't in the mood for that discussion again, especially since I had started the evening feeling like a savvy New Yorker and now felt like a rube.

"Even if someone saw me, how would anyone out there know this number?" I asked.

"Not hard to check the names on the mailboxes downstairs and figure out who lives where," his partner said. "You said this wasn't your place. Your friend in the habit of walking around in her . . . skivvies?"

Lucy and I had been roommates some years back. I still cringe remembering the time she signed for a FedEx package in a teddy, cowboy boots, and a hat Garth Brooks would have been proud to wear. No doubt the FedEx guy remembered, too. I grew defensive on my friend's behalf. "What does that have to do with anything?"

"We're just asking. That's what we do. We'll check to see if she's ever filed a complaint. Technically, this is aggravated harassment." He rattled off the rule book definition.

"Off the record, there's not much we can do. Your friend might consider curtains. Do you want us to file a complaint?"

If I said no and there was a repeat performance, no report would exist of it ever having happened before so I said yes. It was a sharp reminder I no longer lived in the city. In Springfield, I could dance around buck naked and do nothing more than annoy the barred owl that lived in the hemlock forty feet from my deck. And if anything *did* happen, Mike O'Malley would be there in a flash. He'd probably station an armed guard in my driveway. I wouldn't say I had my way with the Springfield police, but after three years and as many adventures, we took each other seriously. More seriously than these guys were taking me.

The cops finished their report. By the time we pulled up to the St. George, it was close to eleven o'clock. J. C. had called ahead to book the room for me, and I assured her I'd be back the following night for reheated ziti — which everyone knows is better the second day anyway.

Climbing out of a police cruiser, slightly disheveled, in a red spandex dress, leather jacket, and flats, I worried I looked like the paid entertainment at a precinct retirement party, but times had changed and the doorman had obviously seen worse, so he held the door as if I were the First Lady arriving for a charity function. I wheeled my suitcase toward the check-in desk.

The hotel lobby was more crowded than I expected it to be at that hour, and I had to weave in and out of a few clusters of people I was sure were staring at me. Then I heard a familiar voice.

"Not crazy about the shoes, but I like the red dress."

I shoved the extended handle on the wheelie down, grabbed the bag with both hands, spun around, and slugged the speaker on the side of his head with the full weight of my suitcase and all the torque in my body. People scattered in fear and the man staggered and dropped to his knees holding his head.

"What the . . ."

There was no blood, but Guy Anzalone was clearly shaken up.

TWENTY-FIVE

The doorman helped Guy to his feet. He no longer treated me as if I were the First Lady but possibly the deranged ex-lover of the man who was still shaking off a nasty blow to the temple.

"You like the red dress, hunh?" I was still seething with the thought that Guy or one of his flunkies had been spying on me, and I was getting ready to deliver the coup de grâce directly to his knees with my sensibly clad tight foot. He saw it coming and sidestepped the blow.

"Wait a minute. I'm sorry! The shoes are fine. It's an interesting . . . look."

A suitcase to the head was clearly not the response Guy Anzalone expected to what he thought was a compliment. He seemed sincere. Could I have been wrong? I held up on my swing.

He continued rubbing the side of his head. "Last time I make any comment about a woman's shoes," he muttered.

The doorman quietly asked Guy if he "should call someone," probably meaning the police. I closed my eyes and willed him to say no. Not three times in one night. I was starting to feel like a streetwalker rounded up every couple of hours. This couldn't be happening.

"Not if the lady agrees to have a drink with me to explain what just happened." I had given more statements that night than a presidential press secretary. I looked at my watch. In twenty-three minutes the day would be over and I could start fresh all over again.

I nodded and let him lead me to a booth not far from where we'd had drinks with Connie earlier this evening.

"I'm surprised you're still here. Where's your wife?" I asked, once we sat down.

"*Now, that's a mood killer. I was hoping you'd start with something like Gee, Guy, I'm sorry, I thought you were someone else* or *Thank you, I'm glad you like the dress.*" He called the waiter over. I ordered a light beer and he asked for a single malt. "No champagne?" he asked, when the waiter left.

"I've had a rough day. I don't feel very celebratory. So where *is* Connie?"

"She's upstairs, trying on outfits for

tomorrow. There's a club I like, near the river. Gentlemen's club. I had a few drinks there and then came back here to tuck Connie in. I got an early appointment in Brooklyn, so I'm not staying in Manhattan tonight." He eyed me from top to bottom, and even without his saying it, I could tell he really did like the red dress. Someone once told me all women should own one and I was considering a future purchase. "I could change my mind and stay in town if I had a compelling reason to do so."

Having just "tucked his wife in," the man had stamina.

"Wanna tell me why you gave me the love tap?"

Unless Guy was a better actor than Ben Kingsley, he genuinely didn't know about the anonymous call to Lucy's. In fact, he was curious when I told him about it.

"What exactly did the caller say? His specific words." For the third time that night I repeated what had happened.

"Why are *you* so interested?" I asked. I thought about Fat Frank and Cookie. Was watching me part of their assignment in looking after Mrs. Anzalone? "Did you have me followed?"

"Why would I do that?"

That was not a satisfactory answer. He

131

finished his drink and the waiter hovered. I was suddenly conscious of not having eaten dinner and my growling stomach gave me away, but the hotel's kitchen was closed. Guy offered to take me to Mulberry Street to a place he claimed made the best gnocchi in the city, but I didn't see myself explaining to Connie the next day how I happened to go out for a midnight snack with her husband who should have been on his way to Brooklyn. I declined and continued plowing through the nuts.

"So did you?"

"Have you followed? That's ridiculous. You're a nice girl. Woman. Bit of a violent streak, but that's not a deal breaker." He was still flirting, but it was a soft sell. Not enough to make me nervous.

"So what does the Tumbled Stone King do when he's not tumbling stone?" I asked.

He had other interests and investments, as Connie had said, but he was vague and that contributed to the feeling that some of what Guy Anzalone did wasn't on the up-and-up.

After ninety minutes, half a beer, and two bowls of nuts, Guy convinced me that he and no one in his employ had called Lucy's, and I eventually apologized for braining him with my suitcase. The weapon in question, sitting on the floor next to our table, reminded me I still hadn't checked in.

"Listen, I'm exhausted. I am extremely sorry for striking you with my bag. As bizarre as this sounds, I have a date to go shopping with your wife tomorrow, so I really should get to bed. Alone." That got a rise out of the couple at the next table who clearly found our conversation more interesting than their own.

"You sure I can't tuck you in, too?"

By this time I didn't even think he was serious. It seemed to be the only way he knew to speak to a woman. I stood up to leave and had to pull down the hem of the red dress, which had ridden up to midthigh. "Let me call Connie. If she says yes, I'll go." I fished around in my jacket pocket looking for my cell, even though I knew I wouldn't be making the call.

"All right, forget it. Go upstairs. Besides, if you stay any longer I might wind up owning another weirdo garden ornament."

"They're not garden ornaments. They're art. And it's an investment. Yours is going to appreciate dramatically."

"Yeah, yeah, like souvenir coins and Lladro and all that other crap she has around the house. I get it."

We still hadn't discussed delivery. I figured

since it involved *manly issues,* like trucks and shipping, it would be his domain and not hers.

"Give me your cell number," I said, "that way we can work out the shipping details."

He hemmed and hawed and deferred to his wife, which was a first in my limited experience with this couple.

"You don't need to call me. And if I want to talk to you, we know how to reach you."

Did they? I didn't remember giving either of them my number. And I did remember J. C's earlier advice — *"Watch your back."* And I felt Guy Anzalone watching it, too, as I walked away.

TWENTY-SIX

There were almost as many Starbucks stores in New York as there were Korean grocers, but the old-time diners and coffee shops were a dying breed, forced out of existence by the purveyors of designer lattes, which took a full minute to order and another five to get. All things being equal, I went with the small businessman.

Connie and I had planned to meet at Andrew's Coffee Shop not far from the Wagner Center and equidistant from the St. George and Lucy's apartment, where I'd assumed I'd be waking up. Even though I'd slept at the hotel, I thought it best to stick to the original plan so I wouldn't get sucked into spending more time on this mission of mercy than I'd planned.

One of the best things about diners in New York (and maybe everywhere) was the dessert case. Gleaming with chrome like Airstream trailers, some were tall with revolving shelves. Others were horizontal and big as meat lockers, only instead of carcasses they held towering carrot cakes, strawberry shortcakes, éclairs, napoleons, seven-layer cakes, coconut cream pies, chocolate cakes with a half inch of icing between the layers and even more on top, and white cakes so artfully decorated all that was missing was the happy plastic couple on top. They were shrines to butter and sugar.

Despite the ball and chain of my suitcase, I got to Andrew's Coffee Shop ten minutes early and slid into a booth under the establishment's Wall of Fame, where autographed pictures of politicians, wrestlers, and neighborhood luminaries looked down on me as I checked out the menu. The dessert case called, as it always did, but the thought of Lucy's red dress and the possibility of fabric fatigue as it stretched across my middle kept me on the straight and narrow. I ordered coffee and waited for Connie to arrive. The night before she'd told me she'd been to Barney's and Bloomingdale's and had gone to Bergdorf's but never gotten higher than the first floor because she wasn't comfortable there. Perhaps she really had gotten out the phone book and started with the *A*s in pursuit of the perfect outfit for the reception. If that was the case, I could be looking at a lengthy expedition that would take us from Chanel to Zara.

My coffee cup was refilled twice and I'd successfully identified all the celebrities in the photographs when I started getting antsy. I called Connie's room at the hotel and she said she was just leaving. Why was she still there? Fat Frank was driving, and Connie swore she'd arrive in five minutes. She would have been on time, she said, but she and Guy had had a knockdown, dragout fight that morning — as much as you can over the telephone. Up until that point, I had had every intention of telling Connie about my nightcap with her husband, but she launched into a theory about his bogus early morning meeting, that ended with her threatening to fling lye in the face of the woman she suspected he was two-timing her with. I thought it best to stay silent before she sent Fat Frank to the hardware store for lye.

The meter was already running. I would give this two hours, even if we only got to the *F* for Fendi. One hour was too short, as if I couldn't wait to get away from her and three hours — well, three hours was too long to spend with a woman who wore mollusks on her boobs and thought maiming a romantic rival was appropriate behavior.

By this time, the formerly nice waitress began to wonder if it had been a mistake to let me occupy such valuable real estate if all I was going to do was guzzle free refills on the coffee, yak on the phone, and study the pictures on the Wall of Fame.

"Do you need a few more minutes, honey?" she asked. This was waitress code for *Are you ever going to eat anything? And My wrist is killing me, why didn't you sit at the counter so I wouldn't have to keep walking back and forth with this heavy pot?*

"I'm waiting for someone." I tried to look hungry to assure her that when my companion arrived, we'd order mountains of food. She glared at the counter in case I missed the hint. I looked, too, and smiled. It was a known fact that smiling, along with saying "I understand" or "I'm sorry," were three of the surest ways of getting someone to shut up and leave. Doesn't always work, but it did this time. She walked away, slightly puzzled, and replaced the coffeepot on the Bunn-O-Matic machine, staring at me and muttering to one of her colleagues behind the counter.

Seated at the counter were a handful of men — solo diners with the look of regulars, there for fuel, not the ambience, and certain that by sitting at the counter they wouldn't have to make eye contact with anyone. At the far end of the line of stools something caught my eye. A denim jacket, covered in patches. I only saw the back of it because the wearer was hunched over his food and the hoodie underneath was pulled up over his head. I'd seen a jacket like that recently.

Just then, Connie breezed into the coffee shop, full of sunshine and profuse apologies and yammering on about the members' reception as if it were prom night and she was hoping to be named queen. That was where I'd seen it, the flower show. The kid whose bag was stashed at my booth was wearing something like it. I jumped up and swept by Connie.

"Hey! Where are you going?"

"Have a seat under Hulk Hogan and study the menu. Whatever you get, order the same for me so the waitress doesn't think I'm a deadbeat. I'll be right back."

As I got closer, I recognized some of the patches on the jacket — Virgin Gorda, Tahoe, Canyonlands, Moab. I tapped the guy on the shoulder.

"Excuse me?"

TWENTY-SEVEN

He spun around on the counter stool as if ready for a fight. It wasn't the kid who'd tried to sneak into the show. It was one of Lauryn Peete's high school gardeners. The one with the rat.

"Oh, hi. Sorry. I thought you were someone else. The jacket looks familiar. Are you Jamal? Ms. Peete mentioned your name." The kid said nothing and gave no sign he recognized me so I kept talking. "Some guy left a bag at my booth. At the flower show. He was wearing a jacket very much like that one. From the other side of the coffee shop I thought you might be him." Still no response. I unnecessarily pointed to the table where Connie and the waitress were locked in an animated conversation. Jamal barely acknowledged, just the slightest move of his chin upward. "Okay, well, you're obviously not him. I'll go."

So far my return to New York had had its

ups and downs. This was one of the downs. At least in Springfield if you spoke to someone, you had a good shot at getting a civil answer. Here it was fifty-fifty. I suppressed a disappointed shake of my head and walked back to my table, where the conversation was not what you'd call lofty. It was a retelling of the time Soupy Sales, another star on the Wall of Fame, had come in for lunch. I was pretty sure it wasn't the first time the waitress had told the story, which was anticlimactic after Soupy's arrival, but it was comforting to know Soupy was "so down-to-earth" despite his exalted status.

Connie and I ordered, mostly to please the waitress, and when the food came, we dutifully picked at it but left most of it on our plates while she discussed fashion. I listened with one ear but was still fixated on another article of clothing — that unusual jacket.

What were the odds two people at a flower show had enough fondness for Moab that they'd stitch a large, horizontal patch from Arches National Park across their shoulder blades? Unless they knew each other — or it was the same jacket. The phrase "odd crop of entrants" replayed in my head. Jamal left soon after, without a glance in our direction.

The call log on my phone still had the number I'd copied from the message board the night before. I dialed it again. This time the message box was full. Well, if the kid wanted his bag, he'd come back to the convention center. Plenty of things were lost and never recovered and, as Rolanda had said, it was probably just dirty laundry anyway. I had more pressing issues to deal with — my new role as personal shopper to Connie Anzalone.

It was hard not to suck in air when she took out her digital camera, and harder still when she whipped out a second memory card, but they were pictures of her garden and she promised we'd view them only if time allowed. Mercifully there were only 114 pictures of her outfits and accessories, but they might obviate the need for an actual shopping expedition, and when I weighed the time I'd spend evaluating them against the time spent selling Primo's sculpture, I decided it was a fair exchange.

With the waitress's vote acting as tie-breaker we outfitted Connie from her existing wardrobe under the watchful eyes of such celebrity fashionistas as Phyllis Diller, Don Rickles, and the aforementioned

Soupy. Connie would look slightly less festive than the late great Fabulous Moolah, an outlandishly dressed lady wrestler who loved the food at Andrew's, but better than all of them, and Guy would be pleased that no additional purchases were required.

As an afterthought the waitress asked what I was wearing. My suitcase was underneath the table, so I heaved it into a neighboring booth, unzipped it, and pulled out Lucy's red dress. I held it up with one hand on my shoulder and the other on my hip. I half stood and leaned against the back of the leather booth.

"What think?"

The men at the counter were ayes. In fact, all the men were ayes, including the busboy, who was too shy to do more than just nod enthusiastically, which rattled the dirty cups and dishes in the gray plastic tub he was holding but threatening to drop. We had one nay, but it was from a pinched, crabby-looking woman eating a jelly omelet, who said, in between mouthfuls, that it looked slutty. Considering the source we took that as a positive.

"The V-neck is a little deep. I may pin a silk rose there, just for modesty's sake."

Connie and Nancy — by this time we were on a first-name basis with the waitress

— thought that was lunacy and recommended lots of gold jewelry instead and perhaps a white fox fur to jazz it up. I promised to take it under advisement.

By the time I left the new friends, still chattering, the two hours I'd allotted for Connie's consultation had been exceeded by forty-five minutes. I was anxious to get back to Lucy's.

I felt foolish for having run out the night before and dropping $250 on a hotel room, when I had a perfectly good place to crash for free. Nothing that bad had happened so I was going back, but this time I had a decorating plan.

In Connecticut I'd head for a Walgreens. In New York, I needed a dollar store. All I needed to do for the rest of my stay was cover Lucy's windows, and the quickest way to do that was with inexpensive fabric and a roll of duct tape.

It was what I'd done in my first apartment in Park Slope, Brooklyn. That apartment was an oversized studio with a wall of windows that overlooked a strip of postage-stamp–sized gardens. It also looked directly into the windows of the building around the block. One unfortunate glimpse of a hirsute neighbor in tighty-whities convinced me that a bed, a stereo, and a full-length mirror did not an apartment make. As my mother would have said, I needed window treatments. That same night, with Lucy's help, I'd duct-taped cheap tablecloths from the local drugstore over the windows. It was early summer, and I can still remember the dancing ketchup bottles and relish jars on the yellow plastic tablecloths because, after all, what's a picnic without happy condiments?

I got used to the tablecloths and they stayed up through October until the inevitable visit from my parents, who were horrified to see their only child living in such squalor. It was as if my mother had found me warming my hands over a garbage can fire.

Not far from the Wagner I had seen a bargain store called Deal-town Discounts. It was sandwiched in between an Irish bar and a Chinese take-out place and the window display was filled with stacks of Pampers, school supplies, personal appliances, and plastic flowers faded from the sun.

The home goods aisle had nothing larger than napkins and dish towels, but I was short on time. Making a duct tape quilt to cover the window was out. I prowled around the store in search of seasonal goods.

Christmas had passed, it was too early for summer merchandise, and, not surprisingly, St. Patty's Day didn't focus on eating as much as it did on drinking, so no table-cloths. Leftover green plastic flutes and leprechaun hats weren't going to cut it. Neither was the store's major closeout item and special of the week, a purple fleece blanket with sleeves that for all the world looked like someone had killed and skinned Barney. Time was getting short. Worst-case scenario J. C. would let me get dressed at her place, but I wanted to give it one last shot, so I kept looking.

"Ain't you going to that party?" It was a young man's voice.

I spun around. It was Jamal. Had he been hovering, waiting for me to finish with Connie? Did he follow me to the store? The thought set me on edge, and he was percep-tive enough to pick up on it. I nodded. Yeah, I was going.

"Don't look so worried. I work here part-time. I just came to pick up my paycheck."

I was relieved. His icy manner at the cof-fee shop had thawed, but not much. Jamal absentmindedly straightened the items on one of the pet food shelves and picked up a box of dog biscuits, shaking it slowly like a maraca.

"What are you looking for?"

I spared him the details of my window treatment strategy. "Tablecloths."

"Nothing new till barbeque season." He seemed to be thinking. "Are they for your tables at the show?" I shook my head. I told him I was desperate and didn't care what the tablecloths looked like as long as they weren't clear plastic.

"Hold on a sec." Five minutes later Jamal came out of the stock room with three dusty packages covered with markdown stickers. I peered inside one of the bags.

"Happy Thanksgiving." There were two large oblongs and a round. They'd do nicely. "How much?"

"Forget it. We've already written them off. You'll be doing us a favor making them go away."

"Are you sure?" I looked around as if there was someone else I should ask. Some grown-up. But Jamal was sure. He even offered me his store discount on the duct tape so my window treatments totalled about two dollars. I'd have to e-mail my mother — she'd get a kick out of it.

As the cashier rang up the sale, I made small talk with Jamal. I tried to stay away from the subject of the jacket but finally couldn't help myself. I asked where he bought it.

"Man, I thought you were different, but you're just like the rest of them. I didn't steal it, okay?" He stormed off, through a door marked Employees Only, and I was left at the counter with a gum-cracking girl whose entire vocabulary consisted of "un-hunh."

Just like the rest of them? That hurt.

TWENTY-EIGHT

Late that afternoon I dressed in Lucy's bedroom, shielded from prying eyes by dozens of cherubic Pilgrims carrying muskets. Soon after, I was out the door in a slinky red dress with a red silk flower pinned to the bodice. At the last moment I pulled on a military-style jacket with a lot of gold buttons for extra coverage in case the flower pin wasn't enough coverage and I grew self-conscious. It either looked chic or goofy, but I had no time to go to the coffee shop for a show of hands.

My taxi crawled to a stop a block from the convention center. Half a dozen limos disgorged their even slower-moving passengers but I was too impatient and hopped out early. It was as if I'd stepped into a movie premiere, only with a fair number of older, less ambulatory people on a green — not red — carpet. I didn't want to make any unfair assumptions, but I did anyway, speculating that the older attendees were horticultural society members and the younger ones were exhibitors and landscapers. There were even a few television cameras, which experience told me would deliver a thirty-second sound bite before moving on to the next small story of the day.

A canvas tent had been installed outside the Wagner Center as a checkpoint, where security guards made sure everyone's papers were in order and gatecrashers weren't trying to worm their way inside. Luckily I'd remembered to stash my badge in my borrowed clutch purse.

Lucy's jacket with its gold buttons and geegaws set off the metal detectors, which continued to sound even after I'd removed it. That sent up a flare to the rest of the security staff, who were on high alert for protesters hoping to disrupt the proceedings.

I spotted Kristi Reynolds in the distance, but she ignored my efforts to catch her eye. She was welcoming a group of well-heeled attendees, including a sour-faced Allegra Douglas and the other woman I'd met in the ladies' room. From the look of pained resignation on Kristi's face, Allegra was giving her an earful. But if Kristi wanted to escape, she wasn't rushing to my aid.

I tried another approach with the security guards. "Rolanda Knox will vouch for me. Call her. What could I possibly have hidden under this dress? There's barely room for me." One guard in particular looked like he wanted to pat me down to find out.

"Touché. She makes an excellent point, young man." I recognized the voice and smiled. It was Mrs. Moffitt, trailed by her entourage. Apparently Mrs. Moffitt and company went anywhere they pleased. Her tacit endorsement of my character was enough for the bouncer at the door, and the four of us — Mrs. Moffitt, Rick, and a man I assumed was Jensen, her gardener — swept in as a group. Our entrance registered with Kristi Reynolds, who finally deigned to look my way now that I was with someone important. Rick and Mr. Jensen escorted us into the members' prefunction area, where the earliest arrivals enjoyed cocktails before the floor was opened and the reception officially began.

"I adore your jacket, dear. It's Balenciaga, isn't it?" The building seemed twenty degrees cooler than it had been during setup, so I quickly put the jacket back on but not before checking the label. Mrs. M., as Rick called her, knew her stuff.

"They keep the room cold for the plants," Jensen explained, "keeps them at attention, otherwise they'll wilt." A certain part of my anatomy was responding the same way.

Jensen snapped pictures with a digital single-lens reflex camera as he spoke. He was attentive to his employer, but she brushed off his efforts to retrieve a gray cashmere shawl from a bag hanging on the handles of her wheelchair.

"May I get you a cup of tea, Mrs. M.?"

"Jensen, you must stop making me old before my time. I'm wearing a long velvet skirt and underneath it a pair of silk long johns." She turned to me. "Now I've done it. I've made them both blush. I dearly love to do that. If you want to get me something, Jensen, fetch me a vodka gimlet and one for yourself. You need to relax. And if none of those young pups knows how to make one, I'll settle for a martini. Very dry."

Jensen hurried off, pleased to be of service. It was clear Mrs. Moffitt had good relationships with her staff. "I believe Jensen has a crush on me, but he's far too old. From the age of forty on, women should start looking for younger men." She patted Rick's hand and promised to stop at my booth within the hour after she had made the obligatory rounds. I repeated the number and aisle twice to make sure they remembered.

I strode toward my area of the exhibit floor, careful not to let Lucy's higher-than-I-normally-wore heels get caught on any of the carpet seams. David was resplendent in a tuxedo that fit too well to be rented. He kissed me on both cheeks. The usually chatty Nikki barely nodded, ignoring me and pouring all her attention into a triangle of baklava and a plastic glass of wine from a nearby bar cart.

When she finally spoke, it was to shove a piece of paper in my direction. "Here. I saw this note on the message board — it's about that bag. I copied the number for you."

"That was thoughtful. I saw it, too. I've tried him twice, but there's been no answer. Maybe *I* should leave a note for *him*."

I grabbed one of my business cards from the Plexiglas container on the table and started writing the kid a note, but quickly outgrew the space on the tiny rectangle.

"Use this," Nikki said. She handed me a five-by-seven postcard that had thumbnail pictures of her most treasured antiques on one side.

"Thanks." I scribbled a longer message and my coordinates, and planned to post it later. Nikki looked pouty and her two-word answers told me something was wrong. She attacked another wedge of baklava. I looked to David for an explanation.

"What's going on?" He was as clueless as I.

"Whatever it is, you have five minutes to move on. I don't want to be stuck between two harridans all weekend. I've already got one on the other side." His light touch broke the strained silence.

"Nothing. Everything's fine," Nikki said, breaking off another honeyed chunk of pastry and shoving it into her mouth. Whatever was bothering her had generated a classic case of anger eating.

She swallowed hard and washed it down with a big gulp of white wine. Uh-oh.

"Go like this," I said, rubbing the front of my borrowed Balenciaga.

Nikki looked down and saw a shiny glob of honey slowly moving down the front of her dress. She foolishly rubbed at the spot with a cocktail napkin, which turned the small sticky spot into a larger one covered with flecks of white paper.

"That's just great. First I have another fight with Russ and he says he's not coming, then I start to feel the beginnings of a cold sore, and now Mrs. Moffitt is going to see me and think I'm a slob." Something

154

akin to a whimper came out of Nikki's mouth.

David volunteered to fetch a glass of water, but the dress was silk and water would only make things worse. Nikki's eyes welled up and her artfully applied smoky eyes were in danger of becoming *Pagliacci* eyes. I risked goose bumps for the next three hours and peeled off Lucy's jacket. "Here, put this on."

She looked me up and down. "Like that's going to fit me?" she said. One lone tear spilled down her face. I could almost hear Pavarotti — it was *Pagliacci* time.

I unpinned the red silk flower I'd fastened to the deep V of my neckline. "Try this."

She still looked like the sad clown in a velvet painting, but her watery eyes now held a spark of hope. I fastened a piece of folded napkin to the stickiest spot and pinned the red flower on top of it. It covered the stain and even added to the look of Nikki's simple black sheath. She sniffled and tried to collect herself.

"For cold sores? I have a friend who swears by lysine. Take handfuls before you go to bed tonight. No nuts, no chocolate, and go easy on the alcohol."

"You're being so nice to me." She was instantly contrite. "You know, my ego's not that fragile."

"Nikki, I don't know what you're talking about."

"If you didn't like my arrangement, you could have just told me. You didn't need to sneak back and change things."

I stood ten feet back and squinted at Primo's booth trying to see what Nikki was fussed about, while she produced a pocket mirror to fix her face and check out the flower pin.

"The pin looks great, but I look awful."

To the naked eye, the arrangement was the same as we had left it the previous night. Except perhaps that *Pink Flamingo,* the tall thin birdlike sculpture, was a little farther to the left than it was yesterday. And maybe *Kelly,* a hunk of hammered metal contorted into an elaborate, abstract spiral, was slightly farther to the back of the booth.

"It *is* different. What a good eye you have," I said, hoping to patch things up. "But I didn't change a thing, I swear. Maybe it was the staff, maybe I was too close to the flow of traffic or the electrical outlets. Who knows? Help me fix it?"

She brightened visibly, then launched into rearranging Primo's creations. "The workmen usually know better than to move things, even *before* the curious incidents in

156

the night started happening. Which reminds me, there was another one early this morning. Dog poop. In the Gramercy Park exhibit."

"Well, at least that you can pick up. Nasty but not really damaging."

"It is when you throw it down a recirculating well. I don't know what smelled worse, the poop or the bleach they used to clean it out. It was reeking when I got here at four P.M."

She fussed with the flower pin, dislodging the paper napkin that had kept the honey from touching Lucy's silk rose. That would cost me, but at least she hadn't said yes to borrowing the jacket.

"I'm going to the members' lounge to fix this. Give me the postcard you wrote for the kid. I'll post it on the bulletin board."

After Nikki left, so did the drama. David and I took our places, waiting for the games to begin. I unearthed my recharged laptop, plugged it in, and pulled up the first page of the quickie slide show I'd slapped together.

"PowerPoint," David said. "Cutting edge."

It was. For a woman who owned a manual lawn mower. Fifteen minutes later, just as the reception was to begin, the lights went out and the entire convention center was plunged into darkness.

TWENTY-NINE

Cell phones lit up like fireflies in the summertime or cigarette lighters at a rock concert, and there was a faint *Close Encounters*-like glow coming from the main doors and the escalator beyond, where the nightly news cameras had been set up. But not enough to see by. My computer kicked into battery mode, so I had slightly more light than my booth neighbors. With no windows or skylights, the enormous space was like a giant cave, except for the few dots illuminating the exit signs.

After a brief moment of alarm — this was, after all, a public building in New York City — there was a ripple of nervous laughter, then the finger pointing began.

"It's those damn lamps," I heard someone say through gritted teeth.

David's unflustered voice came out of nowhere. "I beg your pardon. What makes you think it wasn't your tacky fountains.

Not only are they hideous, eighties, new age crap, they've got everyone around here running for a pee at twenty-minute intervals." That part was true enough, although I never really understood the biology behind that.

David and the fountain lady — his less friendly neighbor on the other side — had been engaged in a custody battle over the community outlet located squarely between their two booths. They were to share the power strip but with an outlet extender, or whatever those things were called. You could plug in as many items as you wanted and not realize you were reaching critical mass until the lights went out. Was that what had happened?

Fountain Lady, whose real name had been rendered unreadable by flowery, overcalligraphied lettering, had a twenty-by-twenty space in which she had attempted to recreate Niagara Falls, in tabletop miniatures, choreographed to canned harp music. By the end of the show, in addition to feeling that we'd all overdosed on diuretics, everyone within thirty feet of her booth would likely feel hypnotized.

In fairness, crammed with floor lamps, table lamps, and sconces, David's booth was also a sensory overload, but we liked him so we minded less. Unfair but true. Since the day before, when one of the fixtures in his booth shorted out and temporarily stopped the waterworks, it had been all-out war between the two exhibitors.

"For heaven's sake," he'd said, in his playful way, "lighten up. The show's not even open yet." She hadn't, and now under cover of darkness the sniping had escalated.

Background noises ranged from giggles to the occasional clatter of a metal object dropping to the purposeful steps and walkie-talkie noises of those trying to rectify the situation. Someone yelped as if she'd walked into a cactus.

Minutes ticked by as we waited for the convention center's emergency generator to kick in. All over there were mutterings of "sorry" and "excuse me" as people bumped into each other as they foolishly tried to get around in the dark. I stayed put, feeling around for a water bottle and eventually just sitting on the carpeted floor of my booth with my legs stretched out in front of me, trying not to wrinkle.

"If I ever do anything like this again, the exhibitor is springing for the chair," I said. "My pals who registered chose poorly."

"That's a newbie's mistake. Everybody does that once. If you're planning to leave that computer on battery, angle it toward the bar. I'm going to get us drinks and I don't want to be bayoneted by a garden ornament."

"I told you. They're art. People suffer and die for art all the time."

"All due respect to Primo — and Picasso — but I'm not ready to die for any art that started life as a bicycle."

I pulled myself to my feet and obliged him by tilting the laptop slightly to the right. It threw off just enough light for David to make his way to the now unmanned bar, swipe a bottle of wine and glasses, and steal back to our booths.

"Success. I don't know what it is, but it was easier to bring it back here and pour it by the romantic light of your laptop. I didn't want to spill anything on myself. Doesn't Nikki sell candles? Speaking of which . . ."

That's right. Where was Nikki?

"Probably in the lounge," I said, "repairing her eye makeup and tearstained cheeks. I hope she wasn't mid–cat eye when the blackout hit."

David dragged over the chair from his booth and we shared it, clinking plastic cups and waiting for the lights to come back on.

"I once heard that nine months after the East Coast blackout, there was a spike in the local birthrate," he said. "It's a sad commentary on our society, when people need to have the lights out in order to do the deed. Although in *some* cases, I can understand the need."

The wine wasn't bad. I held the bottle up to the computer screen and grazed the keyboard with my fingertips to resurrect it from sleep mode. "Looks like Sancerre."

After a few moments of silence, I asked David if he suspected another act of sabotage. We kept our voices down.

"I hadn't thought of that. I was too busy defending myself to the Maid of the Mist. But you might be right. The Javits Curse strikes again."

THIRTY

I didn't believe in curses. Not since I'd read *The Hound of the Baskervilles* in the seventh grade. Someone was intentionally disrupting the show. But who? And why? What was there to gain by making a couple of hundred people uncomfortable? If it was the protesters outside, surely this wouldn't gain any converts to their cause.

After ten more minutes, which felt like sixty, the lights clicked on one hall at a time, to the cheers of hundreds of relieved exhibitors. Kristi Reynolds handled herself well and kept the peace with a brief announcement declaring that, just like in the garden, sometimes the unexpected happened, but a good gardener was prepared for anything. Applause rolled through the convention center like the wave at a sports event. Somewhere a champagne cork popped. Those predisposed to outrage continued to be outraged.

The loudest comments emanated from Allegra Douglas, who was not only outraged but who advocated legal action — although against whom and for what wasn't entirely clear. The rest of us were just happy to get the show on the road.

When the doors finally opened for the reception, members and press poured in, drinks in hand, and irritation and outrage were replaced by the heady anticipation of a successful and profitable event.

"My only complaint," David said, "is that it cut short the cocktail hour."

"The bars look open to me, although this one will be short one bottle of white wine."

"Yes, but here they'll have to stand in line. In the prefunction area, waiters circulate with drinks. The more alcohol, the more sales."

"So, then it's fortunate we're near that bar?"

"Much better than the toilet. Everyone thinks proximity to a restroom is the best placement for a trade show, but they're wrong. Better to be near the booze. One chandelier sale last year paid for my entire show. I credit the Bombay gin." I made a mental note for my next show.

After the initial rush, the attendees spread out, some naturally gravitating toward the display gardens, others to the specimen plants already judged, and still others making a beeline for new products. In that area, as expected, SlugFest drew the biggest crowd. The packaging, kept under wraps for days, had finally been revealed with a flourish — the ceremonial undraping of a mounted poster on an easel. It was a clever rendering of a slug, similar to the chalk outline police used to mark the place where a body was found, only instead of chalk the outline was drawn in silver, like the trail left by a slug. Market research had probably shown anything was better than putting an actual slug on the package, although slugs were making a comeback. There were places on the West Coast where slugs, particularly banana slugs, were considered cute. But most gardeners would be hard-pressed to find any slugs cute.

Lauryn Peete and two of her students were at the bar and I overheard the teacher say to the bartender, "Memorize these faces. Don't serve them alcohol. Not even if they say it's for me. Understand?" It sounded as if she'd said it before, perhaps at each of the bars dotting the floor of the convention center. But the message was delivered with good humor and the kids didn't seem to mind — or maybe they'd already made their own beverage arrangements. Their uniforms for the evening were black T-shirts and black pants, even Lauryn, and for a moment I wished I were one of them and not a woman in a borrowed spandex dress that required her to hold in her stomach for the next four hours.

The high school's garden was a triumph, one of the most innovative at the show, with plants growing out of rusted lard cans and trailing from seemingly abandoned grocery shopping carts. Working streetlights and neon signs flickered all over the double-wide display garden. The centerpiece was the fire escape, flanked on either side by iron bins that looked like mini Dumpsters. Primo's found-object creations would have fit right in.

Nikki was still missing in action but her husband, Russ, unexpectedly showed up in the nick of time to cover their booth and handle queries. Just as she'd predicted, he proceeded to move everything except the sarcophagus. Perhaps the urge to rearrange things was what had brought them together at a support group meeting like AA or Dieters Anonymous. Maybe it was a nervous habit.

I wasn't nervous. After all, my livelihood did not depend on what happened here over the weekend. I'd already made enough on the one sale to the Anzalones to cover Primo's tab at the Paradise Diner for the next two years. And powering toward me with her two suitors in tow was Mrs. Jean Moffitt.

David took my plastic glass and spun away. "Smile."

Rick and Mrs. M. drew near, but Jensen kept his distance, taking pictures of Primo's sculptures from every conceivable angle.

"Thank you for coming back," I said. By example, David again reminded me to smile. I did, but I felt like an idiot, grinning for no apparent reason. It had been a long time since I'd had to glad-hand and wear an insincere expression solely for business purposes. I'd already resorted to flirting to make a sale, so perhaps merely smiling could be considered raising the dialogue.

"Instead of Mr. Jensen taking pictures, I'd be happy to burn a CD for you right now or e-mail you the images," I said, grinning like a beauty queen.

"Jensen enjoys his hobbies. Photography is one of them. He's quite accomplished. They're more for his amusement than my own, although he does keep a record of the significant displays at the shows, so that we don't inadvertently repeat someone else's concept. We wouldn't want to be accused of plagiarism or whatever the botanical equivalent of that would be. What crime would you call that, Miss Holliday?"

"I don't know, ma'am. Graft?" It was weak, but she appreciated my willingness to play along and laughed more than the joke merited.

"Do send your pictures along. Rick will play them for me." She motioned to the bag hanging on the back of her chair and Rick pulled one of his employer's cards out of a thin silver case. For the second time I was close to getting the coveted card. In the meantime I started the slide show on my laptop and she was intrigued enough to stay, even though Jensen had moved on. Mrs. Moffitt asked me to pause the presentation three times for closer looks at the pieces.

"That one," she said. "Go back." I hit the back arrow and then realized the piece she was interested in seeing was the one I'd sold to the Anzalones.

"I'm sorry. I haven't had a chance to update the presentation; that one has already sold."

"I find that exceedingly irritating. I was beginning to like you."

"I just made the sale, ma'am. At the show."
Rick reminded her that I'd offered to play

the PowerPoint presentation for her two days earlier before the show had opened, but she didn't want to wait.

"If Rick says so, then I must forgive you. He is the most honorable and moral young man I know. Sometimes it's quite tedious. May I ask who the buyer was?" I didn't see any reason not to tell her, so I did.

"The Coney Island garden? Jensen mentioned Mrs. Anzalone to me. One of my competitors in the beach garden category. Jensen called it rough but charming."

"That's a lot like the lady herself. Should I find out if the artist is willing to make another piece like the one Mrs. Anzalone bought?"

"Gracious no. I wouldn't want that. Then it wouldn't be unique. Rick and I will test the waters to see how attached the lady is to her purchase." That was his cue to unlock the brake on the wheelchair. Mrs. Moffitt's card was still in his hand and I saw my sale slipping away or, more accurately, rolling away. She motioned to Jensen, who was again nearby, taking photos.

I'd clicked through most of the slides of Primo's work, when I remembered that I had uploaded them in ascending order by price. There were two more pieces after the one the Anzalones had purchased. I cleared my voice and tried not to sound desperate.

"There are two other important sculptures no one else has seen. May I show you?" Exclusivity. It was the old quantities limited, act now routine. Old as dirt, but still effective. And *important*. I'd seen that word used in an auction catalog. What did it really mean in that context? *Important* to whom? Mrs. M. had already lost out on one piece, so she summoned Jensen, who had started to drift to the next aisle.

I waited for his return before advancing the slide show to the last, biggest, and most expensive piece in Primo's collection. Jensen waited a beat, then asked me the dimensions and copied them down in a black Moleskine notebook much like one I owned. He stared at the numbers as if visualizing the item's placement. Rick wheeled Mrs. M. a discreet distance away, and the woman and her gardener conferred. When they returned, they pronounced it perfect for the Montauk garden. How many homes did this woman have? She wasn't going to let this one get away. And neither would her two employees, who would do just about anything to keep her happy.

THIRTY-ONE

While we did the paperwork on the sale, the judges announced the winners of the major display garden prizes. Best Suburban Garden: Fran Strauss, Glen Landing. Best Beach Garden: Pamela Choy, East Hampton. Best City Garden: The Sticks and Stones Garden of High School 240, Brooklyn. Best Country Garden: Mrs. Jean Moffitt, Sleepy Hollow. Best Overall Garden: Mrs. Jean Moffitt, Sleepy Hollow.

I didn't know if the winners had been informed before the rest of us, but Mrs. M. didn't seem surprised and neither was Jensen. All she said was, "I refuse to let them call me *suburban.*" That seemed as much a triumph to her as winning the awards.

Jensen and I ironed out the shipping details and Rick and Mrs. M. rolled away to celebrate and prepare for the obligatory photos.

"That's it," I said to David. "I'm done. I can't take any more smiling for a while. My face muscles need to relax. This is my neutral face. How does it look?"

"Grim but good. Like Victoria Beckham. Does that woman ever smile? With her dough, it can't be bad teeth — must be fear of wrinkles." We agreed that wrinkles or not, if either of us was with David Beckham, we'd be smiling. A lot.

"Take a break," he said. "Get something to eat and explore the show before the hordes come tomorrow. Member night is like visiting the museum without all the tourists and group leaders with green umbrellas. But don't take too long. You've got a few more hours of this."

It was a good suggestion. I knew people to congratulate, but first I went to the buffet table to fortify myself.

Only the most mean-spirited, Grinch-like woman would have begrudged Lauryn and her students the first prize they were awarded for best city garden. As it happened, the Grinch and her friend were standing right beside me, criticizing a platter of pierogie. Allegra Douglas looked as if she'd just eaten a spoonful of sour cream that had spoiled.

"Are you enjoying the show?" I asked.

The friend spoke first. "Oh, yes! Even the blackout was thrilling!" Allegra mumbled a response, but her disgusted look said it all — this was torture for her. Someone was sabotaging her show. Not only had the youngsters from the high school taken a ribbon, but apparently Connie Anzalone had received an honorable mention in the beach garden category ahead of three East Hampton gardeners that Allegra knew well. It was anarchy. Chaos. I left Allegra and her pal stewing over the canapés and went to congratulate Connie and Lauryn.

Whatever else happened at the show, it was Lauryn's night. Most of the television cameras were on her and her students. Every year there was one plant or garden that got all the attention, and this year it was hers.

I hung around, waiting for a free moment to extend my congratulations to her or to Jamal, but she was swamped and I didn't see him anywhere. Another student told me the boy hadn't shown up.

Not far away, Connie's garden was almost as crowded. "Congrats." She was deliriously happy and couldn't wait for Guy to join her later that evening. She had made it through the show unscathed, hadn't needed the bodyguards, and decided that, while tragic, her veronicas had died a perfectly natural death. Not only had her garden been acknowledged, but her backless fish-scale dress was causing quite a stir. A photographer had already immortalized her standing next to a papier-mâché sea horse. On top of that, she excitedly told me that someone named Mrs. Moffitt had invited her to a garden party to be held Sunday evening after the show closed.

"My first real friend at the show," she said. "After you, of course. But you know what I mean. One of *them.*" I did know what she meant. I wasn't one of *them.* Suburban girl in the city. City girl in the suburbs.

"I'm happy for you, Connie. You deserve it."

A second photographer approached and politely asked if he could take our pictures, but I knew he really wanted Connie so I backed away to the perimeter, where I had an overview of the entire spectacle. That was where I bumped into Rolanda.

"So was it all you thought it would be?" she asked.

"All that and a bag of chips," I said.

"I was going to come find you tonight."

"To check my badge again?"

She shook her head. "No, wise guy. The

kid? The one whose bag you have? He won't be coming for it. He's dead."

THIRTY-TWO

Rolanda Knox was not your garden-variety security guard. I knew that the first time I walked into the building. What I didn't know until the reception was that she attended John Jay College of Criminal Justice in the evenings after a full day's work, and she monitored police radio the way other people listened to National Public Radio or watched baby owls on webcams. All day long.

"I always learn something from the scanner even when it's on in the background. I listen, so I know how to observe. Yesterday I heard about a floater found in the Hudson not far from here. White male, twenty-five to thirty."

She repeated it in that staccato, impersonal cop lingo that suggested it wasn't a human — wasn't somebody's kid or friend or lover. It was a "floater," like a raft or pool toy. I guess they had to say it that way.

Otherwise, it would be too hard to think of the victim as an infant, then a toddler, then a teenager, the mental home movies fast-forwarding until the final frame, when it becomes just — a floater.

"He was wearing jeans, Timberland boots, a T-shirt."

"Isn't that every third guy who works at the Wagner?" I asked. "The carpenters and electricians? The show staff?" I didn't want it to be the kid I had joked with, the kid who would have made a cute adult if he'd ever gotten the chance. "Was he wearing a jacket with a lot of souvenir patches?"

Rolanda shook her head. "A T-shirt that said Happy Valley. He was identified as Garland Bleimeister, from Trenton, New Jersey. Wasn't that the guy who left you a message about the bag?"

There was no mistaking the name. Babe had spoken to him. And the Happy Valley shirt had registered with me. I'd had a friend who went to Penn State and wore a Happy Valley hat every time the Nittany Lions had a game, even if he was in another state. *We are Penn State.* Maybe that was why I couldn't reach the boy and he'd never called again.

"What does the medical examiner say? Did he drown?"

Rolanda shrugged. "Don't know yet. Cops don't always like to say right away, but not many people going for a dip in the Hudson this time of year. Not many civilians think to ask about the medical examiner either. You a crime show junkie?"

"No. I just had the bad luck to find a couple of bodies."

My mind was racing. Do I tell Rolanda I saw Jamal wearing the kid's jacket? Do I call the police? What if I was wrong? I didn't know what kids wore these days. For all I knew, some designer at Old Navy had a thing for the national parks and had emblazoned all the park names on their new spring line. Thousands of people could be walking around with the word *Canyonlands* written across their backs or tied around their hips. Maybe it had something to do with the guy who had to cut his arm off. He'd turned into a hero to some people. Why wasn't Jamal here? Was he afraid because the body had been found and it would only be a matter of time before he was apprehended?

"I'd better call the cops," I said. "I still have the kid's bag. Even if it's not evidence, the next of kin will want it."

"If I don't see you later, can we catch up tomorrow?" Rolanda said.

"Sure. I should get back to work. You know where to find me. We can talk in the morning."

"Late afternoon. There's a service for Otis at a Baptist church up in Harlem. A lot of us will be there, so there may be some new faces here tomorrow."

I was drawing a blank.

"Otis Randolph, the janitor who passed." I felt ashamed to have forgotten him. Rolanda and I exchanged cell numbers and agreed to meet tomorrow in the Overview Café, just outside the show's entrance on the second floor of the convention center. If I was too busy and couldn't sneak away, I'd call, and if the service for Otis ran long, she'd do the same. I took my time getting back to the booth. Death has a way of slowing you down, of reminding you there are more important things than whatever you're rushing off to do. Maybe there's a sympathetic, physical reaction, an acknowledgment of a soul leaving the planet.

Back at the shops, where no one knew or cared about the dead boy, business was booming. David's partner, Aaron, had arrived. The wavy black hair and heavy-framed eyeglasses had me itching to break into a chorus of "Peggy Sue," but I restrained myself since I didn't know if the look was intentional or not. The men were chatting up a middle-aged woman and her companion who — judging by the shopping bag and fabric books — could only be her decorator. I overheard something about redoing the country house, so I figured things were going well.

We'd talked about a late dinner and a drink if the three of us had anything to celebrate, and so far David and I had each made a big sale. It was Nikki's turn. But even though I'd only met him once, it seemed ghoulish to party now after having learned of Garland's death. They could celebrate without me. Besides, Nikki was still gone.

The husband had amassed a stack of clear plastic cups on the wicker table he was using as a desk. I counted six. Like wet rings on a bar they told me how long he'd been waiting. They could have been club soda, but his demeanor told me they'd held something stronger. Perhaps it was the muttering, which was not as sotto voce as he thought it was. I took the direct approach.

"So, where's Nikki?" I asked.

"That's what I'd like to know. I wasn't even supposed to be here. I just dropped by . . . never mind." He'd repeatedly called Nikki's cell, but there'd been no answer for the last thirty minutes, the whole time I'd been away from our group.

It was hard to believe she'd just leave. Did she decide she looked hideous in her stained dress and go home to change? Women have done crazier things. I've changed my clothes in elevators on my way out. Maybe she was still in the lounge talking to one of those "big pencils." But even then, wouldn't she drag the buyer back to her booth to close the sale?

"She did this on purpose," Russ said. "She's always complaining that she does it all. I do plenty. She knew I needed to be somewhere tonight, but she resents my trying to leave the business. She saw me here and knew I wouldn't leave the booth deserted. She let me do all the work out of spite."

"I don't think so. She was very excited about this evening. You might want to call security to make sure she's okay. Someone had an accident on an escalator here the other day."

After a brief, testy exchange on the phone, Russ sucked it up and resurrected his charm, but only when someone was within ten feet of Nikki's booth. He was effective when he wasn't fuming and glaring at his cell, willing it to ring. What did I know? I was rusty in the relationship department. Maybe she *had* seen him and stayed away. Between the Anzalones and this couple I was feeling good about being single.

Two browsers, well dressed and drinking, were gently spinning one of Primo's wind devices, so I excused myself and turned on my smile. "May I tell you about the artist?"

Over the course of the next two hours, floor lamps, tufa troughs, urns, four of Primo's smaller pieces — including the wind device — and countless pinecone nightlights were taken away or tagged with sold stickers. Only the mini Niagara fountains remained untouched.

At 7:45 P.M., an announcement came over the public address system that the reception was ending. I crouched down and pulled aside the blue polyester drape Velcroed to the folding table to retrieve Garland Bleimeister's bag.

It was gone.

David, Aaron, and I scoured the area, but the kid's bag was nowhere to be found. "Maybe someone moved it."

"Who'd move it?" David said. "You know how neurotic some of these people are. And the cleaning staff knows better than to touch anything."

Just the same I looked underneath the

tables on both sides of the booth and behind the backdrop curtain. No bag, just knocked-down cardboard boxes and two cases of Trader Joe's water.

"Afraid we'll have a dry spell?" Aaron asked.

"Go ahead, laugh. I can't bring myself to spend five dollars for a bottle of water, even when someone else is paying for it. It threatens my self-delusion that we're living in a rational world."

"Wow. Glad I asked."

"Here. Hydrate." I pulled two bottles from the opened case and tossed them to David and Aaron.

"Do you think he picked it up when you weren't here?"

"Like when? I've been here every hour the show's been open."

"Which leaves the hours the show hasn't been open. Maybe that's why the ornaments were out of place," David said. "Sorry — *artwork*."

They looked so cheerful, I hated to blurt it out and ruin the moment.

"I'm pretty sure the owner is dead."

David stared. "*Dead* as in you'll no longer have anything to do with him?"

"No. Dead as in pushing up daisies. Taking the big dirt nap."

The overhead lights were flashing when a ripple of news spread through the crowd, finally reaching us.

A woman's body had been found in the members' lounge.

THIRTY-THREE

Days before the show had opened, exhibitors and staff had been informed that in the event of police or medical emergencies, we should notify convention center security of the Big Apple Flower Show office and *not* dial 911, which we'd been told would slow down response time. But everyone's first instinct was to call 911, and that's what Lauryn Peete had done when she'd gone to freshen up in the members' lounge ladies' room and seen a lifeless arm sticking out from under one of the doors. She pushed the door open with her foot and saw Nikki Bingham facedown in the stall.

Nikki was unconscious. Her panty hose had giant holes, her knees were skinned, and she had a lump on her forehead the size and color of a damson plum. After the police and convention center security had been alerted, Rolanda Knox called me.

"An anonymous caller to the BAFS emergency line said they heard a fight between a man and a woman in the lounge. But the call was right before the blackout," she said. "No one did anything and no one remembered until afterward."

Rolanda didn't know Nikki's condition. She had been stabilized — or collared and boarded, as the hired EMT staff person had put it. It looked gruesome — and serious — but it was standard procedure for anyone with a head injury even if it turned out to be nothing. Then she'd been taken to St. Athanasius's Hospital in Greenwich Village.

Rolanda and I stayed on the phone until I reached the members' lounge, where she'd agreed to wait for me. By the time I got there, most of the onlookers had gone.

"Maybe there really is a Javits Curse," I said. I hit Call End and shoved my phone in my too small clutch purse. I don't know at what point I decided to tell Rolanda what I knew about Jamal and the jacket, but I had. Somewhere between the news of Garland Bleimeister's death and Nikki's what . . . accident? Assault? Domestic violence incident? I needed a reality check from someone who knew about this stuff, even if it was only through show gossip and eavesdropping on the police radio.

Rolanda looked tired. "Damn. This may

just have trumped the shenanigans at the cat show."

"Interested in a drink?" I asked.

"With you in that dress and me looking like a prison guard? Wait until I change and then, hell, yes."

I sat on a low, gray settee outside the staff locker room. Exhibitors and workers were still trickling out, and the extra police hovered discreetly, probably wondering what I was doing sitting on a bench in the darkened convention center as if I were waiting for a bus.

When Rolanda finally emerged, she looked totally different. Tight jeans, a black leather jacket, and big earrings made her look not just more attractive but younger. And she had unleashed her hair from its tight bun at the nape of her neck.

"What are you looking at? You've seen me in street clothes before, haven't you?"

I hadn't. "Nothing. You look nice, that's all."

"Damn skippy. I'm going for a drink with a white girl in a red dress, the least I'm going to do is put on makeup and some jewelry, otherwise someone might think I'm your date. Or worse. Your pimp."

She took me to a bar called El Quixote that was close by and apparently the place

where everyone knew Rolanda's name.
They'd known Otis Randolph, too. A small
framed picture was behind the bar, wedged
in near the cash register. A popcorn bucket
held donations for flowers. When we entered, the bartender said nothing but looked
me over and, recognizing Rolanda, chucked
his chin at us as a greeting. Without looking
left or right Rolanda headed straight for a
table in the back, which she slipped into
like a comfortable pair of shoes. She ordered
a rum and Coke and I asked for a beer.

"See, I had you pegged for a chardonnay,"
she said.

"Always a mistake to assume. My cop
friends tell me that."

"You have cop friends?"

"In Connecticut."

"And what do they do? Catch bad guys
who park illegally in the handicapped spot?
Oh, no that's right, you said you found
some bodies. I'd like to hear about them
one day."

The bartender brought the drinks himself,
apparently a first, and I put my hand over
the glass to prevent him from pouring my
beer.

"Brian, stop pretending this is a fine dining establishment when all you really want
to do is ogle this woman's cleavage." His

face turned as red as the dress, but the bartender did as he was told and left.

"You trying to impress me, knowing shady characters, drinking from the bottle like one of the masses?"

"The beer stays colder this way. Who do you think I am? I live in Connecticut. Doesn't make me Caroline Kennedy." I took a long pull on the frosty bottle. "So how was your day, honey?"

"By the time I got to the members' lounge, a swarm of people had gathered, getting in the way and probably contaminating a crime scene. Allegra Douglas was rallying the troops, saying we'd all be bloodied and battered before the show ended." *Vandalism was outrageous enough but personal violence was unspeakable.* That didn't, however, keep Allegra from speaking. Nothing and no one could.

"She went on about the old days and how management had sold out and she practically accused that Ms. Peete and her students of vandalizing the show and attacking Nikki. That teacher stayed cool, but I could tell she was still shaken up at having found the body."

"What do you think happened?" I asked. Rolanda gave it some thought but came up empty, shaking her head.

"I'll tell you what *didn't* happen. Some high school kid followed a woman into the toilet just to knock her on the head. No rape. No robbery. No personal connection or grievance. What the hell for? Now if someone had bashed Ms. Douglas on the head, I could understand it." She sipped her drink, pinky up. She talked to Brian over my head. "Less ice next time, baby."

Rolanda was right. There were probably a lot of people who wouldn't mind taking a whack at Allegra, and that number was rising. But why Nikki? What was the motive? Rolanda said she'd been found fully clothed, her handbag untouched, and still wearing an expensive watch.

That was all the news either of us had and I didn't know how we'd get any more. The hospital was only likely to give relatives information over the telephone, and I didn't really feel like schlepping downtown to the hospital to ask in person. But who did she have? No kids and no family here, as far as I knew, just an unhappy husband, who had had a few too many and, depending how long Nikki had been lying there, could have been the head basher.

THIRTY-FOUR

Rolanda and I stared at each other until she broke into a smile. "You want to be her sister? I gots an accent, sho 'nuff they won't believe me."

It was worth a phone call. "*Please* . . . I can pretend to have an accent, too. Can't I be her cousin?" Not sure why I thought that was an easier lie to tell, but I did.

"Stay on the safe side. Immediate family always gets you in. You just found out and you're calling from out of town — that's why you're not at the hospital. That's one of the good things about cell phones. Caller ID can't instantly give your location away. You can call in sick and be partying in Rio."

"I wouldn't count on that. They can do amazing things with cell phone technology these days."

"Yeah, but that's not till way later. Besides, you're just making a phone call. It's not a congressional hearing."

The call went better than expected. I lied through my teeth, and my tentative delivery worked to my advantage, making me sound even more concerned than I was.

Nikki had regained consciousness but was being kept in the hospital overnight for observation. After much prodding, the staff nurse told me she'd overheard snippets of Nikki's statement to the police. Nikki claimed she wasn't struck, she simply fell off the toilet seat and hit her head. The nurse was a little fuzzy on what Nikki was doing balanced precariously on the rim of the toilet when the blackout occurred.

"Can I talk to her?" I asked.

"It's late and she's very groggy."

"Daddy would be so relieved to know I was able to speak with her — even briefly. He's ninety-one and in assisted living but still sharp as a tack." I hated that expression but other people seemed to love it. Rolanda gave me a thumbs-up. I was getting comfortable in my role as Nikki's concerned sister. The "daddy" part worked. I felt guilty deceiving the kindhearted nurse, but she agreed to put the call through and I could almost see her carefully holding the phone to Nikki's ear as we spoke.

Before I said a word, Nikki croaked out some words.

"Show . . . Mrs. Moffffff —"

"Don't worry, Sis. The booth was fine. We made a few sales." She groaned.

"Sarc— sarc . . ." It sounded as if she were hiccuping or about to throw up.

"The sarcophagus? Fingers crossed, Mrs. M. might be interested. Jensen came sniffing around again."

Rolanda pulled at her chin as if scratching an imaginary beard. I didn't know what she meant until she mouthed the word *daddy.*

"And daddy says he loves you."

"Whaaa . . . ?"

The line went dead and I assumed Nikki had fallen asleep and the nurse had replaced the phone in its cradle.

"At least she's all right," I said.

"You've got a future as an actress. Daddy? Where'd that come from?"

"Lord knows. I didn't want to upset her by mentioning her husband and I couldn't say Mommy without cracking up." I twisted in my seat and held up my empty beer bottle to get the bartender's attention. There was that picture of Otis Randolph again, in a dark blue suit, probably the one he was wearing now in the back of a Baptist church. One person falls and it's the punch line to an amusing anecdote. Another falls and winds up dead.

The excitement and concern when Otis's body was found had vanished like a puff of smoke and been replaced by other dramas. If it hadn't been for the mention of the out-of-service escalator, most people wouldn't have known that someone who'd spent the last thirty-six years changing lightbulbs at the Wagner Center and putting down rubber mats when it rained was gone. He was removed from the building like a begonia with aphids.

The unspoken assumption was still that Otis Randolph had gotten drunk on the job and collapsed, falling down the escalator steps, after which, injured, he crawled off to a prefab, fake Amish shed where he lost consciousness and died.

"They said he reeked of Scotch, but I never knew him to overdo it, especially when he was working."

Even though I'd just gotten a refill, Rolanda called for another round. El Quixote was filling up; this time she walked to the bar to pick up our drinks.

The bartender got our order, and over his shoulder Rolanda saw the picture of Otis. "Brian, you ever know Otis to get loaded on his way to work?"

"Otis could put away a few. Sometimes he was pretty happy when he left here, but only after he knocked off. Never going in." He straightened Otis's picture and took a heavy breath. "I heard you mention Scotch, though. He was a gin drinker. Said the ladies liked it because it didn't smell nasty when he kissed them. He was a pistol, even at his age."

Drinking and flirting. At least Otis went out on an upswing. Rolanda rejoined me at the table.

"I don't mean to sound clinical or harsh," I said, "but people don't usually drop dead from a fall and a knock on the head, do they?"

"That's a fact. I was shopping in Sally Army once and a sofa fell on my head. Hurt like hell but didn't kill me. It's true. It was hooked to the wall. Fell and hit me on the back of my head. Didn't even get me a discount." She sucked down her rum and Coke and rubbed the back of her head as if looking for the bump. "But didn't I read in *People* about some actress who died after she hit her head?" she said.

"That was a skiing accident. Very unusual. I understand falls from a standing position are rarely fatal. Think about it. The skull is pretty hard."

"How do you know that? That what you ladies who lunch talk about? How to crack your husbands over the head so it looks like an accident?" Rolanda's notions of suburban life weren't much different from what mine had been before I moved to one.

"That's exactly right. After we finish our watercress and cucumber sandwiches. I used to be in television. The very classy outfit I worked for was just changing its focus from documentaries to all crime, all the time when I left. Some of it rubbed off."

"That was a career misstep. Too bad you left. You coulda done a show about me."

"Could Otis have been hit?"

"By whom? And why?" she said, sipping her drink. "You call the cops about that kid's bag?"

"It's gone. I've looked everywhere. Someone took it."

"Could have called them anyway."

"Hi, there, I had a bag that may have belonged to a dead guy, but I don't have it anymore?"

"I see your point."

"All right. There's something else. Do you remember the jacket the kid was wearing?" She recalled the T-shirt because the words were printed on his chest where his badge should have been, but she had to work hard to conjure up an image of the jacket that had been tied around his waist. "There were all sorts of names and patches on his jacket. I noticed it the day before." I told Rolanda about our accidental meeting at the museum.

"That wasn't mentioned in the police report. Just the shirt. So he wasn't wearing the jacket when he died," she said.

"Unless someone ripped it off his dead body," I said.

THIRTY-FIVE

I leaned in so neither the bartender nor any of the other patrons could hear. "Jamal Harrington was wearing a jacket like that this afternoon."

Rolanda leaned in. "Who's Jamal Harrington?"

"One of Lauryn Peete's students. Sticks and Stones? The high school display?"

My gut and nothing else told me Jamal wasn't responsible for Bleimeister's death. Or Otis's. But what was he doing with the dead guy's jacket? Did he know Garland Bleimeister?

"I wonder who Garland was looking for," I said. "The person he was so anxious to see before the show opened. He asked me to deliver a note, but then Connie screamed and we all took off."

"Doesn't that mean someone at the show should be missing him?" Rolanda said.

"Only if they were going to be happy to

see him. Otherwise, they might be relieved. He gave me a note. He handed it to me while he leafed through the directory to find the name of his friend's company."

"Where is it?"

"Jeez, it's anyone's guess where a slip of paper someone handed me two days ago is now."

"Maybe you stuck it in the directory?" Rolanda asked.

It was possible. I hadn't looked at the book since the show started. Why? I was selling, not buying. Was the note in the jeans I'd been wearing or my card case? A pocket? A bag? The garbage? It could be anywhere in a twenty-block radius, and in New York that might just as well be twenty miles.

"Well, I don't know about that other stuff," she said, "but where's the directory?"

"At the booth, I think. Under the table where the kid's bag was."

Rolanda didn't have a key to the convention center, but what she had was almost as good — a nearly full bottle of Rémy that she'd wheedled out of Brian, the bartender. That tariff got us past Vincent, the night man at the employees' entrance, and Rolanda's knowledge of the Wagner got us upstairs.

199

"Most of the doors are locked from the outside," she said.

Only one door in each hall was open, so the overnight security guard could go in and out, punching his code into the alarm system to report to an off-site company that everything was copasetic.

"Alarm Central's not even in New York. Probably in Indiana somewhere. But they're wired into the local precinct."

I was surprised the center had such a sophisticated system for the flower show, but maybe it had been installed pre-Javits, when the building had been used for shows with more valuable merchandise.

After three beers and nothing in my stomach but a mini-pierogi from four hours earlier I was light-headed. After three tall rum and Cokes, light on the ice, Rolanda was unchanged. "Anthony is on tonight. I'll text him so he knows we're here and doesn't shoot us."

"There's an armed guard at the flower show?"

"Only for the orchids. Chill out, I'm kidding. Of course he's not armed, but why scare the man?" Rolanda's fingers flew over her keypad and two passages of electronic Caribbean music told me first that her message had been sent and then that a reply

200

had been received. She smiled. "He says we owe *him* a bottle of Rémy and he's looking forward to meeting the woman in red."

I pulled my jacket closed and folded my arms over my chest.

The open doors weren't difficult to find, as an eerie whitish-blue light emanated from one rectangle every thirty feet or so. The glow came from the exit signs and the off-hours lighting on the beams, which backlit some of the pigeons still perched in the rafters.

Without the people, the lights, and the buzz, the deserted flower show was like a fairy-tale jungle, albeit a cold one. We didn't need to worry about snakes or tarantulas, just the occasional fluttering of a bird we'd disturbed. And all the vegetation was perfect. No slugs, no deer, no bunnies.

We reached my booth quickly and found the show directory in one of the nearly empty boxes where I'd stashed the box cutters, markers, and double-stick tape I'd used to set up.

"This was where I put the bag."

I fanned through the book. No note.

"Try again. Maybe the pages are stuck together. It's humid in here."

Still nothing, but this time I noticed a dog-eared page. I have a congenital inability to dog-ear pages. I'm a bookmark gal, even if I use a magazine renewal card or a dollar bill.

"I didn't do this. It must have been Bleimeister."

There wasn't enough light to read by, so we took the book and headed for the nearest exit. Two halls down from where we emerged, shadows waved and we heard a sound as if someone had bumped into a trash can. The person uttered a curse I hadn't heard since I was a little girl back in Brooklyn and for which I had never gotten an accurate translation except that it had something to do with going to Naples. Rolanda texted Anthony to see if it was him. It wasn't, but he'd seen the movement, too.

"He says the cleaning staff should all be gone by now," she whispered. I pulled on her arm and dragged her underneath a nearby staircase. Two slim figures made their way to the fire exit, and the heavy door closed behind them with a sucking sound. We exhaled.

"I think I know who they were. Fat Frank and Cookie."

"First it was drinking straight from the bottle. Now you know two guys named Fat Frank and Cookie? Girl, I owe you an apology," she said, "I have got the wrong idea about women from Connecticut."

"They're two men who work for Guy Anzalone, Connie's husband," I whispered.

The Caribbean music started up again and Rolanda fumbled in her pocket for the phone to silence it in case Fat Frank had heard and decided to come back to investigate. "Shoot, I've got to lose that music if I'm really going into this line of work."

It was Anthony again. His text message read:

Someone is in Hall A. Stay away until I know it's safe.

She closed her phone. "He's a tough old bird," she said.

"Older than Otis?"

There was no discussion. I kicked off Lucy's stilettos and we ran to Hall A.

THIRTY-SIX

In the fake twilight of the convention center we couldn't see the men's faces. They barely moved, but we heard the murmur of voices, though it was impossible to tell the nature of the exchange. Was this a friendly chat or was all hell about to break loose? Rolanda took charge.

"Whoever you are," she yelled, "you know you're not supposed to be here at this hour. Show's closed." It was a cheerful admonishment meant to announce our presence and lighten the mood. We padded on the cold concrete floor to where the men stood. As we drew closer, Rolanda saw Anthony talking to a younger man I recognized as Jamal Harrington.

"We're okay, Ro. But, I'll ask you again, sonny, what are you doing here? It's a simple question." Anthony might have been in his seventies, but he was the type of septuagenarian who probably still did one-armed push-ups. He'd have no problem subduing a kid, either physically or through personal authority, if it came to that. But none of us wanted to see that happen.

"Hi, Jamal. Those pilgrim tablecloths worked great." Rolanda and Anthony looked at me like I was crazy, but I wanted everyone to relax and I didn't mind sounding ridiculous if that was what it took. We knew Anthony didn't have a gun, but the jury was still out on Jamal. He must have known what we were thinking, or perhaps he'd had to do it before in another situation, but he held his arms out, carefully opening his hoodie and turning around. It was telling that the action came to him so naturally.

"I was looking for the other guy," Jamal said.

"That's pretty vague, young fella," Anthony said.

"Black dude. The one who was here Wednesday night. Something funny about his right eye. Really big hands like maybe he played sports before he got so old."

"That dude and I were friends for forty-three years. Nothing funny about his eye. He was a veteran. He lost it in a machine shop accident in the army. We worked construction together when this building went up. Still got one of the bricks in the locker room — use it as a doorstop. He played basketball up at the City College courts. Played with Cazzie Russell once. Before we got *so old*. His name was Mr. Otis Cleveland Randolph."

The impromptu eulogy was a tough act to follow. We stood there for what seemed like minutes but was probably just seconds. My shoeless feet were freezing and the rest of me was catching up.

"Maybe we should take this outside," I said. "It's warmer in the hallway and we'll be able to see better." Plus it seemed less confrontational than this standoff in the cold blue light of an empty, hangar-sized room.

We filed outside and, as I suspected, the stress level of the conversation lessened simply by walking into the light. Anthony stuck around until he made sure we were all right. We assured him that we would be. If Lauryn Peete trusted Jamal, I did, too. Besides, if we had to, Rolanda and I could probably take him.

"I'll be poking out of each of these opened doors every five or ten minutes, punching in, so if you ladies need me, I won't be far. Even if you don't see me, I'll be here." He and Jamal understood each other.

"We'll be okay."

"By the way, miss, that's a fine party dress you got on."

(Note to self: permanently borrow red dress from Lucy. I will never be lonely as long as I'm wearing this. How did I get to be this age without knowing that every woman needs a red dress?)

Anthony resumed his rounds. Jamal, Rolanda, and I sat outside the exhibit floor on chairs that only hours before had been occupied by rich old men in tuxedos and woman who, like Connie Anzalone, had agonized over what dress to wear.

"How did you know Otis?" I asked. Jamal looked at Rolanda, then at me. He started to recount the story. Then it sunk in.

"What do you mean *did*?"

He could have been faking it, but I didn't think so. His surprise seemed genuine and was soon replaced by a flicker of panic when Rolanda told him what had happened.

"Oh, man. Now I'm really screwed."

"I'm sure Otis is sorry to have inconvenienced you by dropping dead," Rolanda said.

"I didn't mean it like that. I was outside the members' lounge. Some mean old lady wouldn't let me in. Garland saw me reading a book. One of Toni Kelner's."

"So you did know him."

"I never saw him before that day. He introduced himself. Said he'd read all Kelner's stuff. Me, too. He asked if I could get him into the show."

"Did Garland tell you why he wanted to get in so badly?"

"He had to get in touch with one of the exhibitors who owed him something. He also said he left a bag somewhere and needed to pick it up. I told him I could get it and bring it out for him after my break, but he had to leave to meet his girlfriend. I told him I could sneak him in after dark."

Rolanda was incensed. "What made you think you could?"

"Ain't no thing," he said, smiling shyly, getting a little of his attitude back.

He knew he could because he'd been doing it every night since setup began about a week earlier. "Two cans of Colt for the man downstairs."

Rolanda was pissed she'd sprung for the much more expensive Rémy.

"Why?" I asked.

"I wanted to make sure no one messed with our garden. Ms. Peete went out on a limb for us. People think we're the ones messing with people's stuff, but it's not true. I saw two other men here. A couple of times. Skinny dudes. Creepy."

That sounded like Fat Frank and his partner again.

"Garland and I split up not long after we got into the building. I was cold, so he gave me his jacket to thank me. He told me he'd be heading to someplace warm anyway and wouldn't need it."

"Then I saw you wearing the jacket in the diner and later when you heard Garland was dead, you worried I'd think you killed him. So you skipped the show and sneaked back tonight to talk to Otis Randolph."

"Mr. Randolph saw us together. That's why I wanted to talk to him."

"Or maybe Otis saw you and Bleimeister arguing, so you cracked him on the head and threw him down the stairs to finish the job." Rolanda was going to make an excellent policewoman: she already had the bad cop part down pat.

"Why would I come back if I knew he was dead?"

Good point. Rolanda had to think.

" 'Cause you left some incriminating piece of evidence or wanted to make sure your fingerprints weren't someplace they shouldn't be."

More good points. Except by now there must have been thousands of prints on and around the escalator and the garden shed, where poor Otis had dragged himself with his last ounce of strength.

"We're just talking here," I said. "We're not the police. In fact, you should go to the police."

Jamal wiped his nose on the forearm of Garland's jacket. Or maybe he was wiping his eyes. "Right."

"When was the last time you saw Bleimeister?" I asked.

"Hard to say. I was reading and must have dozed off in the grass shack opposite our exhibit. I figured no one would see me there, but I could still keep an eye on our display." That was Connie's exhibit. So much for Fat Frank and Cookie being good watchdogs — the beach garden had had a non–papier-mâché occupant and they hadn't even noticed.

"Something woke me at about four A.M. By the time I stuck my head out the door, I saw two people running out of the hall, pushing a cart. I couldn't really see, but I assumed it was Bleimeister. I thought he found his stuff and was checking out."

Or maybe it was the person who'd attacked Otis. I didn't want to believe they could be the same person. Bleimeister had seemed like a decent kid. But ordinary people were pushed into extraordinary circumstances all the time. Mike O'Malley, my cop friend in Springfield, said if you eliminated politics and religion most crimes were motivated by one of three things — greed, lust, and revenge. He refers to them as the three basic food groups. And who among us didn't occasionally feel the twinge of one of them?

"Normal people are supposed to contact the authorities when they have information about a crime," Rolanda said. "If you see something, say something." She sounded like she was reciting from a placard in the subway.

"Oh, that's great. Fine. Call the cops. Maybe I can get a job in the prison garden. You think I committed murder for a denim jacket?"

"I don't," I said. "Not even for a leather jacket, but two people are dead. You might be in danger and that jacket might hold a clue."

"How can it be a clue if I've had it for two days and he died more recently than that?"

Jamal's voice was rising from the strain we were all feeling. It could have been an accident, like Otis. Like Nikki. One accident I could accept — but three?

"What else did you and Bleimeister talk

about?" I said.

"Nothing important. I was wearing a Mets shirt. Bleimeister said he was from Jersey but closer to Pennsylvania so he was a Phillies fan. He said he'd outgrown *da shore* and was going away once he picked up what this person owed him." They talked some more. Books, girls, Xbox.

"Oh, yeah, he said most people went to Atlantic City to strike it rich. He'd tried that, but it didn't work. Instead, it looked like one of his old summer jobs might do that. That's it. I don't know anything else."

Rolanda and I were hardly experienced interrogators, but what he said had the ring of truth. Again we advised him to go to the police, not thinking for a minute he'd actually do it.

"Can you talk to your parents about this?"

"I live with my Grams. She's old, diabetic. She'll stroke out. I haven't done anything, except for sneaking into the building. That's no big deal — I didn't break in."

"No other family?" I asked.

"I got a cousin in North Carolina."

"What about Ms. Peete?" He shook his head. The mention of her name turned all his features downward. He didn't want to disappoint the woman who'd put such faith in him.

Jamal was surely one of the last people to see Garland Bleimeister alive and that meant he might know more than he thought he did. Just as we had, someone else could make the same assumption, and they might not be a couple of nice ladies dressed for a night on the town. They could be the same people already responsible for two deaths. I asked Jamal if he'd be around the next day, and he shrugged.

"Man, I don't know what I'm doing in the next fifteen minutes."

"Whatever you decide, be careful. And just to be on the safe side, you might not want to wear that jacket for a while. But don't throw it away. If Garland's death wasn't an accident . . ." I didn't want to finish the thought. Jamal stripped off the jacket and hoodie and put them back on, this time with the zippered sweatshirt over the jacket. He jogged to the fire exit and disappeared down the stairs without another word.

Rolanda and I watched him go. "What part of Connecticut did you say you were from?"

"You realize you're engaging in a form of profiling," I said. "Just because you're from the hood doesn't make you Foxy Brown. Let's go find my shoes. They're borrowed and very expensive."

I passed on a return trip to El Quixote and hailed a cab to Lucy's apartment. My cash and my keys were out well before the ten-minute ride was over, the cash to pay and get out fast, and the keys because that was a New York habit. As soon as the cab pulled away, another car door opened. It was on the driver's side of the vehicle parked in front of Lucy's brownstone. Black car, vanity plates that I couldn't quite figure out; I imprinted the number and tried to read the make of the car in case I had to give a description later on from a hospital bed. My taxi had sped away. I was alone. For a moment I froze, then I saw a familiar hulking figure striding toward me.

Whatever else you had to say about him, Guy Anzalone knew how to make an entrance.

THIRTY-SEVEN

"Did you say anything to her?"

"And hello to you, too."

"Did you tell her?"

"What's there to tell? We shared some cashews in the lobby of a very public hotel with your wife upstairs, not five minutes away. That's hardly the stuff of tabloid newspapers." I was talking tough but not really feeling the part. What was he doing here? How did he even know where I was staying? Had I mentioned it and forgotten in my champagne buzz? Happily, whatever dramatic showdown Guy Anzalone had built up in his mind while waiting for me evaporated. I credited the red dress.

"You're getting a lot of mileage out of that outfit. Most women I know wouldn't wear the same dress two nights in a row." It didn't seem to bother Guy and his eyes moved appreciatively over the spandex. "She was pretty ticked off," he said.

"By *she,* I take it you mean Connie. And that's my fault, *how?* This was a big night for her. Maybe she was disappointed you weren't there." I was cold and hungry and wanted the conversation to end. I glanced up at J. C.'s window and terrace garden. If it had been warmer, she might have had the windows open and would have been able to hear us in case Guy got too friendly and I needed to borrow her door bar.

"Anything else?"

"Why are you so nasty to me? What did I ever do to you besides buy one of those crazy Lego sculptures and compliment you on your dress?"

"I know your wife, and you're hitting on me."

"First of all, I'm not necessarily hitting on you. Second, does that mean you'd say yes if you didn't know my wife?"

Even I had to crack a smile at that one. "Look, I'm tired and hungry, and please — no 'bed' or 'I can fill you up' comments."

He agreed to keep the frisky chat to a minimum and I agreed to walk around the corner with him to Carmine's, a pizza joint he described as not half bad. Given his proclivity for understatement, I took that to mean it was one of the best in the city.

"They still sell by the slice. I can remember when a slice and a Coke was fifty cents," he said. Good manners kept me from asking how long ago that was.

We sat in orange plastic chairs and I looked for a clean place on the Formica table for Lucy's handbag and the flower show directory Rolanda and I had retrieved from the booth.

Our slices came — pepperoni for me, two with extra cheese and a calzone chaser for him; he'd already had dinner. The waiter brought two large Diet Cokes.

"I cut back wherever it hurts the least. I don't want to get too big." He ran his hands over his substantial belly in a way that perversely seemed like flirting.

"That reminds me. I think I saw a friend of yours tonight. After hours at the convention center — Fat Frank?"

"After hours? I'm shocked. Maybe he forgot something. You should be careful. It's not always safe in those big buildings late at night. You could get in trouble."

The slice stalled inches from my lips. I put it down and wiped my hands on a wad of paper napkins.

"C'mon. What am I saying that your mother didn't tell you? You should just be careful, is all."

He'd wolfed down his two slices and

waited for his calzone. "You know, I dated a girl named Calzone once. Nice girl, but too many people made fun of our names. It never would have worked out." He picked up the directory and spun it in his hands, tapping the spine on the table each time the book made a complete revolution.

"You catch any other suckers tonight, or am I the only one who bought something?" I assured him he was in rarefied company and none other than the famous Mrs. Moffitt had been interested in the piece that he and Connie had purchased. She had to settle for something similar but even more expensive.

"I'm glad you didn't show us that one. That was a little slippery of you the other night." He wagged a finger at me. "That's okay. She'll be happy."

He rarely used his wife's name but referred to her as *she* as if that made her somehow less real. He continued to spin the book and I worried he'd drop it on his greasy plate and I'd wind up smelling like garlic for the rest of the flower show, the way Nikki had smelled of fish fertilizer.

"She made me take an ad in this thing. She even sicced this broad on me. Madon', good-looking girl but wouldn't shut up until I took the ad. And she kept harping on

218

certain aspects of my work. I do construction, lend a little money. So what? So does Citibank. Doesn't make me John Gotti."

I assumed this last *she* was Kristi Reynolds. Maybe all women were *she* to him. "You people even look at this thing?" It was a fair question. I hadn't cracked the spine for two days and might never have if it hadn't been for Garland Bleimeister.

Guy leafed through the book and quickly came to the dog-eared page where coincidentally his wife's entry was listed.

"Look at this. It's like she's always there, watching me. 'Brooklyn Beach Garden, Connie Anzalone, Brooklyn, New York,' blah, blah, blah. She changed the name of the garden, but it was too late to fix it in the book. She changed the design, too. I made her add more stone yesterday." He said it proudly, his contribution to the garden.

"Nice touch," I lied.

"These things never tell you the real story. Newspapers neither. You gotta read between the lines." He tossed the book on the table, narrowly missing my plate.

Guy was right. There were six stories on those pages and one of them led to Garland Bleimeister. Someone had to read between the lines. What was Bleimeister's hurry to get into the show before it opened? Who stole his bag and what was in it? And was that why he — and maybe even Otis Randolph — had died?

I picked up the book and started to leave. "Is that it? We're done?"

"We're done. Go home to your wife, Guy. Her name's Connie. Thanks for the pizza. You should pick up a couple of calzones for Fat Frank — that man needs to put on some weight." I pushed my chair back from the table and headed for the door. "My friend will take that order to go."

THIRTY-EIGHT

I made a cup of tea and curled up on Lucy's sofa with the show directory, which I was sure held some answers. It was packed with ads for everything from Guy's fake stone products to tours of Irish gardens to the banks and car companies that had sponsored the show.

In fact, the directory could mislead people into thinking the show was larger than it was. That was a testament to Kristi Reynolds, who relentlessly chased down advertisers. Knee-replacement surgeons? Maybe she was a marketing genius — gardeners frequently had knee problems.

It was no secret that Kristi wanted to give the Philadelphia Flower Show a run for its money. Allegra had said as much in a less flattering way in the ladies' room. But Kristi would have to do better than just a glossy show directory. The Philly event had been around for close to two centuries and was the premier flower show in the country — maybe in the world — with landscape displays, floral designs, exhibits from national plant societies, and individual entries from people all over the East Coast.

The Big Apple had dipped its toes in, but Kristi's greatest strength was public relations, and that's what had kept the show afloat for the two years since she'd taken over from the previous director.

I scanned the ads and four-color images, then went back to the dog-eared page. Counting both sides, there were six entries. Six vendors or exhibitors: Bagua Designs; Bambi-no, Inc.; BioSafe Products; Brooklyn Beach Garden; Buzz Word Honeys and Soaps; and Byron Davis High School. One of them was the place Garland Bleimeister was desperate to go last Wednesday. Maybe the last place he'd ever gone — under his own steam. But as Guy Anzalone had said, their brief descriptions were just the beginning, one or two lines that said what they were selling or why they were here, but probably wouldn't tell me what I needed to know. I'd have to dig deeper if I wanted to get the real stories behind them.

The next morning, a note shoved under my door invited me to breakfast anytime between 6:45 and 9:30 A.M. I didn't remember telling J. C. Kaufman that Lucy didn't own a coffeepot or saucepan, but maybe she'd figured it out when she and the cats had been in the nearly empty apartment when the cops had been there. I'd fallen asleep on the sofa and had dragged myself into bed a few hours earlier, so coffee — especially made by someone else — sounded good.

The red dress was draped over a slipper chair. In the movies, the dress, the shoes, and the underwear would leave a trail, like breadcrumbs, to the bedroom, where a handsome stranger would still be sleeping under warm, rumpled sheets. Would that this were the movies.

I showered, dressed, and patted myself down with the old salesman's mantra "spectacles, testicles, wallet, and watch," a Willy Loman–like routine to make sure you had everything you needed for your day's sales calls. An old salesman had taught it to me on one of my first business trips and, like a song you can't get out of your head, I remembered it every time I traveled for work.

In my case, it was backpack, phone, keys, and show badge. I shoved the badge in the back pocket of my jeans and felt it catch on something. Instantly I remembered what it was. I fished out the plastic badge holder and the slip of paper it had gotten caught on:

I know what you've done. I've found the laboratory you used and I'll tell everyone unless you take care of me. G.

It was Garland's note. The show directory was still on the sofa, where I'd fallen asleep on top of it. I retrieved it, refolded the note, and slipped it into the directory next to the dog-eared page. Then I headed downstairs to J. C.'s.

She must have been listening for me, because the door opened even before I knocked. A warm, biscuity aroma met me at the door.

The pet poison list I'd left for J. C. had made me a friend for life. And the best friends were the ones who could cook. Moochie curled himself around my ankles.

I climbed onto a stool at the wheeled cart that defined J. C. Kaufman's kitchen and sniffed the air as she poured me a large mug of coffee. "Those scones smell heavenly."

"Sleep okay?" she asked. I had a feeling she already knew the answer, since her hearing bordered on supernatural and I'd gotten in late. She probably also heard me stumbling around at three A.M. when I finally made it into the bedroom.

"Not really. Strange doings at the flower show and some crazy dreams," I said. "Beekeepers, giant calzones, and frankfurters doing Radio City Music Hall numbers in my head."

"Drugs?"

"Please. I don't even take DayQuil." I told her about the blackout, Nikki's accident, and the news of Garland Bleimeister's death. Then I pulled out the show directory and Garland's note.

"Does this have anything to do with the linebacker I saw you talking to last night?" So she had heard and seen my conversation outside with Guy Anzalone. She tilted her head as an apology. "Bedroom window faces the terrace and Moochie likes to climb in and out, so I leave it open. I didn't mean to pry. I just wanted to make sure you were all right."

"You were *watching my back?*" She seemed pleased that I'd remembered her catchphrase.

"Some days I'm glad I'm not young anymore," she said. "Have you called the police?"

"Not yet. I haven't had much time. You

know I've called the cops twice in four nights. They're going to think I'm either a cop groupie or a hysteric." I broke open the still-warm scone and watched the steam escape. I brought J. C. up to speed.

"Now that I've found his note, I'll definitely call today. But I'll do it from the convention center. No point in waiting around here. I've still got work to do."

"This boy . . . Garland. He was the one who left his bag with you?"

"Accidentally. But, yes, I did have it briefly. It's gone now. Either he picked it up himself before he died or someone stole it. The sculptures were slightly out of place the other day."

She gave me a long look over the top of her glasses.

"What?"

She tilted her head toward the front door. What was she thinking that I hadn't gotten around to? Was our adventure in Lucy's building the other night more than a run-in with some overzealous menu deliverymen?

"You think someone was *here* looking for the bag?"

"Nothing was taken. I'm just saying — *watch your back.*"

"Lucy doesn't have anything worth stealing, unless the thief is a shoe freak. If there was anything valuable in the bag, wouldn't the kid have been more careful with it? But maybe someone else wanted the bag because they're afraid of what *might* be in it."

J. C. and I exchanged numbers. She made me promise to call the police as soon as I got to the Wagner Center and said she'd stay on the lookout for any strangers in the building. I pitied the poor delivery person who didn't identify himself to her satisfaction. I wrapped a scone for the road and placed it in the outside pocket of my backpack so it wouldn't get crushed. As I did I felt the rumble of my cell and pulled it out of my bag. The caller's number was unfamiliar.

It was a woman. "Is this Paula Holliday? I'm an exhibitor at the flower show. Can we meet? I'd like to talk to you about Garland Bleimeister."

I couldn't think of anywhere near Lucy's for us to meet except Carmine's and it was too early for pepperoni. The caller suggested a place called Jimbo's Bagels a few blocks east. It was in the same general direction as the convention center, so I'd have to pass it anyway.

"Fifteen minutes." I hung up and tried to make sense out of what I'd just heard. "That was someone named Cindy

Gustafson."

"Why is she calling you?"

"I guess I'll find out." I leafed through the show directory. Cindy was one of the six vendors on the dog-eared page.

"Like I said — *watch your back.*"

THIRTY-NINE

Cindy Gustafson fiddled with the lanyard of her badge holder, which was tucked into the breast pocket of her corduroy jacket. It was an old show trick so you wouldn't forget to wear the darn thing but didn't have strangers on the street calling you by your first name and creeping you out when you weren't working.

She stood up and stuck out her hand like an overeager job applicant. From the still life on the small resin table where she'd been sitting — empty coffee cup, newspaper, and bagel — she'd been there a while; maybe that's where she'd called me from.

She was young — twenty-five, maybe younger, close to Bleimeister's age. She had that same dewy look, combined with a surprising coarseness common to those in their twenties. Maybe it was the fashion. They looked world-weary, even if they've never really seen the world and had no legitimate reason to be weary.

"Thanks for coming." She hooked her straight dark hair behind one ear in a move I would see repeated many times in the following twenty minutes.

Cindy said she had met Garland, haunting the corridors of the Wagner Center. "It was Wednesday," she said, "late."

They had talked in the shorthand of the twentysomething — clubs, social networking, jobs, schools. Thinking of his shirt, I asked her if Bleimeister had gone to Penn State.

Cindy shook her head and seemed surprised by my question. "I don't know. I don't remember. Why do you ask?"

"The Happy Valley shirt. I thought maybe he was an alumnus."

"He said that was a joke. He said he'd gotten an education at Happy Valley but not a degree."

"Did you know what he meant?"

She shrugged. Another move I'd see numerous times. Garland told her he'd been at the show earlier and had left a bag at my booth but couldn't get back in to retrieve it because he'd lost his badge. Would she stop by to pick it up for him and meet him later at Dekker's Tavern on the West Side?

"He said he'd treat me to dinner to say thank you, but I got so busy setting up that I forgot. When I called to let him know, he said never mind. He'd made other plans and couldn't meet that night anyway. I thought he was blowing me off because of the stupid bag, but he rescheduled for the next night. He even said dress nice because we were going to a fancy restaurant."

"Where were you supposed to meet him on Thursday?"

"Nick & Nora's. I waited for two hours but he never showed. I even walked back to Dekker's, thinking I'd misunderstood. Then this morning, I saw this."

She pointed to the newspaper. It might have been coffee stains but I thought there were tear splotches on the grainy picture of Bleimeister wearing his Happy Valley shirt and hoisting a can of beer, his arms entwined around two buddies.

I'd only seen Bleimeister twice and the features were indistinct, but the smile was unmistakable. He was the floater, as Rolanda and the paper so sensitively called him. I asked Cindy the same question J. C. had asked me. "Did you notify the police?"

"No. I called you because you were his friend." She looked down and played with a stray thread escaping from one of the buttons on her jacket. If she wasn't careful she'd lose it.

"I wasn't his friend. It was an accident that I had his bag — which, by the way, I don't anymore."

"Did the police take it?" she asked.

"No."

"If you don't have the bag," she asked, "where is it?"

"Beats me. If Bleimeister didn't take it, somebody else made off with it."

"But who? Who'd want a ratty old bag?"

That was the final *Jeopardy* question. Or maybe it was *why* did somebody want the bag? What did they think was in it? And how did Cindy know it was a ratty old bag unless she'd seen it?

"Just for curiosity's sake," I said, "how did you get my cell number?"

"I stopped by last night during the reception, but you weren't there. One of the guys from the next booth suggested I take your business card." The ever-helpful David.

"Look, I am calling the police. This bag business might be something the police can use to find out what happened to Bleimeister."

"Do you need to mention my name?"

"He might have mentioned a girlfriend. Did he mean you?"

"No way." The button came off, as I knew it would, and she shoved it in her pocket. "I have a boyfriend back home. He won't understand my going to meet another guy."

What exactly was I going to tell the cops if I didn't have the bag, didn't mention Jamal, and didn't mention Cindy? Wouldn't they find her when they questioned the people listed on the dog-eared page? Was he pointing to his killer from his slab in the morgue or was that just something you saw on television?

"I may have to. You saw Bleimeister and spoke to him more recently than I did. Depending on when he died, you may have been one of the last people to see him." Just like Jamal, but I didn't see the need to complicate things by mentioning him.

That realization sent a visible shudder through the girl. "Don't worry. Nothing happened. You didn't even meet him. Even the most jealous boyfriend couldn't object to that."

She smiled weakly. "You don't know the half of it."

Jealous boyfriends — another reason to be glad I was unattached.

I dialed 911 and told the dispatcher I had information about the body that had been found in the river. I gave my name and cell number and said I could be reached at the Wagner Center, booth 1142 in approximately twenty minutes. After I hung up, Cindy thanked me profusely, even though I told her she would likely have to talk to them anyway because of the directory and the note.

"Your name's on one of the pages. The cops will want to speak to you. C'mon. Let's get going. Big shopping day today."

I left a few bucks on the table for Cindy's uneaten bagel and grabbed the tearstained newspaper, folding it under my arm. We didn't speak for two or three blocks — hard to shift gears and discuss the weather after talking about a young man who'd just died under questionable circumstances. Although maybe that's exactly what you're supposed to do — talk about shoes or sports. Or work.

"Beekeeping. I've got friends in Connecticut who do it. How do you keep from eating all the profits?" I asked.

"That's easy. There aren't any profits yet. I haven't been doing it that long, and the bees do the work. I just collect the honey every month." She mumbled her answers and didn't volunteer much, so I stopped trying to draw her out and we walked the rest of the way to the convention center in silence and at a funereal pace.

Every once in a while Cindy took a long, deep breath that I took to be a stifled sob. It was more emotion than I expected from her, given that Bleimeister was a total stranger. Maybe she had met him. Hell, I didn't care if she'd answered the booty call — I wasn't her mother. And I wasn't so old that I didn't remember my twenties. Cindy wiped her eyes with the cuff of her jacket, blackening the edges and smearing her liner into extreme cat eyes that Amy Winehouse would have been proud of.

Before we knew it, we'd arrived at the exhibitors' entrance. Not so early that we'd need to bribe the guard, which was good since the liquor stores weren't open yet.

I tried to cheer her up. "Hey, if you ever need to sneak in, you could try giving the security guard a few jars of honey. He's flexible about the going rate."

Cindy mumbled good-bye and made a beeline for the first floor ladies' room to fix her face. I took the escalator and watched Cindy slip into the restroom as I rode upstairs.

David was already at his post, charm machine on and smile affixed, ready to take no prisoners. And I was delighted to see Nikki back on the job — instead of her sour-faced husband. She stood proudly by her sarcophagus, all cheery optimism, wearing a vintage hat with a mesh veil that attempted to cover the purple knob on her forehead.

"Welcome back," I said. "Love the hat."

"Isn't it great? Russ brought it to the hospital for me. He's a dear, isn't he?" I agreed that Russ was a treasure and silently resolved to never, ever get caught up in disputes between married couples.

The story of their reconciliation was cut short by the approach of two men.

"I'm taking a wild stab that those men behind you are not interested in art," David said. It was a good guess. As incongruous as they were, in these surroundings, they could only be cops.

The two men could have been sent by central casting — one was white, the other black. It was either enforced diversity or an unconscious homage to every buddy cop team from *Lethal Weapon* to *Miami Vice.*

"Ms. Holliday?"

John Stancik and Patrick Labidou flashed their credentials and David volunteered to cover the booth while the cops and I found a private place to talk along the wall, where folding chairs had been haphazardly placed for elderly or exhausted attendees. It wasn't even nine thirty in the morning, but I now felt as if I qualified.

Stancik took the lead, while his partner looked around the convention center as if he'd never seen a flower or any kind of vegetation other than iceberg lettuce or confiscated marijuana before. Perhaps he hadn't. There was nothing natural about him, from his beard to his clothing. And while I didn't like to make snap judgments based on what people wore, I hoped Labidou had an undercover assignment later in the day, otherwise hadn't had a closet makeover since 1976. Stancik was younger, better looking in a generic Secret Service man kind of way.

"Did you make a nine one one call this morning about the Garland Bleimeister case?"

"About forty-five minutes ago." I didn't mean it to, but it came out sounding as if I were complaining about their response time.

"Technically," Labidou said, cracking his gum, "you should have called the precinct or the special tips number given on the news, not nine one one."

"I'll try to remember that next time I meet a guy who gets killed."

Labidou let out a low whistle, but his partner kept to the business at hand. "What can you tell us?"

"I met Garland Bleimeister on Wednesday."

"How?"

I recounted the no-badge incident and then with something of a flourish showed the cops Bleimeister's note and the show directory with the dog-eared page.

"He asked me to give this note to someone. Most likely someone on one of these two pages. I never got to hear who the note was for. There was a disturbance on the floor and we all left to see what had happened. He must have sneaked in, so he didn't need me to deliver the message anymore. That was the last I saw of him. I'd been holding his bag, so I brought it to my booth, thinking he'd come by for it, but he never did. Now I know why."

Labidou couldn't resist. "He left you holding the bag?"

"Okay," his partner said, stifling a smile, which was too bad because he had a nice smile that lit up his whole face. "Where's the bag?"

"Gone. Either he came back for it when I wasn't at the booth or somebody else helped himself to it. I understand there have been a number of incidents at the show this year. It could have been stolen."

"Oh, yeah. The Javits Curse," Stancik said.

He flipped through his notepad. "The precinct has gotten calls about that. Mostly some woman named Douglas. Looks like she called more than once. That also checks out with what Rolanda Knox told us."

So she had talked to them. Did she tell them about Jamal? And me?

"Any idea what was in the bag?" Stancik asked.

"Nope. I didn't look."

"Not exactly burning with curiosity, are you?" Labidou said.

I was thinking up a suitably snarky reply when Lauryn Peete stormed over to us.

"Feisty little woman at eleven o'clock and, thank you lord, she's coming our way," Labidou said. "How do I look?" He ran a hand through his hair, but it must have been an involuntary reflex since he was nearly bald.

Every muscle in Lauryn's body looked tense, and there was an angry vein pulsing in her otherwise smooth forehead.

"What did you tell them? You and that horrible Douglas woman. You're all the same. You see a kid with baggy pants and unlaced shoes and right away he's a criminal."

Stancik looked from Lauryn's face to mine. Labidou's gum cracking slowed, then stopped. "Miss Holliday, are you acquainted with Jamal Harrington, *too?*" he asked.

Lauryn took a deep breath and I thought I heard the word *manure* escape from the teacher's lips.

"Why do you ask?" I was all innocence.

"Because he's wanted for questioning in connection with the death of Garland Bleimeister. We also want to talk to him about the death of one Otis Rudolph —"

"Randolph," Stancik said.

"Which we are now officially treating as suspicious."

FORTY

"His parents came in from some place in Pennsylvania to identify the body," Stancik said.

"Some town like Smallville. The mother said Garland started hanging out with some rich kids. He always needed money to keep up with them, so he worked a lot. Especially for one professor who paid pretty well. But that was only during the summertime. The parents weren't sure where Bleimeister had been staying in New York. It could have been anywhere — a friend's place or a bench in the park."

"Wait a minute. I saw him once before Wednesday." I told them about jogging on Tuesday morning and seeing Bleimeister at the small private museum near Lucy's apartment. "He looked as if he might have spent the night huddled in the doorway. I thought he might have been a runaway until I saw him here the next day."

"See, people never think they know anything and then, wham, they do. The Sterling Forsyte Museum — that the one? Transitional neighborhood," Stancik said. "Was that near where you're staying?" I nodded.

"We think Bleimeister might have hooked up with Jamal sometime in the last six months, and the two of them went into business. Kid like Bleimeister could open up a whole new line of distribution for a street operator like Jamal."

"That's ridiculous," Lauryn said. "Jamal is a B plus student with lots of extracurricular activities."

"We didn't say he was stupid. For all I care, he's the editor of the school paper and his mama's got a bumper sticker that says he's on the honor roll, but his name came up, unsolicited, in two separate interviews. People say he's got the makings of a first-rate botanist — or marijuana grower."

Could Allegra and Rolanda both have put the finger on Jamal? If so, it would be the first time they'd seen eye to eye on anything.

"He's got a part-time job," I said.

"So you *do* know him." Labidou acted as if he'd caught me in a lie. "You seem to know both of these boys pretty well. You got a thing for younger men?"

For the first time I wished I had a husband

or boyfriend to trot out to prove to this Neanderthal that I wasn't some lonely woman lusting after young boys.

"He sold me a tablecloth, detective. That was the extent of our relationship. If Bleimeister and Jamal knew each other, why would Bleimeister need to sneak into the convention center to see him? What about the names on these two pages?" I flipped through the book and showed them the pages in question. Lauryn read in between the two taller men. Her face turned ashen.

"What is it?"

"We're High School 240, but our official name is the Byron Davis School. That's how we were registered here. *We're* on these pages."

Like everyone else, I'd been thinking of them as Sticks and Stones or the Gangsta Gardeners. Their school name hadn't even registered when I leafed through the book at Lucy's last night before dozing off. Could we have been that wrong about Jamal?

"Do you plan on interrogating the other people on these pages?" I asked.

"Let's all stay calm. Right now we're focusing on Mr. Harrington."

"Does he need a lawyer?" I asked.

"If he hasn't done anything, why does he need a lawyer? We just want to talk to him.

If either of you ladies sees or hears from him, I strongly suggest you advise him to voluntarily turn himself in for questioning. We will find him, but it will be easier if he comes in on his own. Save the taxpayers a little money. And us, a little aggravation."

Fat chance. Rolanda and I had tried that the night before. Maybe Lauryn had, too. For all we knew he was already on a bus to his cousin in North Carolina.

"Damn. Here comes another one. Are we doing something this morning to attract fine-looking, ornery women?" Coming toward us wearing the least sincere smile I'd seen on anyone since the last election was Kristi Reynolds. She chattered into a headset, but her eyes were fixed on Stancik and Labidou.

"We're done," Stancik said, "but don't forget — either of you sees Harrington, tell him we want to talk. We don't want his body to be the next one we find floating in the river."

Kristi swept the cops off the floor, no doubt doing damage control for the benefit of the morning's showgoers, who were starting to pour into the exhibit hall. Lauryn stammered an apology.

"Forget it. Look, I wasn't ready to indict Jamal because of a jacket." Only then did I realize I hadn't even mentioned the jacket to the police. And if Rolanda had told them, why wouldn't they have said something?

"They're not even going to talk to anyone else, are they?" Lauryn said. "They think they have their man." She shook her head in disgust.

"We don't know that. Not to rub your nose in it, but you were wrong about me. I hadn't said a word about Jamal and you assumed the worst. We could be wrong about them." I wasn't sure I believed it either, but I wanted to raise her spirits.

"I should get back to work," I said. "You know, I've already talked to most of the people on those pages. It wouldn't be so hard for me to ask a few questions. Do a little shopping and snooping at the same time?"

"Would you? I'm going to have my hands full trying to find Jamal and getting him a lawyer." I said I'd ask around and would let her know if I learned anything useful.

"Sell another piece?" Nikki asked, when I returned.

"Dream on — the one in the brown leather jacket? Probably has a painting on velvet in his bachelor pad. Or one of those prints of the dogs playing poker."

"Don't knock those — I've sold quite a

few of them."

I shared as much as I thought they needed to know about my conversation with Lauryn and the cops.

"At least the Javits Curse doesn't seem to have struck this morning," Nikki said, looking around at the relative calm.

Only if you didn't count two possible murders and a drug deal gone awry. I wondered silently if Jamal's absence had anything to do with the disappearance of the curse.

The morning passed quickly with my neighbors depleting their stock of smaller items and keeping their fingers crossed on the bigger pieces. Mrs. Moffitt's Jensen returned and surreptitiously stole another glance at Nikki's sarcophagus. I sold an eight-foot-tall wind device and three table-top sculptures. There wouldn't be much to pack when the show ended, and that would be good news for the folks in Springfield.

Foot traffic had slowed to a crawl around lunchtime. My stomach was sending signals, when I remembered J. C.'s scone still in my bag. It would taste delicious drizzled with fresh honey — and I knew where to get some. I wanted to update Cindy about my talk with the cops, so I found her booth number in the directory and headed for the Buzz Word exhibit.

"Is the owner here?"

A smartly dressed woman in her forties or fifties turned around. She had smooth blond hair cut in an ear-length bob and wore a crystal necklace that might have been Baccarat — a yellow bee on a black silk cord. "That's me. Can I help you?"

"I meant Cindy. Young girl." Oops. "Dark hair, brown corduroy jacket?"

"Let's see — I *used* to be young and had dark hair once, but I can assure you I haven't owned or worn a brown corduroy jacket since I was about three years old and had no say in the matter. That said, I *am* Cindy Gustafson."

FORTY-ONE

"Well, you might have guessed when she said she harvested her honey every month. Perhaps she was thinking of tapping sugar for maple syrup. All the beekeepers I know harvest in the fall."

It wasn't the first time I'd been lied to, and I'd get over it. I should have been tipped off when she mentioned Garland's lost show credentials, but I'd assumed that *he* was lying to her, not that *she* was lying to me. So, who was the girl I'd treated to a bagel earlier that morning and why had she concocted that story about Garland Bleimeister?

The real Cindy Gustafson gave me a good price on six pounds of honey — two pounds each for Lucy, J. C., and myself. She even threw in a set of honey dippers and painstakingly wrapped each jar in colorful tissue paper without using tape, just a few strands of raffia attaching the dipper with the last knot. Ordinarily it would have annoyed the heck out of me that she was taking so long, but even though she wasn't the woman I'd met that morning, her name *was* on one of those two pages. When given an audience, people love to talk about themselves, and Cindy was no exception.

Buzz Word sold artisanal honeys, lip balms, and soaps. The company was based in Bensalem, Pennsylvania, and at present this Cindy Gustafson was the only employee.

When people heard she was a beekeeper, they expected her to be Olivia Walton, churning her own butter and wearing a long dress like the Amish or the Mormons.

"That's tiresome. I prefer Coach. Or St. John, when I can afford it."

Beekeeping wasn't like that — you could have one box or a hundred. You didn't even need much room, maybe four cubic feet per box. Cindy knew one man who had his hives on a roof in Philadelphia, ten boxes with ten frames in each. And it only took a few hours a week, except when he harvested.

Cindy had gotten into it in college. A sign outside the cafeteria asked for volunteers to help with a study on an early outbreak of what they're now calling colony collapse disorder, the thing that is or isn't happening depending on which scientific paper you read. She was fascinated by the rules of the hive — queen, drones, female workers. Things happening at a set time. The orderly transfer of power when a new queen is chosen and nurtured. It was civilized. There were no surprises. She appreciated that.

As a thank-you, the organizers of the study gave Cindy a few pounds of honey and some of the beeswax, which she packaged in colorful tins and gave to friends as presents.

Then the campus store wanted to carry them.

"It supplemented my wardrobe allowance at school, and my parents were pleased that I showed an interest in something other than getting married, but it was just for fun. I took it up again after I divorced. My husband was deathly afraid of bees. He was allergic to bee stings."

The first year all her bees died. The next year she did better, but nowhere near the seventy pounds a year per hive she had planned on, based on her research and the business plan she'd devised. All her items were under twenty dollars, which she had determined was the right price point. She started selling the products at farmers markets, then moved up to county fairs, finally graduating to shows like the Big E — the Eastern States Exposition — and this one.

"People want to spend money at shows. What other explanation is there for the ridiculous number of mops and chamois cloths sold at events like these?" It was David's pinecone-nightlight theory. These people had done their homework.

As casually as I could, I broached the subject of the dead boy, but she claimed to know nothing about him. All I knew was that he was from New Jersey and may or may not have gone to Penn State.

"As it happens," she said, "my younger sister graduated from Penn State, but from your description of the boy, I doubt she knew him. She was an extremely serious student. Too serious. For a time my parents worried that she was putting too much pressure on herself, but it resolved itself. An adviser helped straighten out her priorities.

"In any event, I haven't read the paper for days. Since I got here, it's been all work. This is hardly a huge moneymaking proposition for me, but I certainly don't want to lose any."

"So, your sister is a former denizen of Happy Valley. Do you know of any other use of that expression other than its being a nickname for the Penn State campus?"

She thought about it. "Wasn't that what they called the English expatriate community in Kenya in the twenties?"

That jogged my memory. I'd screened a documentary years back on the unsolved murder of a wealthy Englishman just outside Nairobi during that time period. The press may have even called it the Happy Valley Murder. And now there was another. Very different, of course, but long after the case was solved some well-read magazine journalist would eventually pick up the story and use the headline for Garland's story as a private joke he was sure no one else would get.

"My ex-husband traveled to East Africa frequently for business." She fingered a large chunk of tanzanite on her earlobe. "He bought me these. He was always bringing me something. Unfortunately, the last time it was a rather nasty infection. Just when you think you know someone.

"We moved past it," she said. "I went back to my maiden name and picked up the hobby I'd given up when we married. It keeps me busy."

Cindy Gustafson stowed my purchases in two sturdy black paper shopping bags, and I thanked her for her time even though she hadn't shed any light on Garland Bleimeister. I was still ravenous but didn't need the upper body workout of carrying six extra pounds while I searched for a place to eat, so I headed back to my booth to drop off the honey.

When I arrived, Rolanda Knox was waiting for me. I was not happy she'd blown me off and talked to the cops without me. I thought we were in this together, and I didn't know if what she said dovetailed with my story. The look on my face revealed my irritation.

"Is that your suburban, white-bread version of the stink eye?" she said. " 'Cause when I deliver the stink eye, I usually like to squint a little. Sometimes I adopt a quizzical look if I really want to scare the person."

I placed the honey on the edge of the table where Primo's smaller works were displayed. There was a note on it.

"Some guy dropped that off," Nikki said quietly, not wanting to get between me and Rolanda.

"Guy or *a* guy?" I asked.

She shrugged. "Who's Guy? Tall fellow, tan, outdoorsy. He didn't say his name. Just asked if you were coming back." No one could mistake Guy Anzalone for outdoorsy. Rolanda hovered as if waiting for something.

"And what's the purpose of this visit? Tossing cells? A random strip search for badges?" I asked.

"Will you quit it? I came to talk to you about that thing. Those *boys* we know?"

"You're being surprisingly discreet for someone who blabbed all about it this morning."

"Is that why you look like you're sniffing baby poop? They found me. The janitor, Anthony, called the police late last night as soon as the papers hit the street. The cops were waiting for us at the church before Otis's service even started. His poor mother had to be sedated. Really ruined the moment, having the police at her son's funeral. I left early and came straight here to see you. While I was waiting, Miss Nikki told me something you ought to hear."

"Miss Nikki. I like that."

"Spend a few hours in the old neighborhood and you fall back into the old ways. Tell Miss Paula what you told me."

FORTY-TWO

The last time most of us had seen Nikki had been early Friday evening, before the reception started. She'd been fretting about the stain on her dress and had left for the members' lounge to make sure the flower pin I'd lent her covered it sufficiently and would not impede her ability to sell garden ephemera.

"As I was leaving," she said, "I saw my husband, Russ, coming in at another gate. I knew he'd look after things if I took a little long, so I didn't worry about hurrying back." Maybe that was the reason she had obsessed about the stain — she wanted to look good for the husband she complained about but still wanted to seduce.

"Go on."

"It took me a while to wade through the crowd waiting to come in. When I reached the members' lounge, it was empty. You haven't been in the lounge have you?"

She described one large room with upholstered chairs and small tables arranged in conversational groupings. At either end were the restrooms. There were no doors, just large alcoves with console tables and floral arrangements, leading inside to the sinks and stalls.

"It's not as if you can see in." Rolanda said, clarifying for me. "It's almost like an old-fashioned movie theater."

"But you can hear," I said, prompting her.

Nikki nodded her head. "Yes, if the person speaks loudly enough."

She heard a man and a woman. The woman's voice stayed even, but the man's grew louder and more agitated. At one point, the female voice developed an edge. She said everything was under control and the man was overreacting.

"Don't give me that 'you always' crap and don't tell me to relax. There's a lot of money at stake here. My future."

"I couldn't hear how the woman answered," Nikki said, "but the man sounded like he was losing it. They either got much louder or had moved closer to the entrance of the restroom, so I slipped into one of the stalls. The comments got nastier and I heard scuffling and the sound of someone being pushed. During our worst arguments, Russ

256

would never have followed me into a public restroom to yell at me, much less push me." What a turnaround; Nikki's husband was starting to look better.

"The woman said, 'You look good in a tux. They cover a multitude of sins. They can deflect attention from a weak chin, a few extra pounds, and the absence of . . . well, you know.' That's when I got nervous. I thought, what if he hits her?"

I don't know what I would have done in that instance if I thought another woman was in trouble. I like to think I would have announced my presence by opening the door and acting as a peacemaker — maybe shame the feuding couple by being a witness before one of them landed the first punch.

That's not what Nikki Bingham did. She balanced precariously on the edges of the toilet seat and braced herself in a half crouch against the walls of the stall praying she wouldn't be seen or heard while the row outside escalated.

"The woman said their plan was working and the man should just shut up and execute it. Especially tonight. He'd been dumb enough to bring a kid into their arrangement — and that other poor bastard who worked here — and once again she'd had to clean up after him."

"She called him a loser and he called her a bitch."

"Must be love," I said.

"I couldn't see," Nikki said, "but it sounded as if one of them pushed the other up against the wall or the edge of the sink. They both grunted, and instead of shouting they spit their words at each other. That was scarier. The woman said she'd gotten very good at manufacturing things and could manufacture an accident if he didn't watch his step. She even laughed and said they'd attribute it to the Javits Curse.

"They struggled. Something fell and spilled onto the floor. I saw a lipstick rolling under the door into the stall where I was hiding. I was petrified they'd find me there. Then the lights went out."

It was pitch-black. Nikki heard the others run out and, as she tried to get down, her foot slid off the rim and into the toilet. She twisted her ankle in the bowl, fell over, and cracked her head — first on the lock, then on the tile floor, a trickle of blood sinking into the grout.

"They don't know how long I was out, but no one found me until well after the lights came back on, so what was that, twenty-five minutes?"

"Man," Rolanda said, shaking her head. "I will never say another bad word about those cat and dog people."

"The woman in the lounge said, 'once again.' Do you think the people who were arguing were married or a couple?" I asked.

"If they were, they're headed for divorce court," Nikki said.

"I don't suppose you recognized any voices."

She hadn't. The absence of slang or a hipster vernacular made Nikki think they were aged thirty to fifty with no particular accents or speech patterns to help identify them. Nikki closed her eyes, trying to recreate the experience.

"The woman was wearing heels. I could hear them when she moved from the carpeted lounge area to the tile floor of the restroom. While they were arguing I heard something unzip.

"At first, I worried that it was — you know — his pants, but it must have been the makeup case. That was probably what drove the guy crazy — the fact that he was going apeshit and she was touching up her makeup."

The hospital had kept Nikki overnight and released her early Saturday morning, when she came directly to the show.

"Did I tell you Russ came to pick me up? Wasn't that thoughtful? He brought me clothing and this darling hat."

"That's a little bitty thing," Rolanda said, looking it over. "There were some serious hats at Otis's service this morning. Hats that would need their own cars if they were going on to the cemetery."

"Anyway, they gave me my belongings in a white plastic bag."

Included among her possessions were the stained black sheath, Lucy's now-flattened silk flower, one pair of high heels (right one broken and still soggy), and two makeup bags — only one belonging to Nikki Bingham. She was aching to show us the other, but it didn't seem wise to whip it out right on the show floor. Nikki went to her booth and came back with an English-style trug filled with scented drawer sachets. She placed the basket on the floor of my booth and bent down ostensibly to look for something. Instead she fished out a plastic bag from underneath the fragrant packets and shoved it under the table in Primo's booth.

"I don't want some crazy lady coming after me looking for her lip gloss. I can't think when I've heard a woman sound so driven — and so violent." Nikki, Rolanda, and I agreed to meet later at El Quixote to search the bag for clues.

Was Garland Bleimeister "the kid" and Otis Randolph the "poor bastard" who'd stumbled into something? Or was this just another happily married couple having the kind of knock-down, drag-out fight most people are fortunate enough not to witness except on daytime television?

If I was right that the intended recipient of Garland's note was someone listed on one of the dog-eared pages, I'd met or heard about most of them, most recently Cindy Gustafson, Connie Anzalone, and Lauryn Peete and her high school students. I had about an hour before we were all ejected; maybe it was time to visit the others.

But what was I looking for? An emasculated man? A woman needing to freshen her makeup? I didn't know what I hoped to learn, but my instincts had served me well in the past and I was willing to give it a shot — for Garland and Otis, and for Jamal — but also if someone had broken into Lucy's apartment looking for that damn bag and scaring the crap out of me and J. C., I wanted them to pay. No greed, no lust, but maybe a little revenge. As J. C. had advised, I'd watch my back.

FORTY-THREE

I'd forgotten that I'd already met the Bagua Lady. She'd been the one lingering on the show floor the other night, loading up on handouts at the information booth. It was hardly the stuff of CSI, but all the spiritual merchandise on her shelves made me think she wasn't the type to bitch slap a guy who had followed her into the ladies' room. Then there were the Birkenstocks. Also inconclusive, but I gave her points because of them, although it was certainly possibly to own old-fashioned, hippie shoes *and* stilettos.

I'd already spent almost sixty dollars on honey, so I was not inclined to drop any more dough on chimes or lucky Chinese coins strung together with red twine just to get a few answers. I took the simple approach.

"How's the show been for you?" I asked. It was the standard, innocuous trade show or convention exchange. You never wanted to hear it was fabulous — especially if it wasn't going well for you — but occasionally it opened the door for other, more practical information like, "Way better than Poughkeepsie." Or "Not as good as Poughkeepsie."

"Oh, you know," Terry said. "It's more expensive than the flea markets or craft shows but there's less driving and not as much fun." I took that to mean she hadn't run into any old flames — probably a good thing, given her track record. "I'd rather be outdoors than in all this reconditioned air. Last night was good." Then she shared the details of every sale over fifty dollars. I was sorry I asked and struggled to keep the glazed-over look out of my eyes. I could only assume today had been slow and I was the first person she'd spoken to for any length of time. The more she talked, the less I saw her as Garland's contact. People with something to hide didn't volunteer much, and Terry Ward was the opposite, even drifting off into a personal sidebar about her route selection to the convention center ("I started with MapQuest, but you can never trust them and the GPS told me to turn left but I knew the GW would be crowded . . .").
It was mind-numbing. I needed to change the subject.

"Good idea wearing those shoes. It's brutal standing on these concrete floors all day." That I knew from personal experience. I still had the shin splints from my first Consumer Electronics Show in Las Vegas to prove it.

"You're so right. I even wore them last night for the reception instead of heels. Who could see under a long black skirt? Besides, I'm not here to look sexy. I'm past that. It's all about the sales. And most of the attendees and buyers are women, anyway. We don't need to dress up for each other."

Hers was a philosophy I didn't totally agree with. Was she a killer? Only if you could bore someone to death. It was unlikely Terry Ward was the woman in clacking heels who had preened and reapplied war paint while verbally abusing some poor schlub in the ladies' room. I put Terry Ward on the Probably Not list, then I took pity on her and sprung for two sets of lucky Chinese coins.

The woman at the Bambi-no booth looked haggard. Show life didn't seem to agree with Lorraine Shepard. Traveling from one city to another, sleeping in strange beds and just being away from home and all the familiar things that make it home — your sheets, your soap, a coffeemaker you can trust is clean — took its toll. After a few days, I was even feeling it, but it showed on Lorraine Shepard's face as if she'd been out in the fields picking cotton. She put on a tired smile for the three or four people at her booth, but her pitch had no energy and they smiled politely and then drifted away.

The booth was bare-bones — an umbrella stand filled with baseball bats and two tables covered with a stretchy cloth preprinted with the word *Bambi-no!* in large, bright blue type. Next to the name was the image of a deer about to be brained by a baseball bat. Even to a seasoned gardener with no love for deer, it seemed a tad angry. On the tables were half-gallon bottles of the magic potion. From a distance, they looked as benign as jugs of apple cider, like those stacked in any supermarket once October rolled around. As you got closer the smell became overpowering. Perhaps that's what was responsible for the look on Lorraine Shepard's face and the deep marks etched on her forehead that resembled the pause button or the number eleven.

I hovered, listening to the woman speak with other prospective customers. It was a tough sell. At Primo's booth, people were either intrigued by the art or they kept walking. Here, Lorraine and her husband — the directory listed a partner named Marty — had to constantly battle the skeptics and the naysayers, or worse listen to people recite their own homemade recipes for a concoction that would repel deer. When she did find a receptive ear, two out of three times the listener balked at the price. I found myself hoping her husband was a better salesperson or at least had had a caffeine jolt to combat the afternoon lull.

When it was my turn, I tried asking a question unlike the same few I'd heard repeated in the last fifteen minutes.

"So, Bambi-no — does it have to be reapplied after it rains?" My delivery was perky. I was a real gardener, not a cop pretending to be a gardener. It should have gone well. It didn't. "You are the one millionth person to ask that same question this weekend. Give that woman a kewpie doll." I half expected bells and buzzers to go off.

Lorraine Shepard didn't completely snap, but it was a pretty athletic bend. She shook her head as if it were the dumbest question she'd ever heard, then launched into her prepackaged reply. "Yes. After every rain. Same thing for areas near the sprinklers." She was practically gasping for breath.

"I don't mean to pry," I said, "but are you

okay? You seem a little out of sorts."

Lorraine thanked me. Her husband had been called to a meeting and she'd been on her own all day. She was just tired. I offered to bring her a cold drink or a chair — they hadn't sprung for the chairs either — but Lorraine said her husband would be back soon and anyway the floor was almost closed. No sooner did she say it, than Marty Shepard appeared, staring at my badge and barely masking his irritation that his wife would use what little energy she could muster on someone who wasn't a buyer and who couldn't possibly do them any good.

I jokingly asked if he thought the name Bambi-no would be a problem for gardeners who were Red Sox fans. He was not amused. I spared him the trouble of answering by leaving on my own but not without making eye contact with his wife, who nodded as if to say, *Yes, he's a jerk, but he's my jerk.*

The next name on Garland's short list was BioSafe, the company selling SlugFest. I rushed to their booth just in time to see the last salmon-clad employee flinging off her ugly shirt and tossing it behind a meeting room door, then dashing off.

Everyone else was gone. The door was slightly ajar. I was just your average gardener, hoping to keep the slugs at bay. That was my rationale for entering the SlugFest meeting room.

FORTY-FOUR

The air at El Quixote smelled of beer and barbecued chicken wings. Even without the famous red dress, Brian, the bartender, greeted me as if I were an old friend. He pointed toward the back, where Rolanda was ensconced in a booth that was more private than the table we'd occupied the night before. She was already sipping a drink, so I ordered an Amstel and waited at the bar until he came back with the frosty bottle.

"No glass, right?"

"Thanks."

I slid into the booth opposite Rolanda. The cold beer went down easy.

"Nikki called to cancel, dinner with Russ. I smell a reconciliation," Rolanda said. "You look in the makeup bag yet?"

"I thought we'd share the moment." I pulled the white plastic bag Nikki had given me out of my backpack. Inside was a freebie cosmetics case from one of the department-store makeup companies — a free-with-purchase offer. Spend seventy-five dollars on face cream — which should come with a label *100 Percent Delusional* — and we will give you this stylish, nylon, made-in-China pouch that cost seventy cents. What a deal. I'd fallen for it myself.

"High-end label," Rolanda said. "Our lady doesn't shop at the drugstore."

"We don't know that yet. I've gotten some of these special-offer packages at Marshalls."

"Good tip."

I unzipped the case and upended it over the table with all the drama of someone unlocking a safe from the *Titanic.* The contents spilled out, and Rolanda and I spread our hands to make sure nothing rolled off the edge. It was the stuff that dreams were made of. Whoever left the bag in the ladies' room before the blackout was an equal opportunity shopper. Everything from Maybelline Great Lash to Yves Saint Laurent concealer to Guerlain spray bronzer. This woman was prepared for every contingency.

"That concealer goes for forty or fifty bucks, and it's only slightly better than Almay's," I said.

"Want to leave her a note?"

I thought of the women I'd spoken to that day, starting with my breakfast meeting. Fake Cindy didn't look like she could afford fifty-dollar concealer. Besides, when you're that young, how much do you have to conceal? Let me rephrase that — how much under your eyes do you need to conceal?

The rest of the items were pricey — lipsticks, expensive hair cream, and a tube of brow gel. I took a swig of my beer and pulled out my copy of the show directory.

"First off, there's no guarantee this bag or the argument Nikki overheard has anything to do with Garland Bleimeister, although it's tempting to think so given the reference to 'a kid that had to be taken care of' and the 'guy who worked here.'"

Rolanda was unconvinced. "Weren't they the words Bleimeister used in his note . . . 'I have to be taken care of'?"

It was a common expression, but it was one more thing that made us think the two events were connected. I told Rolanda about my visits with Terry Ward and the real Cindy Gustafson.

"The honey lady had a sister who went to the same school as the dead kid?"

Rolanda thought that was promising, but I didn't see it. "There's probably a big age difference, even if the sister was ten years younger. Cindy's a mature woman, very comfortable talking to me about her ex-husband, his indiscretions, her finances. She even made a few jokes."

"So that's it — if they're funny, they can't be the bad guys? I must have been out that day at cop school."

"Okay, not scientific. I admit it." Still, Cindy had been so at ease with me, it was hard to think of her as a criminal. Or a potty-mouthed, castrating she-devil like the one Nikki had overheard in the ladies' room. Maybe that's what sociopaths do. They get you to trust them and let your guard down before they strike. But I couldn't see her spray painting her face with bronzer. She wore her porcelain skin like some badge of honor, the way women did in the nineteenth century.

"What about Terry Ward? The Bag Lady?"

"It's Bagua."

"What does that mean anyway?" Rolanda asked.

I wasn't really sure. I seemed to recall ba-gua was some kind of map or grid used in feng shui. It told you where things were supposed to be in your house. Not your keys or your eyeglasses, which might be more help-ful — your *chi,* your energy. The good news was, almost anything negative could be counteracted with a mirror, which Terry could cheerfully provide in every price range. I liked the idea of easy fixes but didn't totally subscribe to the practice.

"Shoot, I've got mirrors in every room in my apartment."

"Well, then you're covered," I said. "Terry seems like a nice, agreeable woman. Hardworking, sensible shoes. That's exactly who you have to watch out for. Those nicesounding women in boring shoes. They're the ones who snap. Don't trust a women who doesn't care what she puts on her feet."

It was true — shoes tell.

"She could be in financial difficulties, but didn't seem desperate and didn't strike me as someone who'd do anything illegal, much less commit murder. She also said she'd rather be selling outdoors at the flea market. Didn't sound very cutthroat to me."

"Single?"

"I didn't ask and she didn't say, but no ring." I twisted the ring on my own ring finger; it was one I'd bought myself and I wasn't married, so what did rings mean? Inconclusive.

"Question mark. But if we're definitely adding the makeup case to the mix, I'd say no. At the risk of sounding mean, she had a unibrow. I doubt the woman owns a tweezer much less a tube of Anastasia Beverly Hills brow gel."

Were we really making assessments of guilt or innocence based on health and beauty products? Footwear?

Connie Anzalone's name was the next on the list. She could certainly afford anything in that makeup bag, and hadn't I seen her in full war paint, even coming back from the ladies' room at the St. George, even when she knew she'd be back in her room in half an hour? But her husband wasn't at the show on Friday night. Could she have been arguing with someone else? Who? Fat Frank? Another man?

"Wouldn't her distinctive manner of speaking have registered with Nikki?" she said.

"That was very diplomatic of you and it's a good observation, but *we* know what Connie sounds like. Maybe Nikki doesn't. I've never seen Nikki and Connie together, have you?" Rolanda hadn't. Nikki hadn't even run over that first day to see Connie's meltdown when her veronicas died. She had just repeated the gossip she'd heard in the ladies' room.

As much as I didn't want to believe it, there was something about the woman's cutting remarks in the lounge exchange that smacked of the same casual viciousness I'd heard when Connie and Guy had had their brief but volatile tiff in the hotel bar. And the memory of the lye comment was still, uh, seared in my brain.

"I had drinks with Connie at her hotel. When Guy arrived, I got a glimpse of their relationship. Talk about a thin line between love and hate."

"Were the Anzalones funny?"

"Shut up. This is serious. The husband may be involved in some not quite legal activities. And he's got these two — I don't know, goons, flunkies — at his beck and call."

"Fat Frank and Cookie, I remember. There's legal and there's illegal. Just what does he do?"

"He lends money. Maybe takes bets. Is that illegal or just unsavory?" Rolanda didn't know. She hadn't taken that class yet.

"If my cop friend is right and greed, lust, and revenge account for most of the crime in this world, chances are we can eliminate the Bagua Lady on all three counts. Cindy Gustafson could have revenge on her side of the ledger if Garland knew her sister and something bad had gone down between them. The Anzalones are at least two for three — they have money and there's a beautiful woman involved. It doesn't please me to say this but we may need to put them on the Possibly Involved list."

"Keep your voice down," Rolanda said, looking over my shoulder. "Guess who just walked in?"

FORTY-FIVE

Rolanda slid all the way over to hug the inside of the booth and stay out of sight of the new arrivals. I did the same.

I felt, more than heard, the couple sit down in the booth behind us. First one thud then a softer one that gently rocked the booth Rolanda and I were sharing. Brian came over to take their drink orders and would have asked if we needed refills, but the look on Rolanda's face and a slight move of her index finger sent him away without his saying a word. She mouthed something I couldn't understand and repeated the action three times before I realized the name she was saying — Kristi Reynolds.

I was mildly curious to know what Kristi had said to the cops, especially if she had implicated Jamal Harrington and the other student gardeners because of the trade show mishaps, but I had no reason to hide and didn't particularly care who she was getting cozy with, so Rolanda's precautions puzzled me. But the future cop saw or knew something I didn't, so I kept quiet and stashed the makeup bag.

They spoke softly, but I picked up snatches of the conversation, especially when the man spoke. He had a hearty salesman's delivery and his speech was peppered with excruciating clichés like "Whatever floats your boat" and "I'll scratch your back if you scratch mine." They were the kind of lines that all but ensured his back wasn't getting scratched any time soon. I didn't know how Reynolds stood it.

"What we have here is a symbiotic relationship," he said, his tone getting warmer.

I started to wonder if we should do the sisterly thing by saying hello and giving the poor woman an escape strategy when she dropped the bomb.

"Listen, pal, what we have here is a temporary arrangement. Very temporary. We both know I wouldn't piss on you if you were on fire if you hadn't accidentally seen something you weren't meant to see. So you can stop pretending that we're going to be picking out china patterns anytime soon. The minute this weekend is over, I'm going to make a nice little bonfire with your flyers, your business cards, and that ugly shirt you gave me." Kristi Reynolds spoke the words slowly and, if I had to guess from the tone, they were delivered with a smile, so no one watching from a distance would ever imagine they weren't a happy, flirtatious couple out for a predinner drink. It was eerie.

"Here's the list and a map so you don't screw it up. Thirty-five locations. Make sure you stay away from these ten. Is that clear? If you concentrate on the top five, we should get the response we want."

She instructed the man on how to proceed. Refusing to take the hint, the man still tried to turn the business meeting into a social one and suggested they'd celebrate together when the job was done.

"If that pudgy wet thing on my leg is your hand, remove it now before I stick a fork in it and you never get to date Mrs. Palmer and her five daughters again." She laughed at the end as if they were having a fabulous time and she'd just said something wildly amusing.

Dang, the woman had a way with words! Why didn't I ever come up with lines like that? My bon mots generally came at four in the morning, long after the moment to deliver them had passed.

Kristi excused herself and walked to the bar for another drink.

"That was fast. Hard drinker?" Rolanda whispered.

"I think she wants to get away from him before she goes too far. She still needs him for something and she's giving herself time to ratchet down. That's what I'd need to do after the fork comment," I said. "I'd be hyperventilating."

On her way back, mixed drink in hand, Kristi looked at Rolanda — out of uniform — and couldn't quite place her. Then she came a step closer and saw my exhibitor badge. The three of us nodded politely, and Rolanda and I feigned surprise, as if we hadn't known she was there. I didn't think she bought it.

The next ten minutes passed quickly and Rolanda and I didn't hear much. Obviously Kristi had advised the man to keep his voice down. Was she getting a kickback from his sales or giving him leads? Whatever it was, they were in bed together, figuratively if not literally. I took a page from Kristi's book and went to the bar for a beer but really to see who it was she had been emasculating.

He was about forty years old; thick, dark blond hair; a little pasty; probably ten years and ten pounds past his prime but still the kind of guy your mother's friends would refer to as "a good catch." He wore a sport jacket over a polo shirt and khaki slacks. Kristi and her male companion kept the conversation to a minimum, and after what she must have considered a reasonable amount of time, they got up to leave. I went out of my way to say good-bye, hoping the man would turn around and I'd get a better look at him, but he didn't bite. At their abandoned table were a few crumpled dollars and Kristi's untouched second drink. She recoiled as the man attempted to put his hand on her shoulder, and they left the bar.

"I had a date once that lasted forty-five minutes," I said. "And that was with dinner. Big mistake — knew it right from the get-go. But twenty minutes? That's got to be a new record."

"If the magic's not there, the magic's not there."

Neither of us really thought Kristi and the man in the polo shirt were on a date.

"That color reminded me of something," Rolanda said. I'd thought the same thing the minute I'd seen it.

"Ya think? It's all over the SlugFest booth. I'm guessing that was Scott Reiger."

Once Kristi and her friend left, I showed

Rolanda the literature I had taken from the SlugFest booth. It was long on marketing speak but short on details. The bio pic looked ten years old, but the man Kristi had been duking it out with was definitely Scott Reiger.

"I also made a copy of his meeting schedule."

"Why?"

"Someone once told me you can't believe everything you read. You have to read between the lines. Let's look at that directory again."

In addition to the brief company description, BioSafe, the company that made SlugFest, had taken a four-color full-page ad on the inside back cover of the book.

"Probably not cheap," Rolanda said.

"Especially for a brand-new company with no track record and limited distribution. They do say self-promotion is key for start-ups and newbies."

"More likely Kristi Reynolds threatened to break his kneecaps if he didn't take it."

I took my laptop out of my backpack.

"Eighty percent battery. That should last for a few searches." SlugFest was first. The BioSafe Web site mirrored the booth, the ad, and probably the man — a few catch-phrases; not many details on scientific credentials, ingredients in the product, or how it worked but lots of salmon-colored images that someone must have decided were a warm counterpoint to the less attractive but necessary slug pictures.

As the founder, Scott's bio was the first and the longest. He had an extensive sales and marketing background but not in any gardening-related businesses. Nine months earlier, he'd left an executive position at a well-known pharmaceutical company to start BioSafe. On paper he was the male equivalent of Kristi — aggressive, successful, and single-minded. They'd make a great couple if she didn't stick a fork in him.

"So what does he need her for?" Rolanda asked. "Entrée into the gardening community?"

The way to Kristi's heart was through her balance sheet. All he had to do was write a check for that to happen. Maybe she'd needed him. I googled Kristi next, and the Big Apple Flower Show popped up. She'd been at the helm for two years, taking over from Allegra Douglas. The jury was still out on her performance.

An article in *The Trentonian* made it sound as if she was single-handedly bringing the event into the twenty-first century. A less flattering piece in a New York paper cited the exodus of numerous long-term employees, exhibitors, and community supporters. Referred to as "the always outspoken," Mrs. Jean Moffitt was quoted as saying, "Kristi Reynolds has shaken up our neat little world, but perhaps we were getting too fusty. Too unimaginative. To whom will we pass the torch when all the old-timers like me are planted in the ground if not to the young innovators? Some of her methods may be unorthodox, but if she can sustain us through these few difficult economic times, then I applaud what she's doing."

But not everyone felt the same way about Kristi, including her predecessor, the snarky, chain-smoking Allegra Douglas.

FORTY-SIX

By the time I left El Quixote, the streets were slick with the first drops of rain. Traffic had slowed to a sluggish crawl and people with a single arm raised appeared on every corner. I'd never get a cab. I considered the bus but had no change and no idea what the fare was these days, and I knew better than to go into a store or restaurant and ask for change. In New York this is almost as welcome a thing to say as "This is a stickup."

It's a fact of life in the city that the four-dollar umbrella man is never there when you need him. I turned my collar up, tucked in my hair, and tried to make a twenty-minute walk take ten. The rain had picked up. I was trapped at a light between two better-prepared pedestrians, the shoulders of my wool blazer catching the runoff from both their umbrellas. When the light changed, I stepped off the curb to the furious honking of someone attempting to make a right. Jeez, give me a break — you're in a warm, dry car and I'm in a monsoon. Relax yourself.

The honking continued even after I'd crossed the street. What a jerk.

That's when I noticed the driver had double-parked and his window was sliding down. "Paula! Ms. Holliday, let me give you a ride."

The rain was coming down pretty hard and I had trouble seeing. I moved closer to the curb and shielded my eyes with my hands. It was John Stancik, looking very inviting. "Have you been following me?"

"That sounds a little paranoid. Of course not."

I jogged back across the street and opened the passenger's side door. I checked the backseat.

"All alone. You trust me?"

Why not? Didn't my mother always tell me to trust a policeman? Stancik moved the cardboard tray that was on the floor of the passenger's side.

"You didn't answer my question."

"Station house is five minutes from here. I just got off duty and picked up some coffee. I saw you about two blocks ago."

"But you thought you'd let me get really

wet before offering me a lift?" I got in the car and John handed me a stack of paper napkins from the coffee shop.

"I was trying to decide how much I felt like sparring after putting in a long day." That was fair.

I put on my seat belt, and we pulled away from the curb. "Where's your friend — out looking for a club that still has a disco ball?"

"Give him a break. He's a lot older than you think. He's just very well preserved."

I never knew any cops when I lived in New York. There were thousands of them, anonymous until one of them did something heroic or illegal, or was accused of the same. Most of time they faded into the mosaic of the city. You didn't see them until you needed them. Then, unlike the umbrella vendors, they materialized. Which was a good thing.

In Springfield, I knew them all by name. And their wives' names and their pets'. Some of that had to do with the size of the town; some had to do with my reputation as an amateur sleuth, a fact I kept to myself on the short drive to Lucy's.

The next block was one-way, heading north. Stancik drove farther west, where he'd be able to make a left and go south. We caught one of the red lights.

"Do you know where I'm staying?" I asked, suspicious.

"Wow, you *are* paranoid." Either he had an excellent memory or when we met this morning he'd filed it for future reference. A chill went through my wet clothes.

Without asking he turned the heat on. "Let me know if it's blowing too much. I got two coffees. You want one?"

I lifted the cardboard tray he'd wedged between a large briefcase and the hump in the back of the car.

"Real or decaf?" I asked.

"I got one of each — take your pick."

"That's a strategy," I said. "One for now and one for later?" I took the cup marked regular and popped off the lid.

The light changed and John took the left. After a block, he pulled into an empty metered spot and put the car in park.

"All right. I saw you in El Quixote and thought I might catch up with you when you left. I got one of each to be on the safe side."

My heart started to beat faster and it wasn't from two sips of coffee. Did everyone have that reaction when they talked to cops, or was it only people who worried they'd done something wrong? Had he seen me with Rolanda? Did he know what we were

288

up to? He wasn't saying.

"So were you spying on me?"

"Complete accident."

We made small talk, occasionally blowing on our coffees, although it was more like something to do than an actual safety measure, until the subject returned, as I knew it would, to Jamal Harrington. He proceeded carefully, not wanting to make his offer of a ride seem like a quid pro quo — more information for a warm, dry vehicle and a hot beverage — but it did. Soon after, we pulled up to Lucy's building without my having said much. He left the engine running.

"Apart from your prime suspect — a seventeen-year-old A student with no motive and no record," I said, "how's the case going?"

"Not an A student," he corrected. "B plus. Looks like somebody whacked Mr. Bleimeister on the head a couple of times with a brick or bricklike object, then dumped him in the river. Might have survived the blows if he hadn't drowned." It was a ghastly thought.

"If he was a little slimmer we might not have found him for days."

"What are you saying — heavy people float better? I would have thought the opposite was true."

"You would have been wrong. If we hadn't found him so soon after his death, we might not have connected it to Otis Randolph's."

"Another brick to the head?" I asked.

He nodded.

"M.E. says the two men died within an hour of each other, and the marks on the victims' heads were remarkably similar. Two hours later and there would have been a shift change. Might have gone unnoticed. Randolph stank of alcohol, but there was none in his blood. And it's a million to one that falling down the escalator and hitting his head — even if he'd been an epileptic — would have been enough to kill him."

"Was the wound — ?"

"About the size of a brick with some indentations on it, and above the brim." He looked up from his coffee cup. "That means the top of the head. Not easy to fall and hit the top of your head, unless you're jumping off a diving board into an empty pool," he said.

"And even then you'd have to be an Olympic medalist to hit the very top of your head. Nobody noticed this when Otis's body was found?"

"Cause of death was listed as undetermined."

Poor Otis. What did he know or what had he seen? And what possible connection could Garland Bleimeister and Otis Randolph have had — a sixtysomething-year-old handyman from Harlem and a college dropout from — how did Labidou put it — Smallville, Pennsylvania?

"We know Jamal Harrington was acquainted with Otis Randolph from statements given by Wagner employees, and he was seen talking with Bleimeister on Wednesday. He's a link, that's all. We just want to talk to him. No one's calling him a suspect." The word *yet* hung in the air.

"Isn't that just semantics? Look, I only met him a few times and doubt I'll ever see him again. Show's over tomorrow and I'll go back to my sleepy Connecticut town and plant pansies or whatever it is you think suburbanites do."

Stancik placed his coffee cup in the holder, fished two business cards out of his wallet, and gave them to me.

"What's this for — in case I lose one?"

"I like pansies. One's for Jamal. The other is in case you decide to call me after you get back to Springfield. It's not that geographically undesirable." Very smooth. Had I said I lived in Springfield? Right, he was a cop.

"Thanks for the lift. I'll be thinking of you at three A.M. when the caffeine kicks in."

"Feel free to give me a call."

I turned up my collar and dashed across the wet street into the vestibule of Lucy's building. A note was taped to her mailbox.

Stop in whenever you get home. J. C.

I'd started the day with J. C. Why not end it with her? I'd catch her up on what Rolanda and I had learned, and with any luck there'd be good leftovers.

My shoes squirted water with each step up to J. C's apartment. I slipped out of them and shook off the rain before ringing her doorbell. Just as my finger hovered near the buzzer, J. C. opened the door, having seen me through the peephole. She looked paler than usual and wore the expression of a disapproving teacher. I wasn't greeted with the smell of a welcoming dinner and Moochie and Bella didn't dash out as they usually did.

"You've got company."

FORTY-SEVEN

Was the other cop here — Stancik's partner?

"Are you okay?" I kept my voice down. J. C. glanced in the direction of her weapon of choice. She was either signaling for me to reach for it or indicating she hadn't needed it. Dang if I could tell which it was; I didn't know her well enough. I took a tentative step into her apartment and peered to the right. On the sheltered part of her terrace, inspecting her plants, was Jamal Harrington. He was with a girl. All I knew about her was that she wore no makeup, wore a brown corduroy jacket, and wasn't Cindy Gustafson. I closed the door behind me quickly, as if John Stancik might have followed me up the stairs.

"What the heck are they doing here?"

J. C. shrugged. "Some idiot must have buzzed them in."

They'd been waiting for me on the upstairs landing when J. C. got home from yoga class. She'd threatened to call the cops — by now she probably had them on speed dial — and not even the presence of a fresh-faced twenty-five-year-old girl would satisfy her that they were not up to no good. She'd read the news — that was how confidence teams worked. One looked innocent and softened your defenses, then the other beat you to a pulp and took your stuff. It was only Jamal's detailed description of his winning garden exhibit that kept her from swinging her trusty iron bar and braining him on the spot.

"Just because you can tell a gloxinia from a Glock, I'm supposed to believe you're not thieves or psychos? I'm drawing a blank at present, but haven't some legendary villains had innocuous hobbies?"

"I don't know any legendary villains," the boy had said. "You mean like Al Pacino in *Scarface?*"

J. C. was still poised to strike, if necessary. But Moochie had seemed fond of the boy, and the cat was usually a good judge of character.

"I'm in trouble and Ms. Holliday was kind to me last night," Jamal had said. "I have no other place to go."

With that, J. C. had invited them in.

Jamal and Not-Cindy halted their garden

tour and turned toward the front door when they heard our voices. From a certain angle Jamal could be seen from the street where John Stancik might be lingering, so I motioned for him to come in. He ran toward me and grabbed both my hands as if his savior had arrived. The girl was less effusive.

He straightened up and regained some of his tough-guy demeanor. "Ms. Holliday, Ms. Peete said I was wrong about you. She said you'd help." The boy was polite if nothing else.

"Stay off the terrace for one thing. I just got a police escort home, and my chauffeur may still be outside. I told him I'd probably never see you again, so he wouldn't be too happy with me if he saw you on the terrace. Just for curiosity's sake, how did you find me?"

"Followed you when you left the store yesterday. Then I saw the pilgrims and turkeys on the windows and knew which building and which floor you were on."

The girl said nothing, either getting a new set of lies straight or trying to remember the ones she'd told me over breakfast.

"I don't think I know your friend," I said.

Jamal introduced Not-Cindy as Emma Franklin, the late Garland Bleimeister's girlfriend. At least that was the current story.

"Everything I told you was true," Jamal said, "except I left Emma's name out of it because she asked me not to tell anyone. Because of what happened to Garland. She was afraid."

The girl picked up her cue. "And everything *I* said was true. Except for the honey stuff. All I know about honey is that you press the bear's tummy and the honey comes out of the top of its head."

It was a disarming statement. The girl exuded innocence, sweet stuff gushing out of her mouth as if someone had pressed the right spot on *her* tummy. But she had the ability to get people to lie for her and protect her — including me — and that was a dangerous quality. I wouldn't be doing it again.

"Garland did go to Penn State a few years back, but he never got his degree."

So far, Emma's definitions of *everything* and *true* left much to be desired. I waited to hear the other exceptions.

Not sure that Jamal would show up, Garland had also asked her to retrieve his bag. Without the need for subterfuge or the late-night transfer of alcoholic beverages, Emma had come to the aid of a woman struggling with two cumbersome display cases and a temperamental wheelie cart.

The two of them simply waltzed in together — Emma and a beekeeper named Cindy Gustafson.

"I'm pretty strong. She was nice. She gave me some honey for helping her."

Emma took a large, heavy glass jar out of her bag and I recognized it from the three I'd purchased at the real Cindy Gustafson's booth. Hers was not wrapped. So you decided to temporarily steal the nice lady's identity. Charming. Did you steal the honey, too? Or did you whack your boyfriend on the head with it? The jar was roughly the shape and size of a small brick with some detailed ridges near the lid. I found myself wondering if there was evidence on it.

The girl offered the honey to J. C., who placed it on the butcher-block table. She perched on a counter stool nearby and we waited for the girl to continue.

"Once I didn't have the boxes against my chest, one of the guards saw I didn't have a badge and asked me to leave."

"You were wearing one this morning," I said.

She shook her head and fished around in her bag again, pulling out an empty badge holder she'd picked up near the registration desk and stuffed with a piece of paper she'd written on. She tossed it on the coffee table.

It wouldn't have fooled Rolanda, but would work on a less diligent security guard or a part-timer who wasn't paying attention, and it had worked on me. If this kid didn't watch it, she could turn into a first-class con woman. But why did she do it?

"Why not just tell me who you are and what you wanted?"

"I guess I wasn't thinking straight. I was afraid. I haven't slept in a real bed for two nights. Garland had the only keys to the apartment where we'd been crashing. Then we had to leave. He had my passport. We were going away. Now I don't know who has it. And whether or not they think I know something."

Who were *they?* And what was there to know?

"Just spit it out, dear." J. C. would have made a good interrogator. Or therapist. There was something soothing in the way she drew the girl out. Motherly — now that she'd put that bar down. Or maybe it was the way she now held the jar of honey, which, if it was evidence, was being thoroughly contaminated. It would have seemed strange for me to tell her to put it down, so I asked her to put the water on for tea. She was surprised but put the jar down and did as I asked.

"C'mon, Emma."

"Garland needed money. He started playing cards in his junior year, thinking he could cover his college loans that way. He was good at it. He was also good at spending it. He loved hosting parties with fabulous food and going to four-star restaurants. He was such a steady customer at some restaurants, they let him run up huge tabs. He lived so large they must have thought he was a trust-fund kid and if he didn't pay, daddy would. So not true. His parents had no money.

"Then he started losing. Big-time. The bets got larger as he got more desperate and tried to make it all back chasing one big payoff."

"But it didn't happen," I said.

"He just dug himself into a deeper hole. Eventually he borrowed money from this greasy mob guy. The interest was astronomical, and the number just kept going up, even when Garland made payments. He was winning again but never enough to pay off the principal. I don't even think they wanted that — they just wanted him to pay the interest forever."

Welcome to the world of finance — mob or otherwise.

She explained that Garland's less than

realistic plan was to raise enough cash to get them to Macau, where he claimed to have friends. He was convinced he could win enough dough there to pay back the mobsters and come home with a new stake. And he was expecting someone at the Big Apple Flower Show to give him seed money. There were so many flaws in this strategy I didn't know where to begin, but it was all moot now.

"*Macau?* Couldn't he go to Foxwoods or Vegas, like everyone else?"

"The gamblers knew him at those places. He was afraid they'd know he was broke and get in touch with the people he owed. Besides, he said the food at those places was terrible."

Picky guy. Maybe I'd been too hard on her. Perhaps the tears at the bagel shop that morning had been real. J. C. handed her a box of tissues and got up to make the tea, taking the jar of honey with her.

I wasn't as patient as J. C. and asked the obvious question. "Okay, how does a college dropout with a gambling problem wind up at a flower show?"

"I'm not sure. Garland took some agricultural classes at Penn State. He studied with this wacko professor, who was eventually booted off campus over some unauthorized experiments. Garland worked for him, too."

The girl picked up Moochie and began to mindlessly stroke his fur. "He said taking that job was going to turn out to be the smartest decision he ever made." The cat wriggled out of her grip. Smart cat.

I thought back to the names in the show directory. Bamb-ino and BioSafe probably had scientists on their payrolls, even if they weren't listed in the company literature.

"Were the experiments related to pest repellents? Who was Garland here to see?"

The girl said she didn't know.

"You must know something. People don't just hand out checks for nothing. Who was it? What did Garland have on them?"

"He just said we'd get the money. He said he deserved it. He was entitled to it."

I listened to this young girl calmly describing her murdered boyfriend's shake-down scheme and wondered when exactly her moral compass had gone blooey. *He deserved it.* I guessed whoever had killed the boy thought he deserved it, too. What crucial bit of information was she leaving out?

"Garland said he'd wrap up his business on Wednesday night. He told me not to worry about the bag. If I couldn't get it, a boy we'd met earlier in the day was going to get him into the convention center that night." She motioned to Jamal, who seemed anxious to pick up his thread of the story to clear himself, if only to the assembled group.

"So you and Garland went back to the center," I said. "He left you to do his business and you had a snooze at the beach hut in Connie Anzalone's exhibit and didn't see or hear anything until something woke you — two people running out of the center?"

The boy shook his head. "There were noises before that. Something else happened. One of the Wagner employees — maybe it was Otis — was pushing a large rubber tub or cart, like the cleaning staff uses. He was cursing about how heavy it was and why the hell had someone left it in the middle of the floor 'cause all the cleaning was supposed to be done by then. I didn't think anything of it and stayed hidden because I didn't want to get into trouble. I didn't want to hurt our chances of winning."

Under the circumstances, not winning a flower show contest was the least of Jamal's problems.

"I waited for him to pass and only came out when the sound of the cart's wheels and the man muttering was off in the distance. I didn't see anyone. I checked on the exhibit and went back to the hut, but may have dozed off again. It was later on I heard the other noise and saw the two people."

"Except it wasn't me," the girl said. "I was waiting for Garland at the bar."

How much were these kids playing us and how much of what they were saying was true?

I had the sinking feeling Garland's body had — at least briefly — been in that tub, and that the man pushing it, Otis Randolph, had been killed when he discovered what was inside or how it got there. But by whom?

FORTY-EIGHT

"I'll feel pretty stupid if I let you stay here tonight and wake up dead tomorrow morning." Moochie may have been won over, but J. C. said out loud what she and I were both thinking.

We were still actively trying to convince Jamal and Emma to turn themselves in to the police, but we weren't heartless enough to send two hungry orphans out into a monsoon with no place to stay for the night. That said, we fell a little short of the complete kumbaya chip that would allow rational people to offer their floors or sofas to total strangers. Especially ones who might be involved in multiple murders.

"We can sleep in the hallway," Jamal said.

"The Dons will freak," J. C. said.

Not mobsters or British professors, J. C. explained that the Dons were a gay couple, both named Don, who lived next door and returned from their house in the Hamptons early on Sunday mornings to beat the traffic. A couple of kids huddled in the hallway would send them straight for the telephones. One would call the cops and the other would call their real estate agent. Their apartment would go on the market and that would be unfortunate since they'd just completed a lengthy renovation and a new owner would only rip everything out and the building would once again be filled with dust and tarps and men with carpenter's butt who frightened Moochie and Tommy.

Jamal motioned to the terrace. "Out there's okay. I can move the bench so that it's in the sheltered part so that I can't be seen from the street." Without a word he had assumed it was his presence that was the issue, not Emma's. If anything, I trusted her less than him.

J. C. was not inclined to have anyone redecorating her terrace, even one who'd taken a blue ribbon at the Big Apple Flower Show, but she gave it some thought.

"I will fill a coffee can with kitty litter. If you have to pee, you're not going in my planters and you're not going to go over the side of my terrace. That point is non-negotiable."

Jamal nodded in agreement.

"I may still have a tent from my hippie

days. If I do, it's in the storage room down-stairs."

Some New York City apartment buildings have storage rooms in their basements that can be rented by the owners or tenants. They're the graveyards for baby carriages, abandoned bicycles, and exercise equipment too expensive to toss but too guilt inducing to leave in the owners' apartments. J. C. plucked a set of keys from a bowl on the counter.

"C'mon."

Jamal was relieved. "That's cool. I've never slept in a tent. I think it's a white thing, wanting to sleep on the ground." His comment cut the tension.

That left Emma without a bed and all eyes were on me to offer her the sofa in Lucy's apartment. Lucy didn't have much that could instantly be turned into serious cash, although they'd do well on eBay. The shoes and handbags were expensive — and so plentiful I doubted Lucy would miss any, but it wasn't my place to volunteer someone else's home to a stranger. Particularly one who still had some explaining to do.

J. C. bailed me out.

"I've got bivvy bags. You can both use them." Jamal and Emma looked at her as if she'd offered them Depends. "Short for bivouac?" Judging by their expressions *biv-ouac* must have sounded like a new drug for insomnia or acid reflux.

"They're sleeping sacks," I said. "When you don't need or don't want to carry a tent."

"I knew I liked you," J. C. said. "The girl who lives upstairs, your friend — I bet she wouldn't know a bivvy sack from a flour sack. C'mon, Jamal, you'll have to help me hunt through my things." She walked to the door and picked up her iron bar. The boy seemed hurt that she thought she'd need to defend herself against him. I was a little surprised myself.

"What?" she said, looking around the small apartment at the three people she was now conspiring with. "This?" She rattled her saber. "The gate in the storage room sticks. Sometimes it has to be pried up."

She gently pushed the boy ahead of her on the steps and I overheard them as they headed down to the storage room. "Let's go, Jamal. I'll tell you about the time Teddy Roosevelt and I went hunting in Alaska."

"For real?" he asked, looking back up at her.

"No. Not for real."

They disappeared into the zigzag of the staircase. Emma had said she hadn't eaten since the bagel I'd bought her that morning and I was hungry myself so I jogged down two flights of stairs to catch up with them and hung over the railing. "J. C., okay if we raid your fridge?"

"Be my guest."

Climbing back up the stairs, I hoped for something that didn't need to be reheated. "Emma?"

I tapped on the bathroom door. No answer. I looked outside on the terrace but she wasn't there either. Upstairs at Lucy's the door was still locked. I unlocked it and searched the apartment. Puzzled, I went back to J. C.'s and waited for her and Jamal. After fifteen minutes they returned with their outdoor gear, laughing as if she was a den mother and he an overgrown Cub Scout.

"Did you see Emma?" I asked, as they entered the apartment.

They shook their heads. Jamal went straight for the terrace. J. C. and I followed. Had they discussed an escape strategy or was it the only logical explanation for her disappearance?

The rain had let up a bit. Judging from the faint scrapes on the terrace's painted floor, Emma had dragged the pot of *Pieris* over to the railing, stood on the pebbled mulch, and hoisted herself onto the fire escape ladder that dangled, extended over the front of the building. In the process she'd torn down one of J. C.'s lattices covered with clematis and Boston ivy.

"She said she was strong."

"And athletic," J. C. said, "but that is not a nice girl."

Standing on the terrace, we heard a soft knock that escalated into furious, impatient tapping on J. C.'s partially open door. We must have looked an odd trio to the newcomer, as we stood in the steady drizzle, J. C. with her ever-present iron bar which — now that I knew her better — seemed more like Little Bo Peep's staff than a pugil stick; an inner-city kid holding two bivvy bags and a stack of tent poles as if he had no idea what they were used for; and me.

"Is this a private slumber party or can anyone join in?"

FORTY-NINE

Lucy Cavanaugh put the kibosh on pizza from Carmine's, Chinese takeout, or Thai food, claiming all of the above were loaded with carbs that would expand in her stomach like rising dough and render her new white jeans permanently unwearable. She was given to hyperbole. In the end we settled on the Silver Moon diner, which had something for everyone, even J. C., who thought it a sign of moral turpitude for single women to order in, believing we should either cook wonderful meals for ourselves or go out. On this she was firm. Clearly both women had issues with food; Jamal and I were less picky.

Lucy brought her suitcase upstairs, then came back down in yoga pants and mukluks, drying her long hair, which was still wet from the rain. Three of us jumped as the downstairs buzzer shrieked, announcing our food had arrived, and Lucy jokingly asked if we were expecting to be raided.

"They don't usually ring the doorbell in a raid, dear. Generally, they just knock down the door," J. C. said, as if she knew. By now nothing J. C. did or said surprised me, but it was apparent Lucy hadn't spent much time getting to know her neighbor.

"Go out of town for a few days and all sorts of interesting stuff happens."

"So," Lucy said, "let me get this straight. The cops think Jamal here bashed in some guy's head — maybe two guys — and you're looking for a warm place for him to sleep tonight. The dead guy's girlfriend was here and takes off down the fire escape, and you think *she's* one of the bad guys because she knocked down a plant? If I didn't know Paula my entire adult life, I'd think there was some strange logic going on here."

I picked at a chicken and sun-dried tomato salad that wasn't half bad. Note to self, ask Babe to put this on the menu at the Paradise Diner.

"Not that it isn't always lovely to see you, Lucy, and it *is,* in fact, your apartment, but what are you doing here? I thought you weren't due home for another week."

Lucy had been off on another adventure. This time to a spa that guaranteed a seven-pound weight loss to guests who paid a tidy sum for a one-week stay that included a secret Mayan treatment.

"I'm keeping the world safe from unscrupulous and unhealthy diet factories," she said, one arm raised, the other hand plucking a rippled chip from Jamal's deluxe burger platter.

"Does it work?" I asked.

"Of course it does. The Mayans didn't have a Walgreens or Burger King, much less a decent restaurant in sight. They barely feed you and what they do let you eat and drink has you running to the bathroom all day."

She turned to J. C. and Jamal. "Excuse me . . . but somehow I feel as if we've fast-forwarded and it's okay to mention bodily functions even at this early stage of our relationships." They agreed.

"No probs," Jamal said. "They talk about manure all the time at the flower show."

Lucy didn't recommend the program unless you were going to an awards show or an event where your old boyfriend was expected with his new and younger girlfriend, but even then the weight would all come back the minute you ate a normal meal or drank a glass of water.

"There was more smuggling going on at

that spa than there was in . . . I don't know."

"Tijuana, dear," J. C. said. "So you left early?"

"Hell, no. Seven pounds is seven pounds. I wanted to see that lower number on the scale, even if it only lasted for a few hours. Look, I have proof." She pulled a cell phone out of the waistband of her pants and, after pressing a few buttons, passed around the still-warm phone so we could all be witnesses to her success. "We weren't supposed to bring cell phones — how ridiculous is that? How could I not take a picture?"

"Nice pedicure," I said, handing the phone back.

Lucy yanked off a mukluk and wiggled five perfectly painted toes in a color I would have called Jungle Red. She looked around the room for approval.

"This is okay, right? I haven't offended anyone. I thought having already discussed the smallest room in the house . . ."

She replaced her boot and looked at our plates to see what else she could nibble on, clearly subscribing to the "if it's on someone else's plate, the calories don't count" rule. This time it was a pickle slice from me.

"I know this probably isn't the hot issue — and I'll admit I haven't done much decorating upstairs — but what's the deal with the duct tape and the plastic tablecloths in my bedroom? Did you guys have a party? Not that I mind, but poor Harold will be crushed to have missed it."

"Who's Harold?" I asked. It was unlike Lucy not to share romantic details.

"I never told you about Harold?" she said. I shook my head.

It turned out Harold was Harold Bergstein, the one neighbor she had connected with. He was a former editor at *Glamour* magazine.

"I don't usually read it," she said. "Too many articles and not enough pictures."

Harold lived around the corner and had a direct line of sight into Lucy's bedroom. Given the fact that he was in his eighties, Lucy had never minded the occasional fashion advice in her mailbox and had even left her card once so she could make sure she got Harold's expert opinion right before going out.

"It's a joke. C'mon, the guy can barely see, for Pete's sake. I bumped into him once at the Food Emporium with his caregiver — unless that was some other old guy giving me the eye."

Did I want to know that my best friend was an exhibitionist? Or that she was dancing around in her undies, as the cops had suggested? For an old guy who might have a heart attack if she modeled some of the things I saw hanging in her closet? Lucy didn't see the problem with it.

"He's a friend. All he can see are the colors anyway. I tested him once. All he ever says is, 'I like the green' or 'I like the black.' He's very partial to red."

Sounded like Guy Anzalone was off the hook as my Peeping Tom.

"I have nothing to be ashamed of," Lucy said.

Jamal thought it was a riot. J. C. wasn't so sure. "No, dear, you don't, but we've had enough personal revelations for one evening."

She was right. We needed to decide what we were going to do next. In an attempt to redeem herself Lucy suggested she call a friend of hers, a fledgling novelist who taught writing at Penn State, to see if she knew anything about a professor who sounded like the one Emma had described.

"He may not even exist — that young girl probably wouldn't know the truth if it came up and bit her on the butt." J. C. was still fuming over the lattice she'd have to repair.

"Maybe not, but the best lies are the ones that have a grain of truth in them," I said. "Lucy, do you mind calling her?"

"We're overdue for a phone call anyway. Sarah knows everyone. If this guy was within a hundred miles of her, she either knew him, dated him, or knew someone who did."

FIFTY

Like Emma the night before, Jamal Harrington must have decided he needed to get out of Dodge, because the next morning he was gone. No note. Nothing was missing. He'd repositioned the stone planter that held J. C.'s *Pieris* and taken a stab at fixing the fallen latticework. The tent was down and he'd replaced all the parts in the correct color-coded stuff bags.

"Not easy to do in broad daylight, much less the early morning light of a gray day," J. C. said. We stood in her apartment and she stretched to find something good to say about the boy's unexplained disappearance. Even Lucy, who'd just met him, didn't want to believe he'd been guilty of anything other than being in the wrong place at the wrong time. Probably his sympathetic reaction to the Harold story.

It was the last day of the flower show and I still had a job to do, despite whatever else

317

was going on and a restless night on Lucy's sofa. I hadn't been able to shake the unsettling feeling there was another old dear who had a direct line of sight into Lucy's living room and images of me tossing and turning were going to wind up on some geezer's YouTube page.

I had five hours to sell the rest of Primo's creations, or otherwise pack them up and get them ready for shipping. I hadn't heard from Hank Mossdale, so I enlisted Lucy's help. She promised to arrive just after the doors opened to the public. I found Emma's fake badge on the coffee table and told Lucy to flash it with her customary aplomb if anyone gave her trouble.

"Please, I've gotten into A-list parties with attitude and a smile. I think I can handle the security guards at a flower show." She pocketed the badge. Perversely I almost told her to look for one guard in particular when she showed up — Rolanda Knox. Lucy took a bag of popcorn from the fridge and shoved it in the microwave. So that explained the abundance of Orville Redenbacher's.

"Popcorn for breakfast?" I said.

"Why not? It's a grain."

By the time I left Lucy's, my head was filled with theories about Jamal and Emma.

Where had they gone? Was Jamal meeting her? Even if he and Emma weren't involved in the murder, they were brushing up against some ruthless people who probably were. I didn't want to think either of them was involved in murder, especially Jamal. He seemed like a good kid, but was I prejudiced just because he was a gardener? If he'd been a basketball player or a rap artist, would I be more likely to think he was guilty?

I closed the lobby door behind me and tucked my chin into my jacket against the damp spring morning. As I did, I glimpsed a scene reminiscent of the old television show *Let's Make a Deal.* Three doors, three choices. The only things missing were Monty Hall and a trio of women in gowns.

John Stancik was in a Crown Vic a few cars down on the left. He wore dark aviator glasses, and the newspaper he pretended to be reading was propped on his steering wheel. Even from a distance I could see a cardboard tray holding two large cups, the way a similar one had the night before.

On my right, waiting at the traffic light, was a taxi, its roof light indicating it was free. Having the turtlelike peripheral vision of the experienced New York cabbie, the driver glanced in my direction with the barest tilt of his head. At the slightest encour-agement or eye contact from me, he'd wait and I could jump in and be spirited away.

And in between, parked illegally at a fire hydrant, happily munching a donut, was Guy Anzalone. The cab took off and I was down to two options. Or maybe not.

I turned left and started walking. Going in this direction would add two blocks to the trip but I didn't think either man would drive backward down a one-way street simply to offer me a lift, whatever it was they wanted to discuss — business or personal. I kept my chin tucked into my col-lar as if I hadn't noticed Guy, and he seemed genuinely surprised I didn't run over to his car as if we were headed down to the shore or a weekend in Atlantic City. I wasn't much of a lip-reader but he seemed to be repeating aw, schucks, or perhaps it was the Brooklyn version of that expression.

Stancik was quicker to react and automati-cally rolled down the passenger's side window of the car just as I approached. He leaned across the empty seat to say some-thing, knocking over two cups of steaming liquid onto the dashboard, his newspaper, a small notepad, and the front seat. He did not say aw, schucks.

I intended to keep walking, but the scene

was comical and I took pity on the poor man. Besides, he had given me information the night before — perhaps he'd do it again. I backtracked.

"It's cloudy. Are those glasses supposed to be a disguise?" I asked.

If they were, they did nothing to hide the scruffy brush cut and dimpled chin that I hadn't paid much attention to before but found suddenly vulnerable and appealing as Stancik juggled the dripping items.

"Use the newspaper to sop it up, then I'll throw it in the trash out here." He did as he was told and I pitched the soggy mess in a Doe Fund trash can on the corner.

I strolled back to the car, feeling smug. I drew the line at occupying the still wet seat in the front and climbed into the back, despite the way it looked. "You must be pretty wired. Have you been out here drinking coffee all night?" I asked.

He shook his head. "Just the last hour or so, since we picked up Jamal Harrington. I came back to talk to you." I stopped feeling smug.

According to Stancik, Jamal must have stayed on the terrace until about six A.M. when the neighborhood would be coming to life with the sounds of delivery trucks and people lining up for the soup kitchen at the church next door. He'd stopped at the Koreans and had the bad luck to bump into a couple of uniformed cops hassling a truck driver who was triple-parked while delivering cut flowers to the grocery store. "They recognized his description from a radio call. He slipped into a subway station, but one of the officers nabbed him while he was fumbling with his MetroCard," Stancik said.

"If he was a bad kid, wouldn't he have jumped over the turnstile to get away?"

"When was the last time you took the subway? It's not that easy to do anymore. A lot of those old turnstiles have been replaced. So what did you and the kid you barely know talk about until the wee hours?"

"I had no idea he'd be there."

"You're lucky Labidou isn't here. He'd be making cougar jokes. For someone who doesn't know these boys, you do seem to be in the thick of it."

"I am, now that I'm getting daily visits from the NYPD."

Jamal told the cops about Garland's jacket, so I didn't have much to add except to repeat that he thought Otis Randolph had witnessed the exchange and would have been able to tell the cops it was a friendly one.

"You don't really think Jamal is your man,

do you?"

"I don't *think* anything. I *know* he's been in numerous altercations at his school. He was seen more than once with the victim, and he's got the dead man's jacket, passport, and a large amount of cash. More cash than a high school kid usually carries."

Jamal had said nothing to us about money or a passport.

"Could Garland have forgotten those things were in his pockets when he gave the jacket to Jamal?"

Stancik looked over his sunglasses. "Would you forget your passport and money if you were blowing town?"

I did drive all the way to New Hampshire once without my wallet, but it wasn't the same thing.

"And now," he said, "we have a statement from someone who claims the two men were in business together." He gently pulled apart the coffee-splashed pages of his notepad, but I put two and two together faster and knew who the informant was before he said the name.

"Emma Franklin," I said.

FIFTY-ONE

Stancik was lousy at hiding his reaction. "How did you guess?"

"The Great Holliday never guesses. She knows." I tapped my forehead with two fingers. I was tempted to call Emma a pathological liar but forced myself to exercise restraint.

"I'd be very suspicious of anything that girl tells you. She may have a sweet and disarming exterior, but she is one of the most facile liars I've ever encountered."

"She's a kid from Pennsylvania," he said. "Never been in trouble. Her mother's a doctor, stepdad's in the import business. Are you basing this on something real or some women's intuition thing?"

"You've been hanging out with Labidou too long. He's rubbing off on you. What does Emma say her role is in all this?" I asked.

"An innocent duped by a new and unscrupulous boyfriend who wasn't what he seemed to be."

"How did you find her?" I asked.

"Painstaking detective work. She walked right into the precinct last night around midnight."

"Why would she do that?"

"Fear? Remorse? She had no place to go?"

"Did you hold her?"

"We're not in the habit of incarcerating people who come in of their own free will to make statements."

By the time we'd pulled up at the Wagner, I told the cop everything I knew, up to and including my firm belief that any incriminating evidence found in Jamal's possession had been planted there by Emma — or whatever her real name was — most likely when he and J. C. had gone into the basement to get the sleeping gear and I'd briefly followed them.

"Where is she now?" I asked.

"Anywhere from here to Timbuktu. How should I know?"

"That girl is literally unbelievable," I said, amping up a notch. "She may be Emma Franklin or that may be another identity she's temporarily borrowing. She's like Scheherazade, spinning a different tale every time she opens her mouth."

"Maybe she's doing it to stay alive, too. But it gets worse."

"How much worse could it get? She's pregnant with Garland's child?"

"Not for her. She's suggested that you and some older woman are also involved. That you're in cahoots with this Jamal and maybe even with the people Garland was supposed to get money from. We're gonna assume that the money wasn't a belated Christmas or Hanukkah present. It was most likely a drug deal or extortion."

"Well, now you know she's nuts, right? Right?"

Wrong. I could almost hear him. All he knew was that I, too, had been seen with the dead man. That, according to Emma, and maybe even Rolanda, I'd tried to smuggle Garland into the convention center, that I was the last person to have possession of his missing bag. I'd also been seen at a local diner having breakfast with Jamal and the wife of a man who may or may not be a mobster.

Emma didn't know, but if the cops had asked around further, they'd find that I'd had drinks with the Anzalones the night Garland was killed and telephone records would show he'd repeatedly called me earlier that same evening. I began to see how easy it was to put together a circumstantial case against someone if that's what you wanted to do. And it scared the pants off me. If that was the way a straight-arrow woman from the suburbs felt, I could imagine how a kid like Jamal Harrington felt. Now I knew why he'd run.

Stancik hadn't said another word. He didn't have to.

Losing my temper would be unproductive. "So now I'm Fagin, orchestrating a team of youthful offenders, like the guy in *Oliver Twist*? You've got to be joking," I said, my voice even.

He wasn't. "While I was waiting for you, I ran the plates on that tank idling by the fire hydrant. I hate when people do that," he said, looking up from his notes. Over the top of his glasses, I could see his eyes were chocolate brown. I hadn't noticed before. "What if there's a fire? Anyway, the vehicle belongs to one Concetta Anzalone, wife of Guy Anzalone, who the police in Brooklyn are investigating on usury charges. You've been seen with them on numerous occasions, including one incident at the St. George Hotel, where you allegedly struck Mr. Anzalone with a suitcase. Doorman called it in."

"This is preposterous. I'm getting out

now. If you don't have an actual question for me or a warrant for my arrest, thanks for the lift but I have to go to work. I suggest you do the same."

"Honey, I am at work. I just don't want you to get hurt. You're not in the burbs anymore. Some of these people are rougher than you may be used to. From what we've pieced together, it's not impossible Jamal's crew has been staging these Javits Curse mishaps at the convention center to deflect attention from their real crimes."

"Has anyone questioned these protestors out here about the disturbances at the show?" I asked. Tight security had kept the antichemical, antifertilizer group under control except for one minor incident at the reception on Friday. The cops felt they were in the clear as far as the vandalism went. Management thought it was an inside job — a disgruntled employee or even one of the exhibitors. And the first incident happened before the sales vendors were admitted, so it could even have been one of the display gardeners.

"Right. Maybe it's Mrs. Moffitt."

"No. We checked her out. She's been exhibiting at the Big Apple for a long time. We don't think she'd sabotage the show. We think the first incident might have been staged to destroy some piece of evidence, but now the perpetrator is getting a kick out of being referred to as the Javits Curse. That says kids, not professionals."

I wondered where he'd gotten his detailed show information, then it hit me. "I was unaware of Kristi Reynolds's stint at the police academy."

"Maybe she got there after you graduated. She's a little younger."

Someone once told me the worst wounds were self-inflicted. I hadn't pulled the trigger on that one, but I'd certainly given Stancik the ammo.

"That came out wrong," he said. "That's not what I meant."

"Forget it," I said, hauling myself out of the car.

Just then two fire engines screeched to a halt in front of the Wagner Center. Stancik and I looked at each other.

"Now what?"

We hurried past the thin crowd of protesters, who parted for the emergency vehicles and workers and us as soon as Stancik flashed his badge. Inside the building, the sight of the abandoned security desk had us sprinting up the escalator to the second floor, which was the scene of much chaos and shrieking.

FIFTY-TWO

I didn't know how much water can come out of overhead sprinklers in ten or fifteen minutes, but it was enough to dash dreams and bankrupt a few businesses. By the time the downpour stopped, some hearts were broken. Others thanked their lucky stars that, like a capricious tornado, the deluge had miraculously skipped their aisles or booths and landed next door. All they'd suffered was a light misting, compared to devastated neighbors who'd been washed away in mini-mudslides.

Stancik ran off to find security and to make sure there wasn't a real fire anywhere in the old building. I hurried to Primo's booth and breathed easier when I saw his sculptures had gotten sprayed but were otherwise fine. David's light fixtures had been spared, as had the sumptuous breakfast he'd brought for us. Nikki was less fortunate.

The wooden and wrought iron furniture and tools in her booth could be wiped down, but the dried flower arrangements looked like piles of refried beans, the vintage linens were ruined, and the sarcophagus was filled with water that had leaked through the decorative grate that served as the tabletop. It would be difficult to drain and would probably start to smell soon, since the water that had come out of the sprinklers was hardly Poland Spring.

All around, people wondered how to salvage the last day of the show, one that historically saw an increase in foot traffic from shoppers who knew bargains could be found when vendors were faced with the prospect of shipping home all the merchandise they hadn't sold. This particular day there would be lots of bargains.

In a calm and determined voice (did nothing fluster the woman?) Kristi Reynolds announced that the show would open ninety minutes later than originally planned and that tubs and plastic garbage bags were being distributed by Wagner personnel to help people get rid of any debris. Fans and water extractors were available by calling the building's maintenance number.

Very quickly, the atmosphere changed. Out of the chaos grew a spirit of camaraderie I hadn't seen before at the show, as exhibitors helped one another clean up and improvise in those gardens and booths that had been most severely damaged. In a remarkable display of solidarity Mrs. Moffitt's Jensen got the ball rolling by offering their award-winning specimen plants, window boxes, and container gardens to anyone whose display had been irreparably damaged. She had plenty of takers, and it inspired me to make the same offer for the temporary use of Primo's remaining artwork. Selfishly, I also thought it might even help them sell if they were seen in situ.

Connie Anzalone's Coney Island Garden was unscathed but, wanting to help, she called Guy and the Tumbled Stone King diverted a truckload of rocks and faux flagstone to the loading dock, where Fat Frank and Cookie handed them out like Romans flinging bread into the crowds at the Colosseum or, to use a more recent and perhaps more appropriate analogy, like old-time mobsters handing out turkeys during the holidays.

In some instances, exhibitors joined forces and created one decent display where previously there had been two or three bedraggled ones. As they worked, people shared stories about how their home gardens had survived sudden downpours and freak hailstorms. I was loving my gardening community. In fact, it was the first time I'd felt like part of a professional community in a long time and I was happy to pitch in to help. I called Lucy and left a message for her to come as soon as possible.

Through the frenzied last-minute activity before the opening bell, Stancik and Labidou were clustered around an ever-changing knot of uniformed cops, private security guards, and convention center employees not far from my booth. Periodically workers pointed to the ceiling at the sprinkler heads that had gone haywire and caused all the destruction. A maintenance worker came over with one of the rubber carts.

Five exhibitors asked to borrow small sculptures, so I loaded them onto flat carts and they were whisked away. As I walked the floor, I began to notice a pattern. Not the exhibits that had been ruined — the ones that had been spared. Among them were all Mrs. Moffitt's entries; SlugFest; three major plant suppliers from the Northwest; and, as far as I could tell, any vendors and gardeners with electrical equipment. Perhaps the deluge hadn't hit with the randomness of a tornado.

Like a good citizen I circled back to my

booth to share my observation with John Stancik. I may not be have been as young as Kristi Reynolds, but as my mother would have said, I had a much better personality. I just needed a little lipstick. I swung by the ladies' room before looking for John.

The smoke stung my eyes, and I wondered if there really had been a fire, but it was just Allegra Douglas, puffing away in the first stall. In an uncharacteristic display of thoughtfulness, she tossed the butt when she heard me enter.

"I'm sorry," she said, waving at the air. "I know I shouldn't be smoking here. I'm just so frazzled. How is your booth? Is everything all right?"

Our previous conversations hadn't been that much fun, so I nodded politely and got to the business of primping. Allegra stood there, not saying anything. She seemed genuinely distressed, and I couldn't keep up my cold shoulder routine. I asked if her booth had survived the flood. She shook her head, close to tears.

"It's all under water. It was the way I designed the garden. All the water collected in the middle and didn't run off. It looks like a swamp." I knew she wanted another cigarette and was grateful she didn't light up again.

"Is there anything I can do? Is there anything you can borrow to fix it?"

"From whom? Everyone hates me. I know it. But it's not easy to change when you're as old as I am. What am I going to do — just start being nice at my advanced age? People will think I've gone senile. I'd rather have them hate me than pity me."

"No one hates you. They may think you're a little rigid, that's all. About the rules." God, how I could lie in the name of a good cause. I guess I *had* retained some skills from my former job. "C'mon, maybe I can help." I pulled on her spindly arm and dragged her to her garden.

She was right. It was a disaster. The water hadn't drained, and she had a large murky pond surrounded by a ring of bedraggled plants. With a little luck and a lot of hard work it could look as good as a toxic sinkhole. We had fifty minutes.

"All right. You have three choices: bog garden, amphibian pond, or a high-concept, first garden after the apocalypse, *I Am Legend*/*The Road*–type thing." She just stared. "Scratch that," I said. "Two choices: bogs or frogs. What think?" She went with the frogs.

In fifteen minutes we'd foraged two broken pieces of lattice; more than two dozen stone, ceramic, and metal frogs (they had not sold as well as the hummingbirds and the vendors were happy to part with them for the price of a mention); and three bruised but living water lilies. It was a start. I set her to work, while I went in search of other less obvious materials — an empty six-pack and a neon beer sign. I went to the gangsta garden display, which was in pristine condition.

Some were convinced that was due to the students themselves being the vandals, but I thought it was the wiring in the exhibit. Whoever had arranged for the downpour didn't seem to want electrical items shorting out and potentially causing a real fire or a permanent blackout. They just wanted to screw things up temporarily. Stancik thought it was someone creating a diversion. I thought it was someone with an ax to grind, but a carefully wielded ax.

I was anxious to talk to Lauryn about Jamal, but that would have to come later, in a more private setting. Right then, I needed her help on a smaller but more time-sensitive matter.

"C'mon, Lauryn. This is one of those moments when you get to be the person your dog thinks you are. To be good to someone who's been mean to you. Allegra Douglas."

"I don't have dogs, I have fish," she said, arms folded but a slight curve to her lips. "I also *eat* fish."

"Is that what y'all do in the suburbs?" one of her students asked. "Worry about what your pets think?" It earned the speaker a sharp, critical look from her teacher, who wasn't really hesitating, just savoring the moment. And strategizing. I told her what I needed.

"Not just the suburbs. Trust me," I said to the kids, "you'll feel good about doing it. You'll be making another garden. And this one has a television theme."

I'd said the magic word. And Lauryn knew where I was going with the six-pack and the beer sign.

"Do we need to find someone with a football jersey?" she asked.

"Maybe you can bribe one of the workers?"

With that she and three of the students judiciously picked hardware and plant material from their own display and brought them over to Allegra's booth. I left the kids practicing *ribbit* noises. The girl who had asked about pet habits in the suburbs was telling Allegra about *Frogs,* a cult classic B movie that carried the memorable tagline, "They're not the ones who croak!" Someone

337

went off in search of a jersey or a football and I headed back to Primo's booth.

Amid the sounds of exhibitors, rushing to be ready when the doors opened to the public, and convention center staff, scrambling to put away floor fans and water extractors, Nikki's gasp could barely be heard except by those closest to her, which included me, David, and John Stancik, who'd returned to see how I had fared.

She'd been trying to straighten the decorative grate on top of the sarcophagus when she noticed something colorful through the wrought iron of the grate. Fabric, with patches on it, bobbing in the water.

FIFTY-THREE

John rushed to Nikki's side, instructing her not to touch anything, which I thought an unnecessary precaution since her finger-prints were everywhere. Perhaps it was just cop talk. He left a message for Labidou, who was floating around the building. Stancik peered over the edge of the sarcophagus through the grate. He pulled on a pair of latex gloves and slid the heavy makeshift tabletop a few inches to the right to see what had elicited Nikki's reaction. She took a step back as if something were going to jump out of the stone tub; David put his arm out to catch her, just in case. She'd already cracked her skull once that weekend.

"Is it a body?" Nikki asked.

Perversely, I stepped closer to the sar-cophagus for a better look. I saw a ripple of colors and thought I recognized a scrap of fabric with a familiar image on it, Delicate Arch, a common symbol for Arches National Park, one of the places Garland Blei-meister had visited and memorialized on his jacket. The jacket he'd given to Jamal Harrington.

"Oh, no." The words escaped my lips like a low moan, and before I knew it I'd drawn even closer to the stone vessel. Whatever Jamal might have done, this was no way for a kid like him to end up.

"Stay back," John said. It was spoken softly, a request, not an order, and I complied. "It's not a body. Or a jacket." Stancik used one of the vintage fireplace tools in Nikki's booth and fished something out of the tub — Garland Bleimeister's missing bag. He dumped it on top and we watched the water drain through the decorative grate. Just then someone joined us.

"What's going on? I guess they have to keep it humid at these things, but this is ridiculous. No wonder everyone's hair looks bad."

"It's not the humidity," I said mechanically.

"It's the heat?" she said. "Wait, that doesn't sound right." She threw her head back in a full-throated laugh, cracking herself up. "Love the sarcophagus. Saw one at the Gardner Museum, but I'd never be able to get it up the stairs." Lucy Cavanaugh marched right up to it for a closer inspection.

"Oooh, that bag's never going to be the same. I dropped a backpack in a canal in Amsterdam once. Smelled for days and all my lovely patches ran. To say nothing of the stuff inside. Thank goodness most of it was in plastic bags." She snorted. "Wow, *that* was a long time ago."

Lucy sucked on a Dunkin' Donuts iced coffee and handed me the one she'd brought for me. Skim milk, no sugar. It was just like her to jump right into an ongoing discussion and totally hijack it.

She looked around for an ally or an explanation. "What?" she asked. "What?"

"I don't think the owner of this particular bag will object to its condition," I said. Sometimes clueless but never slow, Lucy nearly gagged on her coffee.

"That's the dead guy's bag?" She gave it a closer look, including the patches, some of which had started to bleed at the edges. "At least he got to travel a bit, before, you know . . ." She trailed off, realizing she was getting into a line of conversation that might be considered in poor taste.

"Detective Stancik, are we going to see what's inside?"

He hesitated before answering me.

"What's the big deal?" I said. "Apparently it's been here for days. I think I was even accused of not being curious enough when your partner asked me about it."

He unzipped the main compartment. Inside, sopping wet but still neatly folded, was a change of clothing, slightly more formal than the T-shirt and jeans he was wearing when we met — black slacks, a button-down shirt, and black slip-on shoes. There was a small Dopp kit with travel-sized toiletries and a washcloth; three water-logged paperbacks; and *Zagat New York Restaurants* with Post-its fringing the pages. In the outside zippered pocket was a soggy deck of cards. What wasn't there was even more telling.

"No wallet, no keys, no ID," Stancik said.

"No phone either," I said.

"How do you know he had a phone?"

"Everyone has a phone," Lucy said.

"He called me. But it was after he left his bag, so he must have had it with him. He had a few bags. Three, I think. Maybe this was the nonessential stuff."

"No wonder he didn't bother to come back for it," Lucy said. "There's nothing here that couldn't be easily replaced if you were trying to get out of town in a hurry."

"I think he left a little sooner than he

planned," I said. "But why all the fuss about a bag with extra clothing in it? Especially if you're expecting a windfall and leaving the country? If it was that important to him, why didn't Garland just come and find me on Wednesday morning after he sneaked in?"

It hit me and Stancik at the same time. Garland wasn't looking for his bag — someone else was. Someone who knew it was missing and wanted to know what was in it. I'd never actually spoken to him on the phone — Babe did, and she wouldn't have recognized his voice. And anyone could have left that note on the bulletin board. For all we knew it was Garland's killer who'd been trying to reach me.

None of us had seen the bag since Wednesday, when I'd stashed it under the table. Nikki thought the grate might have been slightly out of place on Saturday morning after her husband had been there. "I assumed Russ moved it."

"Friday was the morning you thought I had rearranged Primo's sculptures, remember?" I said. "Maybe someone took the bag from under the table in my booth, searched it, and then dumped it in the sarcophagus."

"But why?" Lucy said. "Why not just steal it?" It was an excellent point.

Labidou arrived, carrying a black plastic bag like dozens of others on the show floor. He also held a bunch of battered roses he'd picked up for free. When he saw something was up, he got into cop mode and pushed them on Lucy, who was too confused to respond but was used to men bringing her flowers, so she simply said, thanks, and tried to figure out if she knew him.

Stancik placed the waterlogged evidence in the plastic bag and handed it to Labidou. Still wearing the gloves, Stancik removed the grate. "We'll return this after we've had a chance to examine it. I don't expect we'll learn much but we have to check it for prints. We also have someone collecting the garbage carts, but I don't know that we'll find anything useful after this sprinkler business." As the two men left, I was still pondering Lucy's question, Why not just steal it?

"Either they took what they wanted out of the bag," I said, "or they wanted to make sure that something *wasn't* in the bag. Something that might link them with Garland Bleimeister."

"Then why not toss it back under the table?" Lucy said, absentmindedly whacking the roses against her hand.

Who knew? Fear? Fingerprints? Would

there still be fingerprints on something if it had been floating in the water? The cops seemed to think it was possible, but would a criminal know that? Was it bad timing? If they'd been inspecting the bag on Nikki's table, it might be easier to slip it in under the decorative grate if someone came by. If you were strong.

A handful of rose petals fell, and Lucy bent down to pick them up. Instead of trashing them she tossed them into the water in the sarcophagus. "Oh, sorry."

"Go ahead," Nikki said. "It looks good. Reminds me of a spa treatment I once had." The two women floated the rest of the roses in the concrete tub.

In lieu of the sarcophagus Lucy bought a pinecone nightlight she reckoned would be easier to get into a fifth-floor walk-up. We still had time before the doors opened and I planned to give Lucy a quick tour and drive-by introductions to Connie, Lauryn, and Rolanda, but she dragged her feet.

"Okay, but let's go this way," she said. "We should probably stay away from the security guard at Hall E. I don't think she likes me." That was Rolanda's post. It seemed they had already met.

FIFTY-FOUR

After the morning's excitement the rest of the day was tame. Not many attendees remarked on the extra humidity, thinking, as Lucy had, that it had been ratcheted up for the tropical plants. And if there were booths and exhibits in some disarray, perhaps they were just closing up shop early. Those who did know about the morning's disaster were impressed at how quickly people had bounced back, but for most attendees it was business as usual.

Four of the pieces I had lent to other exhibitors had sold, so Lucy and I would have that much less to pack and ship back to Springfield. I was surprised Hank hadn't called, but he was reliable and I expected to hear from him before Monday afternoon when everything had to be removed to get ready for the next event.

Having lived with them for days, I had decided to purchase one of the sculptures myself. It probably meant I wouldn't make any money for my efforts this weekend, but I was confident Primo would give me a discount. I'd grown fond of the piece, a four-foot oxidized metal sculpture Primo had called *Spade and Archer.* He had used fragments of a shovel and of a bow and arrow. Since my astrological sign was Sagittarius and I am a gardener and a mystery fan, it seemed to have my name on it as well as Sam's and Miles's. I remembered the dumplike backyard at Primo's place and worried that I'd never find the piece again, so I opted to take that one with me in the Jeep when I left the city and not ship it with the others.

At 1 P.M. Jensen swung by with formal invitations to Mrs. Moffitt's after-show party in Hunting Ridge. Connie Anzalone had mentioned it on Friday and I had been faintly jealous, but now David, Nikki, and I had been invited, too. David's unpleasant neighbor with the unsold fountains quietly seethed. Lucy cleared her throat.

"Is it all right if I bring a friend?" I asked. "Maybe two?"

Jensen said yes, and as soon as he left, Lucy pulled me aside. "Speaking of friends? Sarah called just after you left. That professor you asked about? Quite a character. I told her we'd call back since I wasn't sure what you wanted to know."

Sarah Marshall picked up after five rings. According to her, the good professor had had an eye for the girl students. That may have been a contributing factor to his getting the boot, but the school blamed it on his unauthorized experiments on pest repellents. Something to do with toxins, Sarah wasn't sure because the juicier part of the story involved an undergrad, and why stick to boring science when there were more salacious — and easier to remember — details?

"First they pulled the plug on his funding and then they canned him," she said. "I asked about students who might have worked for him. I don't think the school would keep records of his former interns," she said, yawning. "There were lots of them. I'm not sure if I could even get access to them. Especially now. Reporters have been nosing around because of that aggie student who died in New York. Garland something. The prof's name was Lincoln Wrentham."

"How are you spelling that?" I asked.

"With a *W*. Can I go back to sleep now?"

We found a surprising amount of information online about Lincoln Wrentham. At least surprising to me, who prided myself on having the fewest links of most people I knew. Wrentham's last known address was somewhere in New Jersey. No current employer found. No recent papers published. Divorced.

My cell phone rang. It was Sarah, slightly more awake than she'd been earlier. I could hear her drinking something that I took to be coffee.

"Listen, there's something else. Wrentham's daughter went to school here. Some free or discounted tuition thing. She was registered under another name, but when the revelations about her father came out, so did her real identity, and she left when he did. Just as well. It would have been awkward to have everyone know daddy was boffing her classmates."

"You remember her name?"

"Sure. She was in my creative writing class. A-plus student. Emma Franklin."

FIFTY-FIVE

Findthemnow.com found Lincoln Wrentham in Stilton, New Jersey, a small rural community not far from Philadelphia. He was listed with directory assistance as L. Wrentham. When I called it was only my mentioning Emma's name that prevented him from hanging up.

"Is this Professor Lincoln Wrentham?"

"No one's called me that for a while, but, yes, I am. What's this about? Who are you and what do you have to do with my daughter?"

"My name's Paula Holliday. I met your daughter in New York this week, sir, and I think she's in trouble."

The description matched, even as far as her propensity for storytelling.

Wrentham and Emma's mother had met at an airport in Dallas. They were trapped in the Admiral's Club after one inch of snow had halted flights in and out. All the business and golf magazines had been scarfed up by other stranded travelers and the only reading material left was a six-month-old copy of *Parents* magazine that neither wanted. They spent the next three nights in an airport hotel. "It was as typical a late-eighties meet-cute as you could get," he said.

"We were both devoted to our careers and swore we didn't want children, but that changed when we found out about Emma. It was harder for Judith, of course. She went back to work soon after Emma was born, but every time she had a professional setback, she blamed our marriage. My research was bearing fruit and I was offered speaking engagements and appointments all over the country. I started to take them. That led to some indiscretions and our eventual divorce."

"I suppose I was a terrible husband. Judith was bitter. But I was a good father for as long as I had a relationship with Emma. She was nine when we split up. Judith remarried soon after and insisted on changing Emma's last name to Franklin, her new husband's name. I objected, but in the end she got her way. She's a shrink. She was able to convince a judge it would be traumatic for a child of that age to have a different name from her mother and her step-father. I only wanted what was best for Emma, so I knuckled under. Later on, I learned she told Emma that I'd wanted nothing to do with her and that's why they changed her name. She's poisoned that girl against me for years."

At some point, the former Mrs. Wrentham read that the professor was developing a formula that could revolutionize farming and gardening: a foolproof pest repellent. She told Emma that her biological father stood to make a fortune and that the girl was entitled to part of it. It was her inheritance.

"Judith became obsessed with the millions she thought I'd make."

"So *did* you discover a foolproof pest repellent?"

"*Et tu,* Ms. Holliday? Foolproof and safe are two different things. But it's not ready for general use. The unintended ecological consequences could be disastrous. No responsible person would bring something into the market until it had been tested exhaustively."

Clearly we were dealing with a person who didn't give a rap about the unintended ecological consequences if they'd killed one or maybe two people to get the formula.

Emma had gone to see him about a year ago.

"I don't know how she found me. I haven't made a secret of my whereabouts, but we haven't exactly stayed in touch. She asked for two hundred and fifty thousand dollars. I asked her what kind of trouble she was in, and she said no trouble — she joked that it was just back allowance plus interest."

The girl seemed to think that would be pocket change for Wrentham, but despite what her mother had said, he claimed not to have it. He'd bought a small farm and set up his own research facility with the settlement the school gave him, and he lived modestly continuing to test his formula.

"Emma will inherit whatever I own at the time of my death, but if I dropped dead tomorrow, it wouldn't be in the millions of dollars as she and her mother think I'm sheltering. I'm afraid I'll disappoint them again," he said. "Lately, I've felt she was very close to me. I just hoped that as she got older, she'd want to hear my side of things, perhaps learn to forgive."

"Her proximity might have been more than a feeling, Professor Wrentham. Did you ever employ a young man named Garland Bleimeister?"

"I did. I hire seasonal employees to help

353

with the gardens and bring produce to the farmers markets. Garland was with me for three summers. Good boy. Although I know he had his issues. He ran down to Atlantic City more than I thought a boy his age would. At first, I thought it was for women."

"Sir, I'm sorry to tell you this, but Garland has been murdered."

"I heard."

"And Emma is somehow involved."

He hadn't heard that. Wrentham agreed to take the next available flight from Philly to Westchester Airport, where Lucy and I would pick him up.

"How do you know when the next flight is?" I asked.

"I can be there in — two and a half hours. I have friends."

"He's smart, single, straight, and has friends with private planes?" Lucy said. "If he can cook, I want him."

"I didn't ask. So Emma and Garland were a couple, but she keeps that from Daddy. Garland needs money and Emma thinks she'll just ask Daddy, but that doesn't work. And," I said, "given her mother's influence — some might say brainwashing — Emma thinks he's holding out on her. She and Garland steal Wrentham's formula and offer it to someone who'll pay handsomely but keep their names out of it by claiming to have invented it himself. They don't want a long-term relationship, just a nice, simple payoff. And who knows — maybe Emma thinks her father will never find out and she can go back to the well at some point in the future after she dumps Garland."

"Isn't that like kids nowadays?" she said. "No work ethic."

"Their buyers — and it's got to be either the SlugFest or the Bambi-no people — initially said yes and then must have reneged on their agreement to pay, otherwise Garland would be lying on a beach somewhere instead of on a slab at the morgue."

"Who's got the most dough?" Lucy asked.

"Neither of them is rolling in it. The Slug-Fest guy looks a little more prosperous, but looks can be deceiving. And Bambi-no looked like a mom-and-pop operation. What if the payoff was contingent upon one of them getting a fat licensing agreement at the show?"

"And Emma?" Lucy said.

My guess was she pulled the strings but stayed in the background.

"I think she sicced the cops on Jamal as a diversion because she was still trying to make a deal. She didn't want the buyers arrested — even if they were killers — until she got her dough."

"I can't wait to meet this girl — preferably with a plate-glass window between us."

"In addition to being an accomplished liar, Emma is a remarkable and gutsy young woman. Her father's been called a genius and her mother is a vengeful psychiatrist. That could make you feel smarter than everyone else. Too smart to get caught," I said. "Let's hope she's smart enough to not get herself — or us — killed."

FIFTY-SIX

"How do you know they'll both be there?" Lucy asked.

According to Jensen, Scott Reiger and the Shepards were both invited and had said yes. That was all we had to go on. Jean Moffitt's party was a big event in gardening circles. It would be telling if the SlugFest or Bambi-no exhibitors *didn't* show up.

"Do we bring a house gift?"

"No time to shop. Besides, the woman probably has everything she wants," I said, packing my things. "There doesn't seem to be much of a waiting period between her admiring something and acquiring it."

"I know where we can get some lovely plastic tablecloths. Gently used." Lucy had ripped down the Pilgrims and turkeys as soon as she'd gotten home, and they were now crumpled in the corner of her bedroom, the duct tape still attached.

"It's a good thing I travel light," I said,

"because *Spade and Archer* will be taking up a good chunk of the backseat." Lucy looked at me blankly.

"The sculpture. Primo's piece?"

I'd been told people wore everything from overalls to long dresses to Mrs. Moffitt's post–flower show shindigs, but the red dress was not going to make a third appearance quite so soon. I opted for something more conservative: my all-purpose black jacket and black slacks. Lucy was more adventurous and when the phone rang, we knew her outfit had passed muster with Harold, who'd been delighted to learn Lucy hadn't sold her apartment to a paranoid woman with bizarre taste in window treatments.

The umpteenth white jacket Lucy cinched over her green floral dress was the charm — Harold agreed, although he did ask if she had it in red — and she modeled for him in her tiny bedroom. It walked the line between sweet and creepy.

"I can't believe you're taking fashion advice from an eighty-year-old man, whatever his past CV. I may need to rethink your position as my fashion guru."

"I don't always take it." She looked at my outfit. "Wouldn't you like to borrow something more festive?" she asked. "You look a little downtown for a garden party." I stood in front of the full-length mirror. She was right. Next to her, in her sunshiney outfit I looked like our high school gym teacher on her way to a funeral.

"We're just taking a short drive out of New York City. We're not going back in time. Besides, there may be a confrontation at this party and I don't plan to be wearing white gloves and a big hat if there is."

"If it's more than verbal sparring, I'm not sure I'll be much use." She tossed me one of her castoff white jackets, which made me look like the staff I was expecting Mrs. Moffitt to have. All I needed was a carnation. *Hi, I'm Paula your waitperson.* Beverage? I eyed the military jacket that I'd worn to the Friday night reception.

"I've been hustled, haven't I? Go ahead," Lucy said. "It's you. But it's still downtown. Take a scarf. Something bright." She rummaged through a fabric-covered box and tossed me a piece of red nubby silk with a dragon pattern on it that was so long it could have been worn as a sari. I wrapped it around my neck five or six times as instructed. Harold would have approved. J. C. heard us in the hallway and cracked the door just a bit until she was sure it was safe to open it all the way.

"Where are you two off to?" she asked.

"Garden party at Jean Moffitt's."

She motioned for us to come closer — the Dons were home and the walls were notoriously thin. Stancik and Labidou had returned, asking her about Jamal and the girl, and the Dons were on high alert.

"It's a good thing I didn't know anything. That way I didn't have to lie." She looked around, although it was just the three of us in the hallway.

"At least I didn't know anything when they asked me."

She asked us in and closed the door behind us. Sitting on her sofa was Emma Franklin.

"Let's see," I said, "who are you today? Runaway princess? Alien life-form?"

"Go ahead," she said. "I deserve it. I'm a liar. I've always been a liar. Ever since I was a child. I used to make up stories about my famous father and how he was doing top-secret work for the government and that was why he couldn't live near us and I had to change my name. Later I said he was in the witness protection program. What was I supposed to say? That the great man dumped me and my mother so he could indulge his appetite for nineteen-year-old girls?"

Lucy and J. C. were softening. I could see

it around their eyes that had morphed from skeptical slits to moist, round pools. Any minute, one of them would put her hand on the girl's shoulder and she would own them. She'd be off and running, spinning another tale that had elements of the truth in it, but could not strictly speaking be called *the* truth. I reserved judgment until I heard all of this version.

She had spent over a year stalking her father by the time she finally approached him. "Can you imagine," she said, "after all this time, he said he wanted to get to know me." Wrentham was sounding like less of a rotten, philandering dad. When he refused to simply write her a check, she devised the plan to steal and sell the formula that her mother had been telling her about since Emma was a little girl.

"*The formula.* God, I heard about that so many times I thought *everyone's* father had a formula. I knew what a formula was when most kids my age still thought it was something you gave to babies." She took a deep breath and went on. "Last summer I contrived to meet Garland Bleimeister," she said. "It wasn't hard."

She said she'd zeroed in on Wrentham's weak-willed employee, a sweet, malleable boy with a few addictions of his own — food and poker. She convinced Garland to steal the formula.

"He'd already been doing it. Sort of."

For the past three years whenever Garland took the professor's produce to market, he also stashed a couple of contraband containers of the pest repellent.

"He sold a concentrated solution for a hundred dollars a jug out of the back of his car."

"To consumers?" I asked.

"No. To one person. I don't know who. The buyer diluted and repackaged it. Garland didn't think my father would ever find out."

"And it wasn't much of a leap to go from stealing a few jugs to stealing the formula," I said.

She nodded.

"He would use part of the money to pay off his gambling debts and he thought we'd use the rest to go away. I just didn't plan on things turning out the way they did."

"Were you really going to go away with him?" I asked.

She let out a sigh. "I honestly don't know."

When Garland didn't show up for their Thursday dinner meeting, Emma thought he'd gotten cold feet, and she resolved to go through with the plan herself. She didn't know he was already dead, and the buyers didn't know Garland had a partner until Emma contacted them.

"Then I saw the paper with the news that Garland's body had been found. Once I realized they'd killed him I just wanted out of here, but I needed to make sure there was no way for them to connect me to him. I didn't care about the formula. I could go back to my father anytime — as long as I was alive. I tried to make people think Jamal was Garland's partner." It was the first time she looked or sounded contrite. "I just needed to check Garland's bag. He had said you probably still had it and I wanted to make sure there was nothing in it that connected me to him."

"So was the magic formula in there?" I asked.

She shook her head. "Garland had it on a flash drive. He kept it with him always. Maybe deep down he knew it was the only thing that kept me sticking around."

"So you didn't even have the flash drive and were going to try to make a deal?" Her expression barely changed, as if to say, *yeah, so?*

"Did you take the bag and toss it in the sarcophagus?"

"No. I was going to go back to the convention center for it, but I got nervous. I started to wonder if Garland had talked to you about me. That's why I called you and pretended to be Cindy. To check you out and see what you knew."

"I'm the least of your problems. You do know these people probably also killed a janitor at the convention center."

"Okay," Lucy said. She stood up and slapped her hands on her thighs. "Now we call the cops. Killer shoes, killer apps. These I get. Real killers, no."

"Let's just hear the rest of Emma's story," I said. "Why are you here? What do you want?"

"I'm scared. Now the people we approached keep contacting me."

"You've still never met them?"

She shook her head. She insisted she didn't know their real names either. They went by Mr. and Mrs. Rose.

"How did you and Garland hook up with them?"

"He said he met the man at some market where he used to bring the produce. They want the formula bad and want to meet me."

"Just don't go," Lucy said. "There's a concept. Don't go into the deserted building. Don't go into the woods at night. Don't open the door when the scary guy is coming up the stairs. It's simple."

"You don't understand. What am I supposed to do — never open the door again? They know who I am now."

"How'd they find you?" I asked.

"I don't know. . . . Maybe there was something in Garland's bag. Who knows? I got a text. I thought it was from Gar. It was his number."

So whoever it was had Garland's phone. I called Stancik and got plugged into his voice mail. Then I called the precinct to see if anyone knew where he was.

The desk sergeant said he was in New Jersey chasing down a lead; after that he was heading to some fancy-schmancy party in Westchester. "Stan's probably leaving us to start a private security company for rich people."

"Is Labidou with him?" He was. That meant it wasn't purely a social call.

"Emma, where are you supposed to meet Mr. and Mrs. Rose?"

She showed me the address. "Looks like we're all going to the same garden party."

"Okay if I join you?" J. C. asked.

"Sure. You can remind us to *watch our backs.*"

FIFTY-SEVEN

It was a tight fit in the Jeep with me, Lucy, Emma, J. C., and *Spade and Archer*. One sharp turn and I could skewer a passenger.

"Someone rest your hand on that thing so it doesn't flop around too much," I said.

"I'll do it," J. C. said. "I feel naked going into a questionable situation without my iron bar anyway." It was rare to hear from a woman who missed her weapon.

A phone rang, and three women fumbled in their bags. I stuck to the driving. The party had started without us, but with as many guests as Jean Moffitt invited I didn't think we'd be noticed or reprimanded if we arrived fashionably late.

The phone kept ringing. It was mine. Lucy retrieved it from my bag, pushed Answer, and held it to my ear so I could keep driving.

"I just landed."

I'd almost forgotten about Wrentham. I

got off the phone and said nothing to the others but Lucy remembered that he was flying into the Westchester airport.

"Okay. We have to make a stop and we're gonna need to make room for another passenger back there." The airport was thirty minutes away as long as I didn't make a wrong turn. Lucy quietly reset the GPS.

We stopped for gas and a much-needed pee break. Emma and I made an uneasy truce and positioned *Spade and Archer* on the roof of the Jeep while the others went to the restroom. We wedged an old fleece jacket that I kept in the car for emergencies underneath the piece to keep the noise level down and to prevent the sculpture from bending. Then we threw a tarp over the whole thing and attached it with bungee cords.

"I hope this works. I'd hate for it to fly off on the highway when it's not even paid for."

"Why do you have so many of these things?" Emma asked, holding one of the cords as if it were a snake.

"After duct tape, a bungee cord is the single most useful thing you can buy for a dollar. Sometimes two for a dollar. C'mon, get in the car. There's something I have to tell you."

Fifteen minutes later J. C. and Lucy

emerged from the service station bathroom newly primped. J. C.'s black sweatshirt was loosely thrown over her shoulders and an unnecessary but fashionable belt hung around her slim waist over a white cotton tank top that they'd just bought, three to a pack, in the mini-mart. Her lips were slightly pinker than they'd been before.

"Is that what you two have been doing? Shopping and playing with makeup? Jeez, I could have used some help here."

"Where's Emma?"

I pointed to the median, where Emma was balanced on a concrete block clutching an unlit highway light.

"How'd she get over there?" Lucy asked.

"I activated the ejector seat. Whaddaya think? She ran off when I told her we were picking up her father at the airport. I don't know where she thought she was going, but she realized pretty quickly there was nowhere to go. She's on foot, on the highway, and now she's paralyzed with fear and can't move.

"All right," I said. "There's not that much traffic. One of us just has to bring her back." But the service station was around a slight turn and that made it dangerous and difficult to see oncoming traffic for more than a few seconds — especially if the vehicle was doing more than sixty, which was a good bet on this road at this hour. J. C. would have volunteered if I'd let her, but I wasn't about to.

"Hey," Lucy said, "I just met the girl. I like to save my infrequent acts of heroism for people I've known more than forty-five minutes."

"I'll go. There's something else you can do." I looked around the service station for traffic cones but didn't see any. Improvising, I unwound Lucy's long red scarf and handed it to her. "See that tree right near the curve in the road? Stand on something and tie this to the highest branch you can reach. I don't need them to stop, but people will slow down a bit when they see it. At least I hope they do. But don't stay there. You'll get killed."

"Great, if one of them hits me, that'll really slow things down for you."

"Not necessary. I'll go get her after the first car that slows down and sees me."

Lucy ran to the far end of the service area. She didn't give herself enough credit for bravery. She clambered over a large tree of heaven ailanthus and attached the scarf. She gave me the high sign. Two cars passed, but only the first had slowed down. Not good.

"What can I do?" J. C. said. I was running

low on ideas.

"In my truck I've got a big yellow lantern." I told her to go down to the end of the service area where Lucy was still waiting for more instructions. "Just click it on and off a lot so drivers will know something's up. I don't need that much time."

"You mean like Morse code?"

"Do you know anybody who *really* knows Morse code? Besides, even if they did, they wouldn't be able to read it going seventy miles an hour. Just flash it a bunch of times. Wait a minute. I have a better idea." I ran to the Jeep, drove to the end of the service area, and backed the car over to the side of the road as close as I dared to the highway. I put the hazard lights on. Between the red scarf, the hazard lights, and J. C.'s faux Morse code, anyone who didn't slow down would have had to be crazy.

I ran back to the spot opposite Emma and waited for my chance. Yes, there was honking and some name calling, but it only lasted a few minutes. I bolted into the road and yanked Emma back to the service area. Lucy drove the car back to our end of the parking lot.

FIFTY-EIGHT

"Gee, Emma, we're going north, not south. Get in the car." She did as she was told. We crawled down to the on-ramp and got there just in time to see Lucy's silk scarf fluttering in the breeze and ultimately flying away like a giant bird.

"You owe me big-time."

"That was a five-dollar purchased-on-the-street-from-a-Senegalese-guy scarf and you know it."

Lucy and J. C. were an impromptu tag team, explaining to Emma that no matter what her father had done, she should at least hear him out. I didn't know if it was working on her, but the brainwashing was getting to me.

"Okay," I said. "I know you both have Emma's best interests at heart, but she's a big girl. Apart from the fact that she did just run into traffic — which is a major no-no at any age, by the way — she's a grown woman. She knows adults make mistakes. She's even made a few herself recently. If he can forgive her, maybe she can forgive him. Maybe they can patch things up, but it's up to them, not us. So, lay off."

"I'm sorry," Emma said. "Really. I've never met women like you before. You're amazing. You're so normal."

We rode in silence for the rest of the way, until we reached airport arrivals. When we pulled up to an attractive, older man with a thick mustache and longish gray hair Emma burst into tears. She jumped out of the car and ran to hug him.

"I can definitely see the appeal," Lucy said, watching the reunion from inside the Jeep. "We still need to confirm the private plane business, but I hope she tells him how amazing we are. The *normal* part will be harder to sell."

J. C. leaned forward from the backseat. "I don't disagree with you, dear."

Wrentham and Emma squeezed into the backseat and we resumed the drive to Jean Moffitt's. The iron gates guarding her home opened automatically, revealing a small table manned by uniformed staff to welcome guests.

"I think I own that jacket," Lucy said, looking at a parking attendant.

"You do. I just tried it on and it made me look like a busboy. That's why I borrowed this one instead."

"Please don't tie that one to a tree. I didn't pay for it myself, but it would have been very expensive if I had."

Valet parking gave me a ticket and a map of the gardens and grounds. An official greeter, also in black pants and a white jacket, looked for our names on his clipboard. I was listed with two guests, but Lucy exercised some of her famous charm and it didn't matter that I showed up with four. Wrentham, Emma, and J. C. showed them IDs, and they took our names.

"Has a Mr. Stancik arrived?" I asked.

Another quick perusal of the guest list. "I don't see him on my list — oh, wait, there he is. A last-minute addition. He hasn't arrived yet, madam."

I asked about Reiger and Shepard, and they were both in attendance. Our group walked a few steps onto the terrace and we were surrounded by offers of food and drink.

"We are perfectly safe," I said. "This is a huge party. All we have to do now is stick together and smoke out Mr. Rose. The police are on their way. Just don't go off anywhere on your own." I scanned the crowd for familiar faces. Turning around, I realized J. C. and I were already on our own. Lucy had followed a tray of hors d'oeuvres to a massive buffet overlooking a large pond. Emma and her father had disappeared.

"You did tell them we were perfectly safe," J. C. said.

"And they listened to me? I was trying to make them feel better. We're on a ninety-acre estate. Someone could die here and not be found for years."

J. C. promised to stick close and we set out to find Kristi Reynolds, who might lead us to Scott Reiger, who I'd recognize but J. C. wouldn't. "Look for a salmon-colored shirt," I said, "he's been wearing them all week. It has his company name on the breast pocket, SlugFest."

Guests spilled over from the sunrooms to the terraces to at least three different levels of the property. The area was almost as crowded as the convention center had been. Spotlights surrounded what the map called the Great Pond, and their reflections glittered in the water like the phosphorescence you sometimes see on the beaches in the Caribbean.

"Ms. Holliday." It was Jensen. "Mrs. Moffitt would like to welcome you and your guest personally." I had a feeling he'd said that two hundred and fifty times that evening, but I didn't care — he made it sound genuine and it was classy. He led us through a gaggle of people clustered around Mrs. M.'s chair, and we shook the papery hand and exchanged a few generic pleasantries.

"Tell me about your guest. Do we have the honor of meeting the famous artist herself?" J. C. did look artsy in her gussied-up sweat suit. I said no and left her to explain who she was. I took my drink to the fringes of the terrace, looking for the SlugFest man and the Bambi-no couple, when I felt something squarish and hard pressing into my back. I stiffened.

"Okay, where's your badge?" Rolanda Knox playfully jabbed me a second time with her cell phone.

"That's hysterical. You're lucky I didn't swing around and knock you off this terrace."

"Are you surprised?" She entwined two fingers on her right hand. "Mrs. M. and I are like this. It's my third year."

I *hadn't* expected to see Rolanda at the party but I wasn't unhappy about it. "I'm glad you're here. *They're* here," I said.

"Who — poltergeists?"

"All of them. The vandals, the blackmailers, the killers."

"You left out the cyborgs, the Visigoths, and the Sharks and the Jets."

"They may be here, too, I'll have to get back to you on them. I just arrived."

I gave Rolanda the shorthand version of the previous three hours and told her to keep her eyes peeled for Stancik and Labidou, who should have already been there. Off to one side I saw Scott Reiger and Kristi Reynolds locked in conversation. If Rolanda and I hadn't heard them going at it the previous night, we might have thought they were getting on, but we'd heard the vicious things she could say with a smile. Lucy swung by with two glasses of something.

"Hello, hello. Take this. Sorry, I would have brought three if I had known." She looked up into Rolanda's face and the breezy demeanor evaporated.

"It's okay," Rolanda said. "You don't need a badge for this party."

"We're watching Scott Reiger," I said. "He's one of the two guys I think could be our man. Out of nowhere he comes up with a perfect pest repellent? Not a scientist — not even a gardener. Remarkable."

"Two years ago that sleazebag was hawking fat-burner pills eventually banned by the FDA," Rolanda said.

"How do you know?"

"I overheard one of those girls in the ugly pink shirts. She also told her friend that Reiger asked her if she wanted to come into the convention center after hours to make a few extra bucks."

"Sex?" Lucy asked.

"That's what the kid thought, but Reiger said it was something else. She thought it sounded fishy, so she passed."

Two people had pushed the cart that we thought had held Garland's body. Was Reiger in on it with Kristi? One of his employees? Or was it Shepard and his wife? The long-suffering Lorraine?

"Is Kristi the one with the fake tan? What a diva," Lucy said. "I saw her in the powder room. She had way more stuff in her arsenal than I do and that's saying something. Most of it was still in boxes, too. Who tries new makeup at a party?"

Someone who just lost her makeup bag?

"Was she with anyone?"

"No, but she was yakking on the phone. To a man, I'd guess. I overheard her say the curse was over. She was laughing. I assumed she was talking about her period. My older sister used to call it that as a joke, I think."

I didn't know about Kristi's cycle but I thought she meant the Javits Curse; and the only way she could possibly know it was over was if she had orchestrated it.

FIFTY-NINE

"At the El Quixote, Kristi mentioned thirty-five locations," I said. "Maybe they weren't distribution outlets. What if they were sprinkler zones? She kept telling the cops it was an inside job. She wasn't lying."

"Can you turn off separate sprinkler zones?" Lucy asked.

"Why not? I do it all the time in people's gardens. You can also turn off individual zones on an alarm system."

"But why would she sabotage her own show?"

In the course of mingling I'd seen most of my show acquaintances — Connie, Nikki, and David. Lauryn and Cindy Gustafson. I looked around for the one person I knew who might have the answer. She was near the valet parking, having a smoke.

Lucy, Rolanda, and I headed for the entrance as casually as we could for people who really wanted to be sprinting. My new friend, Allegra Douglas, was just stubbing out her cigarette in a portable ashtray when we got there.

"Nice party," I said. Chitchat over. "What happens if the Wagner Center is no longer deemed fit for the Big Apple Flower Show?" I asked.

"It would be unfortunate. Lots of people at Wagner will be put out of work. Maybe the building will finally come down and new construction go up. Someone makes a lot of money on that. On the director's recommendation, the board probably moves the show to Javits; Kristi Reynolds quadruples her budget and doubles her salary. Shall I go on?"

"Can one lost show do that? Surely there must be other events at the Wagner Center?"

"None that are subsidized by a billionaire's widow who's passionate about gardening. If Kristi can convince Mrs. Moffit that BAFS needs to relocate, that building will lose its staunchest supporter."

"Then why not sabotage her plants instead of other people's?"

Allegra was shocked by what we were suggesting. "I suppose there's a limit to even Kristi's hubris."

"Thank you, Allegra."

Since we were back at the entrance, I

asked the attendant again if Stancik had checked in. Still not there. Where the hell was he?

We moved out of earshot and I tried to think how we could find the Wrenthams. Then I remembered he had called me from the airport. His number was the last one on my call log. I hit reply. It rang close to ten times. Finally someone answered. The sound I heard was something between a gasp and a moan.

"Professor? Is that you? Where are you?"

He didn't speak but I held on, waiting for something, background noises, anything. Then I heard it — *ribbit, ribbit.* "Are you near one of the ponds? Can you tell me which one?" I thought I heard rushing water but couldn't be sure if the sound came from the phone or a nearby fountain. His voice sounded a little like Nikki's after she'd been sedated, but Wrentham's had the trace of desperation in it, and a little gurgle that might have been blood.

"Hang on, we're going to find you."

I pulled out the map they'd given me when we'd arrived. "Lucy, can you get us a couple more of these?" She ran off and was back in less than a minute. There were three ponds on the property and three of us.

"We really shouldn't go off on our own.

Rolanda, how about if you get Lauryn Peete and get her to search with you?"

"How about if I get my gun and go by myself? All right, I don't have a gun with me, but that little thing? I'd sooner get Connie Anzalone. At least she's got some meat on her bones. And I know she's not afraid of anything."

"Just don't go by yourself," I said.

"I won't."

I told her to head for Mary's Pond on the right-hand side of the property. "Don't do anything crazy — we're just looking for the Wrenthams. If you see Reiger or Shepard, stay away. One of them is dangerous. Do you have Stancik's number?"

"Yeah, it's on my phone."

"Good. Don't be afraid to use it. Be careful. I want to come to your graduation." Rolanda took off in search of a partner. She would make a good cop one day, if she got through the night.

I looked at Lucy in her flowered dress and tight white jacket, rumpled and stained with sap from the tree she'd climbed, and she reminded me of a little girl who'd gotten her Sunday dress dirty. "You stay here and wait for Stancik." I fished around in my bag for one of Stancik's cards and gave it to Lucy. "Call him every five minutes until you get him. In fact, plug the number in now. Tell him what's going on and tell him Wrentham may need an ambulance."

"Where are you going?" she said.

"To find J. C. so we can look for Wrentham and his daughter."

"You'd rather go into battle with an old lady than me?"

"Who's going into battle?" Climbing out of his black tanklike Escalade was Guy Anzalone. The happy teddy bear threw a few pretend punches in my direction.

"Thank goodness you're here," I said.

"I been waiting all weekend for you to say that."

I took him by the arm and led him to the left side of the parking area away from the bright lights. I toyed with the idea of telling him I needed his help, that two lives might depend on it. Then I took a different tack. I whipped out the map and pointed to Horse Pond, on the left-hand side of the estate.

"Meet me there in ten minutes, you big hunk of burning love. I'll be listening to the frogs near the pond." I appropriated a long-handled flashlight one of the attendants had set down. "Take this. Wait for me. And watch your footing. There may be landscaping I don't know about. Watch where you step."

"I like a woman who knows what she wants when she wants it. Ten minutes. And one of your frogs will soon turn into a prince," he said. He took off to the left, waving the flashlight from side to side as he walked.

Lucy sized him up in less than a minute. "I get it. He's got a certain Flintstonian charm."

"It's not that. He doesn't know it, but he's helping us look for the Wrenthams."

SIXTY

The sky was turning blue-black. We were going to need another torch; Wrentham would be harder to find as the night wore on. What I didn't want to think about was where Emma was. And where "Mr. Rose" was.

I had the lantern that we'd used on the highway in my car, but I could tell from *Spade and Archer* strapped to the top that the Jeep was buried in back of the lot. Guy's Escalade was still front and center. I ran to the attendant just as he was getting in to park it.

"My husband forgot something in the trunk — I'll just be a minute." The attendant helpfully popped the trunk lid. A plastic orange crate held Guy's emergency kit — jumper cables, a flashlight, a piece of carpet, and some flares. Next to the cables was Guy's sample case, with tumbled blocks and, for comparison, a few pieces of the real thing. I dumped all but two of the stones and put the flashlight and flares in the case. You never knew. Nothing else useful was in the trunk, just a lot of old magazines, a map of upstate New York, and a pair of foam stadium seats from the Mets' new home, Citi Field.

"Mr. Rose — I can't believe I just got it. It's not the flower, it's *Pete* Rose. Bambino's founder is a baseball freak."

I slammed the trunk shut. Lucy and I took off with the map and the stuff from Guy's car. I carried the sample case like a handbag, albeit an ugly, heavy one, and slipped past the crowds that were shrinking closer to the house as it grew dark and the gardens were less visible.

The Great Pond was the biggest, and it would take the longest to get around. As much as I'd snickered about Terry Ward's sensible shoes I was glad to be wearing mine. So far Lucy's canvas wedges were holding their own in the soft, moist soil near the pond, but they started to make sucking noises as we got closer to the water.

"I will sacrifice the red scarf and these shoes, but, please lord, do not let anything happen to the jacket Paula is wearing."

"Sshhh. I think the lord has more pressing business right now." We crept around slowly until we were close to one of the spotlights. Lucy's white jacket shone like the moon. That was good if one of the Wrenthams saw us, bad if it was Shepard. I told her to take it off. In deference to her prayer, I took mine off and gave it to her to wear. If it fell in the mud now it would be her doing.

A third of the way around the pond we heard another sound from my phone. Wrentham was trying to say something. Either we were getting closer to him or the killer was. Then we heard footsteps, someone slogging through mud. *We'd* moved into a muddy area. Was I hearing my own steps echoed on the phone? Were we that close to Wrentham? Or were they someone else's footsteps? We stopped moving, but the sounds continued. I thought I saw movement in the reeds, so we crouched down and waited until it passed. Two glowing yellow lights emerged from the reeds and I held my hand over Lucy's mouth to stifle the scream.

"Raccoon."

There was a storage shed twenty-five yards behind us, a custom-made version of the expensive prefabs sold at the show. I motioned to Lucy to creep back to the shed and stay hidden until we knew what was going on. And we did that until her cell rang.

"Where the hell are you?"

Lucy handed me the phone. "It's for you," she whispered.

It was Stancik. He'd tried my cell, but it had been busy. He was returning Lucy's call.

"I heard from Emma. She's hiding somewhere on the Moffitt property. She thinks a man named Mr. Rose killed her father," he said. "She's terrified."

"I can identify with that. Except I think Wrentham is still alive. I can hear him breathing. And I think Mr. Rose is Marty Shepard, the Bambi-no guy."

"You're right. We found his wife stranded in a ditch off the Hutchinson Parkway. She was babbling about a red dragon flying through the air that caused her accident. I think she must be drinking that crap they're selling. Where are *you?*"

"On the right side of the Great Pond. Wrentham's on the phone — not with us. I'm not sure where he is except there are frogs there."

"Where the heck is the Great Pond?"

"Didn't they give you a map when you entered?"

"Only one guy was at the table; the rest were scrambling around the parking lot. A lot of ticked-off people walking around in the dark, trying to find their cars."

"Okay, forget the map. It's the large pond in the center directly opposite the terrace where the band is playing."

"Stay put, you lunatic."

"Did he just hang up on you?" Lucy said. I didn't bother to answer. I handed Lucy her phone and pressed my own to my ear. I still heard breathing. That was good. I tried to think of something positive to say.

"Hang on, Lincoln. There's a beautiful woman here who wants to go to bed with you." It was the only thing I could think of to keep his spirits up. The last thing I wanted to do was mention his daughter. For all I knew she was lying on the ground beside him. The beautiful woman remark got us a grunt and I took that as a positive sign.

When we got to the shed, Lucy reached for the doorknob, but I grabbed her hand first. I wanted as much notice as possible if I was walking into a space already occupied by a killer. On my hands and knees, I crept to a side window and half stood to peer in. The shed looked unoccupied. Just then something drifted onto my hair and made me look up.

"Jeez!"

Standing over me with a flaking, rotten tree limb in her hands was Emma Franklin, poised to take a crack at my skull.

SIXTY-ONE

Emma dropped the branch and her hands flew to the sides of her head. She mouthed *I'm sorry. I didn't know it was you* over and over again until I took her by the shoulders to quiet her down.

"It's okay. It's okay. Keep quiet. Your dad's going to be fine."

The three of us scurried inside the shed, took a deep breath, and crossed our fingers for Stancik to find us before Shepard did.

"Are the police bringing a lot of men?" she whispered. It was a child's question. Presumably they'd alerted the local authorities, but where the heck were they? Where were they when we spoke? I didn't know, so I didn't say.

"Why did you leave?" I asked, once she was breathing normally.

She'd gotten another call from "Mr. Rose" just as we entered the Moffitt property. He'd seen her arrive and said he was ready to make the drop-off if she'd meet him on the far side of the Great Pond.

"My dad said we should meet him so that we could reason with him. Explain that the product hasn't been completely tested yet, and there could be serious problems." So much for reasoning.

He'd already dispatched Garland and Shepard was expecting Emma to be alone, not accompanied by a man claiming to be the scientist who'd created Bambi-no. Emma said Shepard/Rose was unmoved by Wrentham's concern for the planet. He said he'd been selling a diluted version for three years and no one had died yet and that was good enough for him.

"He said he could make a fortune in the two or three years it was available before the government pulled it off the market, and after that who cared? Marty Shepard would be living on an island by that time — preferably somewhere in the Caribbean, where they had really good baseball players. Who's Marty Shepard?" Emma asked.

At that point Shepard had revealed the Louisville Slugger he'd had hidden under his coat and moved in the girl's direction. Her father stepped in and took the blow, one crack on the side of his head that took him down fast. The girl ran off and hid until she thought it safe to call Stancik. I handed her my phone.

"Talk into the phone, Emma. Your dad will be able to hear you. Whisper. Tell him you're okay. It'll help him to hang on until the police arrive."

Emma, Lucy, and I sat huddled in the shed, Emma cooing into the phone, her estrangement from her father forgotten. In the distance the party noises were growing fainter as revelers either went indoors or left. Someone once said time is too slow for those who wait. Maybe it was a poet. Maybe it was an old rock and roller. In any event, it was too slow for us.

"Think I should turn the flashlight on?" We ran the risk of Shepard seeing us, but how long could we just sit while the life ran out of Lincoln Wrentham? Three votes for yes. We took an inventory of the shed. A tractor and a classic wooden canoe dominated the space.

"Can there *be* two slower vehicles than these?" Lucy said. "I thought rich people had Jet Skis and cigarette boats."

"They're at her other house. It's not so bad. That's a top-of-the-line tractor. It costs more than my car and can probably go twenty or twenty-five miles an hour."

"Is that fast enough to outrun a crazy man?"

"Depends if it's a crazy man with a gun or a crazy man swinging a baseball bat," I said.

The problem was, we'd be exposed. And I wasn't sure the tractor could go at top speed with three people hanging on. The canoe was even slower but we might be able to crouch down and hide in the hull. It was only a mile or so, but either option was preferable to running back to the house in the dark.

We didn't have time for another vote. The shadows rippled outside the window and we killed the light. I told Lucy and Emma to stand on either side of the double doors and gave them hunks of Anzalone tumbled stone ready to use as weapons. Where was J. C. with her door bar when I needed her? I got on the tractor to see if the keys were there and I could figure out how to start it.

Shepard kicked in the double doors and stood silhouetted in the doorway with the faint light behind him illuminating the bugs and mosquitoes circling him. He was holding a baseball bat.

"You in there, little girl? I don't want to hurt you. I just want that formula. Your boyfriend said it was on a flash drive. Just toss that sucker out and I'll go away, I promise." Right.

He stepped into the shed and Emma, nervous, struck first, but she didn't make contact. He turned and raised the bat to strike her, and from behind Lucy connected with a sharp blow to the back of his head. She screamed while doing it and then dropped the brick, which wasn't heavy enough to put him out of commission for long. He was on his knees but getting up, so I turned on the tractor, temporarily blinding him with the lights.

I reached for one of the paddles in the canoe, aimed the front edge of the blade at Shepard's neck, ran toward him, and pushed hard. He clutched his throat and hit the deck again, falling to his knees. The three of us jumped on the tractor and tore ass out of the shed, running over some part of Shepard's body in the process.

Halfway to the main house the spotlights turned on us and we were guided back to safety.

SIXTY-TWO

"It was a lovely party, Mrs. Moffitt. I hope I'll get to visit again in the daytime, when I can see a little better."

"You're quite welcome, Detective Stancik. Maybe you can come back when Paula returns to advise us on where to place another sculpture. We've decided to purchase a second piece."

Jensen wheeled his employer away to bid good night to the last stragglers. Few had noticed a disturbance earlier in the evening. And when police cars and an ambulance arrived, they were quite ready to believe as they'd been told that one of the older guests had suffered heart palpitations and was being looked after. Not exactly true. Wrentham and his daughter were on the way to hospital.

"When did you know it was Shepard?" I asked.

"We looked through your show directory

and checked out all the people on the dog-eared page. Reiger had had some shady dealings but Shepard was a flat-out fruit-cake. Mrs. Shepard gave us an earful when she wasn't going on about the dragon she saw."

It wasn't the first time Marty had started a business, based on nothing more than a slim premise and a catchy baseball name. The Shepard basement was littered with promotional merchandise from failed ventures, including the Batter-Up Cookie Company. He'd refused to listen when Lorraine told him cookies were made from dough, not batter. Besides, cookies in the shape of bats weren't as appetizing as those that looked like balls, bases, or even catchers' mitts. They looked like exclamation points, and Lorraine drew the line at Marty's suggestion to put *Louisville Slugger* on them in black icing because the Louisville Slugger Company was very much in business and she didn't want to get sued.

And it was labor intensive. The list of reasons not to do it went on and on, but Marty wouldn't be deterred. She wanted to be supportive, so they compromised on the words *Play Ball.* But it was hard to write on a cookie the width of a breadstick and most of them wound up looking like they said

Playbill, which was not much of a draw to twelve-year-old boys.

"After the cookie company, there was the Sacrifice Fly Swatter," Stancik said. Lorraine had wisely resisted the urge to tell her husband a rolled-up magazine worked just as well. Cartons of the flyswatters were in Shepard's basement, too, but he could never make them cheaply enough for the numbers to work.

Then somebody else came out a few years later with the Talking Fly Swatter, and that sent Shepard over the edge. He drank for an entire weekend and stayed in the car whenever they went to Walgreens that summer, refusing to go inside and see their mountainous display of flyswatters that mocked him by repeating things like "Gotcha!" and "No fly zone!"

"Don't you understand?" he'd said. "It was my idea and someone else is making millions." It was nothing like his flyswatter, but there was no reasoning with Marty. Lorraine Shepard was a patient woman, but she was close to telling Marty it was three strikes and you're out.

At a farmers market Marty saw a kid selling unlabelled pest repellent from the back of his truck. Marty saw him the next week. And the next. The fourth time, he bought all Garland's inventory and made a deal to purchase whatever the kid could get him.

For two years he cultivated the boy and tried to figure out himself what the hell was in the noxious mix. Then one day out of the blue Garland offered to sell him the formula for $250,000. Marty said yes, even though he didn't have the money. He got a third mortgage, but it wasn't enough. He dragged his feet for months until he was able to convince a laboratory on Route 1 to analyze the mixture. They came to within 90 percent of its ingredients, and that was good enough for Marty. He told Garland to take a hike.

He sank a big chunk of what would have been Garland's money into prototypes of packaging, test marketing, and a trip to Minnesota to pitch it to a distribution company, but they blew him off when he'd arrived for the meeting. He'd fix them. He'd sell it himself, then they'd be sorry.

Marty spat nails when he saw the Slug-Fest booth right near them at the show. He'd already been looking ahead to the next item in the product line and had been toying around with the word *Slugger*. This time without the problematic *Louisville*. Then when Garland showed up demanding his money, things got really ugly.

"Shepard never knew who made the original formula," the cop said. "When Garland told him it was a renowned scientist and he'd pull the plug on Bambi-no once the boy confessed his involvement, Shepard decided to kill him. It might be years before the scientist realized it was his formula on the market. By then Shepard would have already gotten rich and disappeared."

"Wouldn't Garland be incriminating himself by confessing to Wrentham?" Lucy asked.

"You didn't meet this kid," I said. "He was charm personified. He probably thought Wrentham would send him away with a slap on the wrist. What happened next?"

"They saw Garland on Wednesday and arranged to meet later that night. Shepard's not saying anything without his lawyer present but we think they met in the convention center because the Shepards assumed it would be deserted. One of them struck him from behind with a large heavy object."

"This may sound crazy," I said, "but could it have been a two-pound jar of honey?"

"A two-pound anything can kill you if it lands in the right spot."

"One blow?"

"There were more. I didn't want to get too graphic the other night. They put his body in the garbage tub to get it out of the building. Otis Randolph must have come along while doing his rounds."

"That was when Jamal heard him muttering and moving the tub?"

"Right. Now the Shepards had another problem. It wouldn't take long before Otis wondered what the hell was so heavy in that tub. We think they killed him when he realized what was in the cart. Now they had two bodies to dispose of. They staged Otis's body to make it look like an accident. Shepard even poured Scotch over it to make it seem as if Otis had gotten drunk and fell off the escalator."

"That was handy," Lucy said, "having a bottle of Scotch?"

I explained that alcoholic beverages were the currency of choice if you wanted to sneak into the convention center at night.

"They took Garland's body down to the loading dock and threw him in the back of their SUV. Then they dumped him in the river."

We were joined by a motley group of people coming out of the woods on the Moffitt property. While the local police were searching for us and for the Wrenthams, they also stumbled upon Guy Anzalone, battered and scratched but refusing a doctor's care. He

401

was walking sheepishly behind his wife and Rolanda Knox, who had found him practicing frog noises in the gazebo near Horse Pond. He had not yet turned into a prince.

Marty and Lorraine Shepard are awaiting trial for the murders of Garland Bleimeister and Otis Cleveland Randolph. They have separate attorneys, each of whom is claiming that his client is innocent. Marty searched the entire convention center — including the bag found in Nikki's sarcophagus — looking for the flash drive that Garland claimed to have. It was never found. The Shepards, whose grip on reality slipped quite a bit, continue to refer to this chapter of their lives as the Curse of the Bambino.

Emma Franklin and **Lincoln Wrentham** have reconciled. She is nursing him back to health on his farm in New Jersey. No charges were ever filed against her. He continues to test his formula, but as of this writing there is no foolproof pest repellent.

Kristi Reynolds lost her job with the Big Apple Flower Show when it was learned she was responsible for the Javits Curse, which she staged in the hopes of moving the show to a larger facility. Civil charges have been filed and criminal proceedings will likely follow.

Scott Reiger stumbled upon Kristi Reynolds as she was holding a blow dryer to Connie Anzalone's veronicas. She convinced him to help her with the Javits Curse the same way women have been convincing men to do things for centuries. She reneged. He did not get a distribution deal for Slug-Fest when it was discovered to be simply a watered-down version of Slug-B-Gone, a product no longer on the market. He has been banned from all future Big Apple Flower Shows.

The SlugFest booth worker who posed as a photographer and helped Reiger vandalize the show was released into her parents' custody. An article in *New York* magazine about her involvement has prompted a number of media offers that her parents are considering.

Jamal Harrington was completely exonerated of any wrongdoing. He is still living with his grandmother. **J. C. Kaufman** is helping him get an internship at one of the networks. The two have a standing Wednesday night dinner date. She's watching his back.

Lauryn Peete is still teaching and was recently awarded the New York City Golden Apple for best high school teacher.

Connie Anzalone forgave the Tumbled Stone King. She never found out who he was waiting for in Mrs. Moffitt's garden but suspected it was a promiscuous feng shui expert her friend Doreen DiMucci had warned her about.

Rolanda Knox graduated from John Jay with highest honors and now has her sights set on a law degree. Paula and Lucy attended the ceremony and party at El Quixote. **Harold Bergstein** chose their outfits.

Fat Frank and Cookie were so taken with the Big Apple Flower Show that they have decided to exhibit next year.

Allegra Douglas was reinstated as the head of the Big Apple Flower Show. She has invited Connie Anzalone to join the steering committee. A grant in the name of Otis Cleveland Randolph has been funded by an anonymous donor. It will be awarded annually for the Best Nontraditional Garden.

Any memories of lying unconscious in a bathroom stall, waking up in a hospital, getting drenched by overhead sprinklers, and thinking she'd found a dead body vanished when **Nikki Bingham** sold her vintage sarcophagus to **Mrs. Jean Moffitt.** Nikki pronounced this the best Big Apple Flower Show ever.

Paula Holliday finally read the note Nikki gave her at the show. It was from Hank Mossdale. He'd arrived early, but was ejected when a security guard discovered he didn't have a badge. He suggested they have dinner soon. She was to wear the famous red dress.

ABOUT THE AUTHOR

Rosemary Harris is past-president of Sisters in Crime, New England, and currently vice-president of Mystery Writers of America, New York. She has worked in marketing at Crown and American Express and as a producer for Disney/ABC and WNET. She lives in New York City and Fairfield County, Connecticut.